BERMONDSEY PIE & MASH

CHRIS WARD

BERMONDSEY PIE AND MASH

2016 Chris Ward

All rights reserved

The right of Chris Ward to be identified as the Author of the work has been asserted by him in accordance with the Copyright, Designs and Patents act 1988. No part of the publication may be reproduced, stored in a retrieval system, or transmitted, in any form or by any means without the prior written permission of the publisher, nor be otherwise circulated in any form or binding or cover other than that in which it is published and without a similar condition being imposed on the subsequent purchaser.

ISBN – 10: 1537775510

ISBN – 13: 978 – 1537775517

This is a work of fiction. Names, Characters, businesses, places, events, and incidents are either the products of the Authors imagination or have been used in a fictitious manner. Any resemblance to actual persons, living or dead, or actual events is purely coincidental.

A huge thanks to my dear wife Helen for a fantastic edit

EDITED BY HELEN WARD

CHAPTER 1

It was the morning of June the third, a baking hot day with crystal-clear blue skies and glorious sunshine. Lexi had been waiting for this day like no other; he was coming back to her, her other half, the half that made them both whole. She had woken early and had had a hearty breakfast of two soft poached eggs on brown wholemeal toast with crispy back bacon, washed down with two cups of strong filter coffee. She had then spent twenty minutes luxuriating in a cherry-bomb infused bath instead of the usual two-minute rushed shower. It was a morning to savour and to relish every moment; the anticipation was exquisite and at the same time, strangely a little nerve-wracking.

Lexi was still petite, still very striking, and still very sexy. She had chosen a sexy black lace underwear and a dark ocean blue Chanel trouser suit with a multi-coloured Hermes silk scarf. She was looking in the enormous gold framed mirror in the substantial entrance hall adjusting her light auburn hair. She had had it cut short the day before, which was just how he liked it; she felt like a million dollars. She suddenly heard the squeal of tyres on the shingle and hurried to open the heavy mahogany wooden front door and almost tripped as she rushed to meet the car pulling into the long driveway. She was so ecstatic she was near to tears; she hadn't seen him for three long months. The Senate investigation had been long and arduous, but it was all quickly forgotten as the huge silver Mercedes limo slowed to an almost presidential halt right in front of where she was standing. The back door of the car flew open and he stepped out. He was in his usual dark blue suit and crisp white shirt which was open at the neck. She rushed forward and almost knocked him over as she threw her arms around him and squeezed ever so tightly.

"And I'm pleased to see you too, Lexi!" laughed Paul Bolton.

Lexi disentangled herself from Paul, took a step back and looked him up and down.

"Are you alright? How's your gamme leg? How was the flight? Does Oliver know you're back?"

Paul took hold of her shoulders, "Lexi! slow down!" He pulled her close and kissed her passionately on the lips, she responded in kind, having missed him so much she didn't want to let him go.

She whispered in his ear "You're safe and you're home now; I thank God for that"

He nodded and smiled.

The driver and the huge bodyguard were waiting for him to move.

He took Lexi's hand and made for the front door.

"Oliver, Becca and the kids should be here in about an hour." he stopped and turned to stare intently into lexis eyes; he was close to tears, "I've never been happier than now, I love you so much and I am so delighted to be home."

Lexi flung her arms around his neck and kissed him long and loudly on the cheek.

The huge Bodyguard and driver looked at each other without any change in facial expression.

Lexi laughed, "We're like a couple of teenagers, for God's sake!" she stopped as a tear ran down her cheek.

Suddenly she became serious, "You promised, you haven't forgotten?"

Paul took a deep breath and looked thoughtful. "I haven't. No more travelling and I must leave everything to Oliver."

"Good," Lexi smiled broadly, "so let's go and grab some lunch, unless of course you have something else in mind?" She gave him one of her cute looks with eyebrows raised.

"Paul smiled again and laughed, "I want to take my time with *that,* so you must wait until Oliver leaves us alone later tonight."

"I just thought a quick … no, no, ok; but if I have to wait, it better be good!"

Paul laughed as he grabbed her firm bottom and squeezed, "It's going to be well worth waiting for; trust me."

They stepped through the door into the cavernous entrance hall still laughing and giggling.

CHAPTER 2

The woman strode through the automatic opening double doors into the building marked VISITORS ENTRANCE.
She was tall and confident, attractive with long blond hair, she was dressed to thrill in a short black skirt and an ever so slightly tight, crisp, cream coloured shirt that accentuated her large and well-rounded breasts. She walked with a purpose, swinging her black Michael Kors Selma bag, then she stopped almost exactly in the middle of the reception counter.

She gave the man behind the counter a superior look, "Good morning, I have come to visit my son."

The man dressed in white cotton trousers and white shirt smiled at her.

"Your name please madam."

"Travis, Doctor Sharon Travis."

"And who have you come to visit please?"

"Mr Callum Bolton."

The man in white looked at her closely; he knew the Bolton patient, and he felt sorry for the woman. Bolton was an infamous killer who he knew would never be released from the hospital.

He picked up a clipboard and asked, "Have you ever visited the hospital before?"

Sharon gave a wry smile, "Two visits a year for ten years but I'm very well acquainted with the procedures," she smiled and added, "I know everybody and...," she paused, "I don't recollect seeing you before?"

"Just transferred in from a unit in Kent. Short staffed and all that; you know what it's like nowadays."

Sharon just smiled at him. Her brain was always collecting minute pieces of information; new member of staff, short staffed generally; it all went into her box index labelled Broadmoor High Security Psychiatric Hospital for the criminally insane. She looked closer, he was a big man, broad shoulders, massive chest and handsome enough, she wondered if he had a huge thick heavy cock.

"Your wife must be missing you," and this time, she smiled at him playfully.

"Left years ago; not many can hack being a prison guard's wife."

Sharon feigned concern, "Poor you! It must be hard. Do you live in the grounds?"

"No, I..." suddenly, another guard with a much slighter build and dressed the same in all white, appeared from an almost hidden door behind the counter.

The guard behind the counter promptly put on his professional face again. "Please fill in the form and return it to me when you've finished," he handed Sharon the piece of paper. As she moved away, he admired her cute tight arse swaying gently from side to side.

She knew the drill; she took the form and went to sit in one of the cheap red plastic chairs by the huge windows. She had filled them in so often she could do it automatically.

Within a minute or two, she was finished, and she rose and handed the form back to the guard behind the counter who was now alone.

She whispered conspiratorially, "I know it's against regulations, but can I ask your name please."

The man said nothing for ages, but he had already noticed her splendid figure and was in a good mood.

"Tony, Tony Bridge"

Sharon exclaimed, "Really? Callum's dad's name was Tony!"

The man smiled at her, staring at her breasts, and licking his lips at the thought of touching them, kissing the nipples, and sucking them, wondering what it would be like to juggle the two ripe melons in his hands.

Bridge held his hand out pointing, "Doctor Travis, please continue through the door marked screening."

He had managed to pull himself together yet again, but little did he know it was already too late.

Sharon went through the screening door and was directed to a cubicle where she handed over her gold rotary watch, Samsung mobile phone, Black Selma bag and gold jewellery. She was then thoroughly body searched by an ugly, fat, sweaty woman guard who also dressed in white. She passed the test and was told to sit and wait until she was called. She sat down, and her mind wandered back to when she had worked at the hospital and met Tony Bolton who was then a patient. The sex, the violence of the escape - it was a different life, a different world, she could hardly remember anything in detail but knew she had been there.

She still lived in Canada and earned a respectable living as a psychiatric consultant Doctor, which enabled her to fly British Airways first class over to the UK twice a year to visit Callum. She massaged her face as she thought of Callum being locked up and how it had hit her hard, and whenever she thought that he would never be released she plunged into deep depression and floods of tears.

"We're ready for you Doctor Travis," said a young man who also dressed in the obligatory, almost blinding white, beckoning her to follow him.

She stood up and walked steadily down a long, seemingly, a never ending white painted corridor. The smell was always the same; she could never forget its disinfectant, an over powering smell of disinfectant. The guard held a heavy security door open for her to go through. She entered and tried to focus. She must try to be bubbly and happy for his sake; he detested it when she was miserable, and especially hated it when she cried.

She saw the space and there behind the glass was Callum, her son, her little boy; tears filled her eyes, she could see him smiling, and she bravely smiled back. She sat down in front of the glass and placed her hand on it, he did the same and they just looked at each other smiling.

"Hello Mummy, how are you?"

"Very well thank you, Callum."

"You look great."

Sharon threw her head back and laughed. "I can always rely on you to give me a boost. You do realise I'm nearly, well never you mind!"

"You don't look a day over twenty-one, mummy."

Sharon laughed again and then suddenly stopped, tears again filled her eyes, "Seriously for a minute, how are you keeping?"

"Mummy, I've been here ten years, I'm used to it now, it's like home; I have my friends and everybody is very nice to me."

Sharon thought about the drugs they shovelled into him daily.

"Well, I must say you do look well, but could do with a bit of fattening up. How's the food?"

"Same as usual, awful," and he nearly split his sides laughing.

"When are you going back?" He asked after the fits of laughter

She took a few seconds to answer, "On Saturday, so three days left. I'll be back in to see you on Friday."

"Thanks for coming mummy, I really look forward to it, and so appreciate it."

"You're my son, I miss you so much," tears flowed down her cheeks. "I'm sorry, I know, I can't help it."

"Don't cry mummy, I won't be here for ever."

Sharon cried even more, she knew they would never let him out, he was too dangerous; and he was only thirty-one.

***

It was getting dark and Sharon was straining to watch the staff entrance that led out to the car park off Kentigern Drive in front of the hospital. She was praying it wouldn't be much longer because if it got too dark, she could easily miss him. It got to six-thirty and it happened quickly. The black iron security gate swung opened, and several men and women appeared. He was one of them; he was wearing a long brown wool coat that made him look even bulkier than he had in the visitor's suite. He got into a clean, shiny light blue Ford Focus and pulled out onto the Drive. Thankfully, he drove slowly, turning right onto upper Broadmoor road, and two minutes later, he turned right again into White City Lane, a small cul-de-sac. He stopped outside an insignificant-looking, small terraced house, got out the car and approached the blacked-out house. He turned a key in the front door and let himself in; soon, the hall light came on, in, what Sharon assumed was the lounge. By the look of it, she thought he lived on his own. She parked further down the road and leaped out of the car. She was on a mission and was determined.

She was soon at the cheap white UPVC front door. She pressed the bell and waited, her heart was pounding as she saw him coming towards the door through the small glass panel.

It seemed like an eternity and then the door opened.

He recognised her almost instantly. "What the...?! My God! You shouldn't be here! Leave or I'll call the police."

"Tony, let me just talk to you for a moment, please," she was raising her voice and it worked.

He was horrified and realised it could turn into a nasty scene; he decided on a course of action. he grabbed her arm.

"Jesus keep your voice down, will you?" he almost dragged her into the tiny hallway.

"What the hell are you doing here? This is against all the rules! You could get me sacked!"

Sharon started crying. "You don't understand; I don't want anything, just a shoulder to cry on, that's all. Please don't send me away."

He took a deep breath as he put his arm around her shoulder; it felt good just to touch a woman.

"Come into the lounge, I'll put the kettle on." He deposited her on an old green sofa and shot off to the kitchen. He made the tea in the old-fashioned way: he poured boiling water onto teabags in the cream coloured china pot. He then placed china cups and saucers and a side plate of chocolate digestive biscuits on a silver tray and then made his way back to the lounge. He pushed open the low-cost wooden internal door and shut it with his foot. He turned and nearly dropped the tray. Sharon was lying naked on the sofa. Although getting on in years, she still had a young woman's body, long slim legs and her breasts were glorious mountains reaching to the skies begging to be caressed, kissed, and licked.

"I noticed how you looked at me. So now, you not only get a great view, but you can also touch, and then I'm going to lick your balls and suck your cock and drain you. Come to me."

He was mesmerised; he could smell her perfume and sex. He hadn't had a woman in months, and here was a gorgeous, delicious naked woman right in front of him begging for it. He could feel his already massive erection and was unsettled. He put the tray down on the coffee table and went to her. She opened her legs and he slid on top of her, and he was lost forever.

CHAPTER 3

Detective Inspector Karen Foster was driving slowly around the Sutton one-way system. She came back up Throwley Way towards the traffic lights; they were red as she drove straight through and then turned sharply right into the police station. It was one of the largest in Surrey; as well as all the customary police activities, it had a very serious intelligence capability. Karen headed up the war against organised crime and specifically, child trafficking and modern-day slavery. She was counting down to retirement, having done twenty-four years with one to do to make it twenty-five. She could of course stay in the job but felt there were other things to life than policing. She parked her new, but dirty grey Ford Mondeo in a white line-marked bay and made her way into the back entrance of the station.

She was feeling good in her new Marks and Spencer beige trouser suit with fresh dark green shirt. "Morning chaps!" she said cheerily.

The two officers at the reception desk, dressed in the official uniform of blue trousers and white shirts, looked up an answered loudly, "Good morning Ma'am!"

She walked passed them, smiling and muttering, "Who the hell said it was a GOOD morning?" It was a June Wednesday morning and she felt quite well for a change. She had stopped drinking during the week for a month, and no longer had the shakes or the very strong urge for booze when she woke up. There was no doubt it had gotten out of control and had begun to affect her work. She had just caught it in time before it had become a serious issue, and she was thankful for that, considering the many years working for the Met and Surrey Police forces. Karen made her way to the lifts and was soon on the fifth floor where she had her own separate office, and her own team, in an open plan design next to her.

"Good morning all!"

"Don't know what's good about it" she heard someone mumble, and she chuckled to herself.

"Team meeting in ten and who's getting the coffee?"

There was a general muttering as the usual argument started as to who's turn it was to get the Detective Inspector her coffee.

Five minutes later, the newest recruit to the team knocked and entered her office.

"Your coffee, Ma'am."

"Thank you, Roberts, very kind of you."

He was about to open his mouth to say he hadn't had a choice but decided against it. He liked DI Foster; she was incredibly experienced, fair to all the staff and she liked a drink, which to the average copper, was passing the likeability test with high grades.

"Will there be anything else, Ma'am?"

"No, you may go."

He nodded and let himself out.

Karen sat back in her black leather swivel chair and sipped at the scolding hot coffee. She was more content than she had been for some time. She was back living with another woman. Nina was Moroccan and a slim beauty. They had met in a bar which was where Karen met just about everybody she knew. She could never decide if she preferred women or men, and she chopped and changed on a regular basis. She thought back to the two female loves of her life, Esme, and Chau, both women of beauty and so damn sexy. She shook her head and picked up the latest intelligence reports which had been placed on her desk early that morning and started to read.

***

"So, where's Jeff?"

Jeff Swan was her assistant and had worked with her in various locations for twenty odd years.

Karen was sitting at the head of the impressive modern twelve-seater table; there were seven present: Roberts the new boy, Nicola, and Jenny two admin officers, Terry, Andrew, and Robert who were the trafficking team, and Paul who was the modern slavery officer. They were all dressed in suits but looked more Asda than Marks and Spencer.

She looked around the table. "Well," she held her hands out in front of her, waiting for an answer.

"Just late in I guess," Andrew piped up.

Karen looked up at the round white cheap plastic clock on the wall; it was ten am.

"Paul, phone his mobile please; meanwhile, we'll get on."

Paul stood up and ambled away from the table, punching Swan into his phone contacts list.

"What's the latest on the Roman case? This was code for a case concerning trafficking of young women from Romania into the UK for sex purposes.

Terry, the lead officer answered, "Surveillance has commenced on Alexandru Dalca and Ciprian Albescu, two very nasty pieces of work. We're working on mobile phone mapping which should happen in the next couple of days. As usual, there are no landlines in any of the flats. We believe they've brought in about ten girls who are now working in multiple brothels in the Tottenham North London area."

Bermondsey Pie & Mash

Paul shouted out, "He'll be here in five Ma'am!"

"Thank you, Paul."

Karen turned to Terry, "I want to know what is happening to the money. There must be shedloads of cash; so, where are they hiding it? Or probably more likely, which banks or businesses are they using to launder it?"

Karen stopped and twiddled the blue biro in her fingers, then she added, "Also, speak to our contacts in all the banks in north London. I want updates on any dodgy accounts that receive multiple cash deposits that do not fit the business profile. Check for multiple deposits by anonymous people into business accounts. Ask them to check for bulk purchases from chemists that could be rubbers," she looked across at Roberts. "That's contraceptives and the real name is... "

"I know what a condom is Ma'am," he said, going red in the face, and shaking his head in embarrassment.

"Of course, you do, let's move on. I also want as much info as we can get on the girls, where they're working, etc. When we strike, I don't want to miss any, you all know how I detest these bastard traffickers; I want to make sure we have a watertight case to put them away for a very, very, long time."

"Couldn't agree more, Ma'am. Bastards all of them, and these two are particularly nasty; they control the girls with violence and if that doesn't work they get them hooked on heroine. I can't wait to arrest the smug little shits."

There was a silence which seemed to last forever but was only seconds; it was broken by the door opening, and Jeff Swan entered.

"Sorry, I'm late boss," he was the only one who could call her that.

Karen looked at him, her Mr dependable. He was medium height with thinning hair and looked scruffier than usual. He was wearing a brown coloured suit that looked as though it hadn't been cleaned for years, and his tie was all eschew on his greying white shirt.

"I need a chat when we've finished."

Jeff nodded and took his place at the table.

"Let's move on," Karen fiddled with her pile of papers. "OK so..." She stopped and lifted the top piece of paper and looked at it closely. She couldn't believe it, an intelligence report headed PAUL BOLTON RETURNS TO UK. She read it quickly.

Mr Paul Bolton of Virginia Water, Surrey, has been deemed a racketeer in the USA and has been deported back to the UK. The FBI say that Mr Bolton was running a casino operation in Las Vegas and underpaid taxes to the tune of twenty million dollars on profits. Mr Bolton agreed to plead guilty and pay a sixty million dollar fine for indemnity against prosecution. A senate hearing took place and Mr Bolton has left the USA for good. Mr Bolton still has nightclub interests in London. We believe Mr Bolton has taken a step back from running the Den Nightclub and has passed that responsibility onto his only son Oliver.

She shook her head. Paul Bolton, the Paul Bolton and Lexi. She thought of Katie dying in the Nadler hotel, Callum Bolton rotting in Broadmoor… the memories went on for ever. She passed the sheet of paper to Jeff. She almost went to work for Paul, she'd always liked him and Lexi, and Duke, who was so riddled with machine gun bullets he was unrecognisable. It was a long time ago, a different time; she had moved on, but the urge was there, the urge to pick up the phone and say hello. She wondered if it was the same beautiful house in Virginia Water. She would think about it, and maybe after the meeting…

Jeff handed her back the paper with no expression whatsoever. She had expected a reaction, something; he knew the Boltons, he knew how she had helped them with confidential police intelligence information.

"Take five," Karen pushed her chair back, making a scraping noise on the wooden floor and made for her office door. "Jeff, join me please."

Everybody around the table was looking at each other, wondering what the hell was going on.

Jeff stood and followed Karen into her office.

"You were late."

"Got stuck in traffic."

Karen laughed, "Bollocks! What's the real reason?"

"Usual stuff; massive argument with the misses. Might be time to call it a day."

Karen couldn't give anybody advice on relationships.

"You two have been like this for years, sort it out or split up for Christ's sake." She shook her head and then they both laughed at the same moment.

"So, Paul Bolton's back?" asked Jeff, "How long's it been?"

Karen thought for a second, "Must be getting on for ten years. I wonder if he's changed."

"You're going to call him, aren't you?"

"I have to, I can't resist it. I want to know how Lexi is and their son Oliver. Memories, Jeff, you know what it's like."

"I know. Well, call them now and get it over and done with."

"I need to collect my thoughts first, but yes I will."

Jeff moved towards the door, "Can't wait to hear the gossip," and he smiled at her.

Karen smiled back, and she was almost shaking with anticipation of making the call.

Jeff left the office, and as she went to pick the phone up it rang. Five seconds later, she was charging out the office shouting for backup.

CHAPTER 4

"Nana! Nana! Nana!" The two identically dressed boys in shiny black leather shoes, blue corduroy trousers with red braces on blue shirts, ran as fast as their little legs would carry them towards Lexi and Paul, who were standing on the top step outside the front door. They crashed into Lexi's legs and hugged for all they were worth.

"We want sweets Nana! We want sweets!"

Lexi knelt so she was at eye level with them, "Matthew, Robert what is the missing word?"

They jumped up and down, "Please! Nana, Please!"

Paul was shaking with laughing. Lexi grabbed their two little hands and proceeded back into the house.

"Becca! Come and give an old man a hug!" Oliver and Becca were carrying some shopping bags towards the house.

Becca was wearing skinny blue jeans and a white frilly see through blouse and white bra. she put her bags on the step and held her arms out and gave Paul a hug and a kiss. Then, Paul put his arms around Oliver and kissed him on the cheek also.

"Welcome! Welcome! Come in! it's so good to see you both."

Paul had dressed casually in green corduroy jeans and a white shirt. He was over the moon to see Oliver and Becca. He had liked Becca from the moment Oliver had introduced her to the family. Becca had given up her job at British Airways and looked after the boys, full time.

They strolled into the house. "So, how was it, old man?"

Paul looked thoughtful and winked, "We'll talk a bit later."

Oliver understood; it would be in private, later in the evening.

Lexi made a fuss of the two boys, and everybody chatted endlessly until tea time when a selection of delicious crust-less brown bread sandwiches and cream cakes were served. It was soon seven pm and Paul and Oliver disappeared to the office.

They sat facing each other at a large modern glass table.

"So, it's all over?"

Paul nodded his head sorrowfully, "The last month was fucking hell, sitting around with nothing to do and FBI all over the casino. I'm glad it's over."

There was a brief silence then Paul added angrily, "That bastard Babich and his poodle Carter have a lot to answer for."

"Ethan Babich and Steven Carter will get what's coming to them, don't worry about that," Oliver said reassuringly. "They've stolen fucking millions from us and they'll pay for that. What do you want to do?"

I've been thinking about it and I want to go back to running clubs, it's what we've always done, and we do it so well. How's the Den doing?"

"It's taking record money and making first-class profits. We should have kept some of the others."

"No point dwelling on that now; we got a fair price for them. So, money is no object then. I'll leave it to you but let me know the overall picture on a regular basis."

"Thanks dad, it's going to be an exciting journey again, I'm already looking forward to getting started."

"Remember, it's always about money. Look behind the excuses, the reasons, and you'll find money lies at the root of everything; and thank God, we have millions stashed away all over the world. Make it work son, and if you need help of any kind, you know where I am."

They stood and embraced, kissing each other briefly on the cheek.

Paul looked at his son proudly, "My last words of wisdom: family is everything, remember your brother George, don't take any chances, surround yourself with good loyal people and look after them. That's it, now let's go and see the ladies and have a last drink before you go."

Oliver and Becca left at eight thirty, later than they had planned but it had been such an enjoyable fun day. Paul and Lexi saw them off and then retreated into the lounge to relax.

"Do you want a drink?" asked Paul.

"No, I want you to come here and kiss me"

Paul smiled, "It will be my pleasure Mrs Bolton."

He sat next to her on the comfy red sofa, and as he leaned across to kiss her, his mobile, which was on a small coffee table, began to ring.

"Probably Oliver saying they've left something behind," He said as he grabbed the phone and pressed the green button.

"Did you forget...?" He started to say then stopped and listened for a couple of seconds and then looked at Lexi and whispered to her, "You'll never believe who this is."

Bermondsey Pie & Mash

He paused then said into the phone, "I'm putting you on speaker-phone so Lexi can hear and talk to you."

Paul touched speaker on the phone and placed it back on the table.

"Say hello to Lexi."

Lexi was looking perplexed and then the voice rang out, loud and clear.

"Hello Lexi, it's Karen Foster, how are you?"

Lexi couldn't believe her ears and her mouth opened wide in surprise.

"Karen! Oh My God! How are you? What a surprise!"

"I meant to call earlier but, well, you know, it's never that easy to…"

Paul interrupted, "You should have taken the job Karen! What are you doing now?"

"I'm still a bloody copper of course! What else could I do? I'm working in Sutton nick, trying to shut down child trafficking gangs."

"You know me Karen, I can't abide those fucking people," he turned to Lexi and whispered "Sorry." He turned back to the phone, "Foreigners, I suppose?"

"Yes, Romanians."

"Bastards they should all be shot" he knew Lexi didn't like bad language but he couldn't help it.

"Karen, you must come down to see us as soon as possible."

"I'd like that very much Lexi. How is Oliver?"

Paul cut in, "He's a fine young man, and I hasten to add, mostly due to Lexi. He's married with two boys. You may remember he was attacked at Heathrow; he married Becca, the British Airways girl who helped him."

"Oh, I'm so happy for you both, Grandparents. Who'd have thought it!"

"I know. When are you coming down then?"

"Are you still in Virginia Water?"

"Yes, same house; you must come." Lexi was so excited.

Paul turned serious for a moment.

"How did you know I was back?"

There was a second's silence.

"Can't answer that Paul, could get me into trouble."

"I understand, the FBI have probably told the whole world. So, Karen, what about your personal life? have you settled down yet?"

Karen sort of laughed.

"Well, Karen, I want to know as well." Lexi knew Karen liked men and woman and wondered…

"I'm with a lovely Moroccan lady now," Karen laughed again. "She's really very nice and we get on really well."

"Bring her down with you we'd love to meet her."

Paul gave Lexi an ARE YOU SURE look.

"I'll think about that. Look, it's late; I'll check my diary and come back to you soon."

"Make sure you do Karen otherwise there'll be trouble"

Everybody laughed.

"Speak to you soon Karen," and Paul touched the red button.

He took a deep breath, "That woman! Why can't she find a good man, get married, and live a normal life?"

"Because she likes women and men and can't make her mind up. Now stop dithering; get over here and kiss me before I fall asleep."

Paul smiled at her, "You aren't doing no sleeping tonight, baby."

Lexi laughed loudly. "And you better forget all that ghastly American slang you've been picking up."

CHAPTER 5

"You'll do as you're told, you fucking bitch!" The huge man slapped the young girl hard around the face, sending her sprawling across the bed.

***

Simona Dumitrescu was sixteen; she had dropped out of senior school and had been working in a hairdresser's in a small town called Ploiesti in central Romania. She worked there for three months and got so fed up, one day she decided to take a day off work and travel to Bucharest, the capital, which fortunately was only thirty kilometres away. Simona persuaded her best friend and ex-classmate Ana Funar to go with her, telling her they would meet some rich cosmopolitan handsome men, get married and live like queens. They had caught the slow local train from Ploiesti, and an hour later were arriving at Gara de Nord, the main station in Bucharest. They rushed out the station and were soon wandering the streets, admiring the wonderful architecture and at mid-morning, they stopped at a small, quaint coffee shop.

Alexandru Dalca was tall and well-built, with dark hair and a designer stubble. He was dressed in his trademark dark blue Levi jeans, white shirt and black leather jacket and was sat in the main Bucharest station, slowly sipping his Cafea Filtru. He was bored, pickings had been poor recently and they had orders but no girls. He always sat where he could see the local trains pulling in. They were commuter trains, but he was looking for specific people, young girls who were travelling to the big city for some excitement, girls who had run away from home and were lost, girls who had come to make their fortune in the supposedly gold lined streets of Bucharest.

He sipped again at his coffee and then became more alert as another local train pulled into the station. The crowded train spilled its contents onto the platform, they were mostly men in suits, and then he saw them. They stood out like a sore thumb, and were conspicuous by their age and clothes - two young girls of about fifteen or sixteen. He stared like a hungry lion, eye-balling its prey prior to attacking. The girls had backpacks, that told him they were visiting for the day. He licked his lips and began to rub his fingers together. he pushed his coffee to one side as he stood up and continued to stare. They were wearing blue jeans and cream coloured puffa jackets, slim and quite tall, both had dark long hair and were pretty, perfect for him and his customers. The girls headed out of the main Station entrance and he began to follow.

At mid-morning, the two girls stopped for a coffee break and to rest their feet.

"The coffee is lovely Ana. Aren't you pleased you came with me?"

Ana shrugged, "It's alright, but I could have stayed in Ploiesti and drank coffee."

"Cheer up! We are in the big city, let's enjoy ourselves."

The door to the cafe opened and Simona noticed the tall handsome well-built man enter. He went to the counter and ordered coffee and a cake. The lady behind the counter turned to make the coffee and the man looked around the few tables and smiled when he caught Simona's eye.

"Good morning, how are you today?"

"Very well, thank you"

"You are on holiday?"

"Here for the day."

"That's good. Where are you from?"

"Ploiesti."

"I know it, not too far away. So, what are you doing today?"

"Just looking around, you know."

He nodded and turned to the counter. He then turned back and deposited a plate with two cream cakes on it in the middle of the girl's table.

"You must have cakes with your coffee," he smiled and then laughed.

The two girls also laughed and smiled, the dance had begun.

"That's very kind of you. Why don't you join us?" Ana asked boldly.

"It would be my pleasure."

Alexandru Dalca was pleased, so far everything was going perfectly according to plan.

"So, do you girls work in Ploiesti?"

"I work in a hairdressers and Helena is a hotel receptionist."

"Good jobs that pay very well, you are lucky."

Simona laughed, "They are not well paid! You must be joking! Do you live and work in Bucharest?"

"Yes, I work for the biggest model agency in the country."

"Simona was beside herself. "Really? How exciting very exciting!"

Dalca smiled. "It is a job, nothing more. I search for new talent to work here and abroad in Europe and America."

The girls were wide eyed; they had met a real charmer who worked in the modelling world!

"I wanted to be a model," piped up Ana. Simona gave her a surprised look. "I was told I was not tall enough."

"No, I do not believe it, you are pretty, well you are both pretty enough to be models, and tall enough." He turned to the waitress. "More coffee and cakes"

"Here is my card," he handed them a card each which said Star Model Agency and gave an address in Bucharest.

"What do your models do?" Asked Ana.

"They model clothes of course, what did you think?"

"Is that everything they do?"

"Well, some do clothes, some underwear, like sexy knickers and that kind of stuff, and some do adult work."

Both girls went quiet then Ana said, holding her breath, "Are you looking for models now?"

"Always looking, you never know when you might bump into some pretty girls who want to make lots of money."

Simona gushed, "How much money can the girls make?"

"Everything is paid in dollars; a good model can earn one thousand dollars a day in Bucharest and a lot more in London for instance."

"You send girls to London?"

He laughed, "Of course we send girls to London, Paris and Rome; that is the business I work in."

The girls were transfixed and excited by all the talk of big money and travelling.

"Well, I have to go. By the way my name is Alexandru Dalca. It's been nice talking to you." He pushed his chair back and went to pay.

Simona looked at Ana and both knew what the other was thinking. It was Simona who invited the hunter closer to its prey.

"Mr Dalca, before you go we..." she looked at Ana who nodded. "We wondered if we could audition for modelling with your company?"

"He didn't speak and shrugged his shoulders. "I hadn't thought that you might be interested but yes of course, you are young, slim and pretty; why not?" He flung his arms in the air and laughed. The he paused and said pointedly, "Please excuse me I must make a call."

He stood up, opened and shut the door, and stood outside the café and made a call on his mobile.

The door re-opened and he entered. "We are lucky, the photographer is in the studio and we had a cancellation; what do you say?"

Simona was slightly concerned, "Audition now?" She turned and looked at Ana who nodded.

"OK, how far away is the studio?"

"We grab a taxi and we are there in ten minutes; it's exciting, isn't it?"

"Do we get paid anything for the audition?" Ana asked tentatively.

"What! of course not! it is an audition; you must persuade me you are worth taking on, and if you did, then of course we pay you. If you travel abroad, it is all expenses paid and the five-star life, hotels, nightclubs, beaches, a lovely well-paid life."

The door opened and as if by magic a taxi driver appeared. "Taxi for Mr Dalca."

It wasn't just a taxi, it was a huge black Mercedes; the girls were wide eyed.

The Mercedes sped around the ring road and then entered a modern looking industrial estate. They pulled up outside a small industrial unit that had a nameplate which read, Five Star Studio.
"We are here, let's go!" Dalca jumped out the car and the two girls followed. They all entered the front door and were met by a receptionist.

"Hello Mr Dalca, Gavril is waiting for you in studio 3."

"Thank you Diona. Follow me girls."

Dalca strode along a corridor and then entered a door marked studio 3. The girls followed him in and were immediately impressed and surprised. The room was smallish but looked like an incredibly professional film studio. There were cameras and lighting everywhere, huge white backdrops on a stage at the far end and at the side, a table and chairs and a coffee machine.

"Girls, grab yourselves some coffee while I speak with Gavril."

The receptionist appeared and helped them with the coffee machine. Both girls were pleased there was a woman present.

"So, girls, I expect you would like to freshen up?"

They hadn't really thought about it, but both said yes at the same time. Diona took them to a side door and opened it, inside was a very modern luxurious bathroom.

"Come back when you're ready."

Simona locked the door and they both jumped up and down with excitement, hardly believing their luck.

Simona said excitedly, "He wouldn't have bothered to bring us here unless he thought, we were… you know, alright."

"I guess. What if they ask us to model underwear?" asked Ana with little frown.

Simona went wide eyed. "Oh God I hadn't thought of that! it's a good job I wore my best matching pink lacey set then. What about you?"

Ana had to think, "Plain white cotton. You mean you would do it straight away?"

"Why not? I want this job and I'll do just about anything to get it."

The girls had a pee, did their make-up and hair and were ready. They opened the door and re-entered the studio where Dalca and another man in his 30s, and Diona, were waiting for them. Multiple lights were on and it all looked so exciting. Dalca introduced Gavril the photographer to the girls.

As soon as the introductions were over, Gavril said, "OK girls let's warm up first. Both of you on the stage and flirt with each other and me."

Simona and Ana stepped onto the stage and stood still, looking uncertain.

"Move around laugh, smile, jump, stick your tongue out at the camera, have fun."

Gavril moved around them, continually snapping away with his hand-held camera.

"Come on, have fun! Now hug each other, kick your legs back…, good! Good!"
Ten minutes later Gavril called a halt. "Take a break, girls!"

Gavril went to speak to Dalca in the corner while Diona made the girls fresh coffees.

Dalca then joined the girls and Diona at the table.

"There's a problem."

The girls couldn't speak but Diona asked, "What is it, Mr Dalca?"

"We have too many girls doing fashion, we need girls who will do underwear."

Diona turned to Simona and Ana and back to Dalca. "It's such a pity, they are lovely girls."

Simona said quickly, "We don't mind doing underwear, it's only like being in a bikini."

"You sure? We don't want to pressure you into anything you're not comfortable with," said Dalca.

Ana spoke this time, "It's no problem, we will enjoy it."

"Ok Diona, get the girls ready please."

"Follow me girls." And she took them to another door on the other side of the studio.

"Wow!" Simona had never seen so many racks of clothes.

"So, look, get undressed and let me see what you are wearing and whether we need you to put something else on. Are you natural, trimmed or smooth?"

Neither girl spoke, not really sure what she meant.

"Diona raised her eyebrows, "Ok, do you shave your pusseys?"

Ana swallowed, "I do." She turned to Simona who laughed, "Yes I do as well."

"Thank goodness for that!" cried Diona and they all burst out laughing.

The girls then undressed and looked good enough in their own knickers and bras.

Diona led them back into the studio and they again stepped onto the stage.

Dalca liked what he saw and imagined having them both at the same time; he would make sure he did as soon as possible.

It seemed like hundreds of photos were taken and then Gavril called a halt. "That's a wrap then!" and he started to pack away his camera.

The girls stood there, not sure if they had finished or not.

Diona called to them, "Get dressed we have finished." She led the girls back to the room with the rack of clothes where they got dressed and were soon back at the table sipping more coffee.

Gavril returned from somewhere and sat down with Dalca, Diona and the girls. He laid a large print of photos onto the table and smiled.

"They are good, very good indeed."

The girls scooped up the images and took a great interest in them. They were both laughing and making cooing sounds as they looked and at each photo closely.

"Is that really us? They look fantastic!" Simona said happily.

Gavril smiled, "Obviously, by a brilliant photographer, but if I'm honest, photoshop had a hand in them as well."

The girls had no idea what he meant so calmed down and sat quietly with big smiles on their faces.

"So, girls, we will drop you back in the city centre and give you a call, maybe in two days' time."

"Please give Diona your home phone numbers, we need to speak with your parents for consent to join the agency."

Simona was instantly worried nobody had asked how old they were, and she was scared if they knew their how young they really were, it would mean no work.

"Can we speak with Mr Dalca alone for a moment please?" Simona asked.

Diona and Gavril left and went out of the studio door.

"So, what is it?"

"Well we eh..." Simona was apprehensive

"Spit it out, I've heard it all before."

"We are both sixteen, is that OK?"

"Sixteen! Shit! You both look eighteen! Anyway, don't worry; I'll take care of it."

"You sure?"

"Yes, it is not a problem, trust me."

"We trust you Mr Dalca" said Simona, "Yes we do," and she looked at Ana who nodded.

"Good, so maybe we better not phone your parents. Look, it's best you phone me on Thursday at two pm. We can then give you an answer, ok?"

"We would like to work for you, we can work very hard," Simona said pleadingly.

Bermondsey Pie & Mash

The hunter was being invited to eat his prey, it would soon be all be over.

Before 9am on the Thursday, the phone call came, and Dalca told the girls the agency would give them work. They were also very lucky that a contract had come in for underwear work in London the next weekend. They would be away for two nights and be paid two thousand five hundred dollars each.

The girls were ecstatic and couldn't believe their luck, the hunter had his mouth open and was licking his lips ready to devour its prey. They told their parents they were staying at each other's houses and made all the necessary arrangements. They took their passports and arrived at the Henri Coanda International Airport and met up with Dalca.

"You are excited?"

The girls were buzzing and couldn't stop laughing and smiling.

They checked in and then sat in the coffee shop.

"Where are we going to stay?" asked Simona excitedly.

"The five-star Dorchester Hotel on Park Lane of course; only the best for my girls."

The girls enjoyed a glass of wine and a meal on the Romanian TAROM Airways flight and were looking forward to their first visit to London.

They landed at Heathrow and proceeded through Customs with their EU passports, with no issues at all. A silver Mercedes car was waiting to pick them up.

Dalca introduced the driver to the girls, "This is our representative in London, Ciprian Albescu."

Neither of the girls liked the look of Albescu, he was hard looking and didn't smile.

The car sped out of the airport and they headed towards central London. They couldn't take their eyes off the views out the rear car windows. Sights they had seen on post cards suddenly came alive right in front of them - black taxis, the huge red buses, it was all so new and exciting. It seemed like a long journey and it was, but suddenly, they finally slowed down in front of a block of flats in Green Lane, in North London.

"We stop to see someone for ten minutes before we go to the hotel," Dalca announced.

The flats were not that nice from the outside and the girls couldn't wait to move on to the hotel.

The lifts weren't working so they walked up three flights of dirty smelly concrete steps and followed the men into flat sixteen and were shocked at the state of the flat. There was a horrible smell of stale food, sweat and the toilet. Dalca led them into the lounge and told them to sit on the dirty, old grey sofa. Something had changed in his tone, something had changed in the whole situation. Both girls were silent and worried, it got worse when Albescu entered and asked in a harsh tone holding his hand out.

"Give me your passports!"

Neither girl moved.

"Give me your fucking passports! NOW!"

The girls fumbled in their bags and both brought them out and handed them over.

"When do we get them back? Asked Simona. "And your language is horrible."

He didn't answer, he just left the lounge and shut the door.

Ana turned to Simona, "I'm scared. What is happening?"

"Do not worry, we will speak to Alexandru; the other man is a pig."

"But why do they want our passports?" asked Ana, looking very worried.

It suddenly dawned that they were about to be eaten alive by the hunters.

"Ana, listen to me, whatever happens, do exactly what they tell you." Simona was also terrified but was strong and began to pray silently.

Two minutes later the door opened and both men appeared.

"Leave your bags and follow us," ordered Albescu.

The two girls hesitated but then stood up and followed the men. They followed them down the narrow hallway and into a large bedroom. They both knew they had made the biggest mistake of their lives and now they were going to pay. The hunters were going to devour their meal and keep going back for more.

Albescu was the one in charge. "We make videos first and then we all have good time."

Simona and Ana couldn't move.

"Mr Dalca, please we are not used to this, we are both virgins. Anything but this, please."

"You'll do as you're told, you fucking bitch!" The huge man slapped the young girl hard around the face, sending her sprawling across the bed. He had found it was good to make the girls aware of their precarious situation early in the relationship.

"First, you do lesbian together, then some fucking with boys, and then gang bang videos. Get undressed before I smash in your skulls!"

The girls were shaking but did as they were told. A new man appeared who gave them direction and filmed with a large camera he rested on his shoulder. He told them to just follow instructions and they would be looked after.

They were given some wine and then held down and injected with something which they later thought was a tranquilliser of some sort, and then the filming started. The lesbian part of it wasn't too hard but then young big cocked boys came in and took their virginities and fucked them senseless in every conceivable position. It seemed to go on for hours and then they had a break for thirty minutes. Neither could speak, Ana cried and called for her mom. Then the gang-bang filming started, three men on each girl fucking them in every hole, again it never seemed to stop. Finally, it was over, and they were told to just put knickers on and sit on the bed. Plain cheese sandwiches and orange juice were brought to them, and they ate and drank. They thought it was over but it was only just beginning. Albescu and Dalca were next; they took their time abusing and fucking both girls. After that different men came into the room intermittently throughout the night up to three am the next morning. They had to do unimaginable things with filthy smelly drunken men who treated them as pieces of meat. It was finally all over and they were told to sleep because the next day was going to be very busy.

There was no respite. The next day, it started at twelve o'clock midday and went on, and on, and on. Two days later, the girls were taken to a new flat, a ten-minute drive from Green Lane. It was pleasanter than Green Lane but the basic duties had not changed. They worked from midday through until two or three in the morning. They noticed an improvement in the clientele, cleaner, better dressed, not so drunk; they thought the pay for their services would be higher, not that they ever saw a penny of it. They lived on the premises, sharing a bed in a tiny box room. They didn't talk much, they didn't have time; as soon as they finished work they slept. They would get up late, have some food and a shower and it was back to being fucked whichever way the client liked it. Two days later, Simona made a personal vow; she was tough, she was over the original trauma, and she vowed that whatever it took, and however long it took, she and Ana would escape, and at the same time, they would pay back the bastards who had tricked them and ruined their lives.

CHAPTER 6

Sharon Travis had cancelled her flight back to Canada. She had moved out of the three-star Canberra hotel and into the box like terraced house in White City Lane with Tony Bridge. She pretended she hadn't wanted to and relented only after making Tony actually beg. He knew she was leaving very soon and wanted to have as much sex as possible before she went. He was obsessed with her to the point of near mental breakdown; nobody in his life had fucked or sucked him off like she did, she was an extraordinary woman.

Sharon collapsed in a wet heap on the crumpled white-sheet covered bed.

She gasped for air, "You're an animal, that must be the fifth time."

"Haven't had any for months and you are a stunningly gorgeous woman."

"Thank you, Tony, you're to kind," she said as she reached out and took hold of his half erect cock.

"So, when will he be ready again?"

"Very soon but he could do with some help."

Sharon moved around and smiled seductively at him, she then lowered her mouth and took him in, he groaned loudly.

"Oh, God that's good!" he groaned.

Sharon could feel it growing as she sucked, she let go and ran her tongue up his length then once again took him in.

"Jesus, you are so damn good," he groaned again.

They had been at it for two hours; both were covered in sweat, even Sharon's hair was matted with semen and she was sucking as though her life depended on it.

"Oh, God yes, keep going, faster, faster, yes swallow it, swallow it all!"

He came again, and again, bucking and thrusting into her mouth, and she loved it as much as him because she was doing it for her boy.

It was the second night when things came to a head, they had fucked for an hour and he was laying on the bed once again exhausted. She had not mentioned Callum once since she had moved in but that was about to change.

"So, Tony we're having a hell of a time, aren't we?"

"You bet we are, I can't get enough of you, in fact I think I'm actually in love with you."

"You're very sweet Tony and that is an interesting thought, but I can tell you it's never going to happen, and I'll be out of your life for ever very shortly."

Tony's face turned sour. "Don't say that Sharon, I don't think I can survive without you."

"Come what may Tony, all, no, most of us survive. Think about it Tony, even my son Callum survives, locked up in that lunatic asylum, probably never going to see the light of day ever again, think about that Tony."

He did; he looked thoughtful, he bit his lip until he tasted blood and then he blurted it out.

"Why don't we get married? I'll come to Canada with you."

Sharon just sat there naked and then she opened her legs and lifted her arse. "I think you just like my lovely trimmed pussy, isn't that right Tony?" she swayed her arse from side to side, "What do you say Tony?"

He couldn't take his eyes off her, the pleasure, oh, the pure pleasure. "I say let's get married and escape to Canada."

"I like that word escape, it has a nice ring to it, what do you think Tony?" She was still moving her arse provocatively from side to side. She moved her hand down to touch herself and moaned.

"The thought of you coming to Canada is quite exciting but there is always a price to pay for everything, don't you agree Tony?"

He couldn't take his eyes off her. "Yes, anything you say Sharon, anything at all."

She took a deep breath. "Good, then we will all go to Canada together. What do you say to that, Tony?"

He gave her a quizzical look, "All?"

"My darling Tony, have you not caught on yet? You, me, and my son Callum of course. Now do you understand?"

He was silent for what seemed an eternity. "It will be difficult, but of course there is always a way."

Sharon closed her eyes "That's what I wanted to hear Tony, thank you. Now come here and use your tongue for something other than talking so much."

CHAPTER 7

It was the second week in June, a Friday, lunchtime at one o' clock.

"Why in God's name are we meeting here?" asked Sam Woodman glancing at the surroundings.

"Orders from on high, apparently, Oliver Bolton likes Pie and Mash with Liquor," replied Ben Jones.

Six heavy-set hard looking men, all wearing dark suits had entered Manze, the famous Pie' Mash and Eel shop on Tower Bridge Road at midday. The shop had been there since 1892 and some said the food hadn't changed in all that time. Ben had been visiting Manze for ten years and was right at home. He had ordered double pie and mash and the others had followed suit. They sat in two booths at the back of the shop; Ben wanted to be able to see the entrance and who was coming in. He ate his food slowly, savouring the taste that never altered. He glanced around, so many things changed all the time but Manze didn't. The same shiny green and white tiles, the iron fixtures suspending the marble topped tables, and finally the church type pews to sit on; yes, maybe a bit uncomfortable but original.

He glanced at the door and then the counter; he saw the usual women who had worked there for years, resplendent in their green overalls with checked trim on the collars and cuffs. He laughed to himself, it was like going back in time, and there was nothing wrong with that. Suddenly, Steve Thompson, sitting next to him, nudged him with his elbow and motioned to the door. Ben looked up and saw two men enter the shop. It was them alright; the bodyguard in front looked like he could handle himself and the man behind was well built and looked like it could be Bolton. Ben slid out from the table and stood waiting.

He extended his hand and Oliver shook it "Ben Jones."

Oliver made steely eye contact. "Oliver Bolton, good to meet you Ben; you come highly recommended. So, how's it going?"

Ben laughed, "Well, I've been coming here for over ten years so I'm right at home, but I'm not sure about some of the others. Let me introduce you to the team. Steve, Sam, Bill, Chris and Fred."

The team had stopped eating and were staring at Oliver.

"I'm going to get some food and then we'll talk."

Oliver went to the long counter and ordered double pie, mash, and liquor with a cup of tea.

Two minutes later he squeezed in next to Ben and tucked into his food. Between mouthfuls he started talking.

"So, we are opening some new clubs and we need a high-quality team of people on security; the jobs are well paid, and you should realise we know what we are doing having had clubs before. The Den, our original club in Soho is doing very well and we want to open about twenty more and replicate that success."

Ben looked at Oliver and listened to him and jumped to his first of a few misconceptions. He thought Oliver was soft, he wondered if he'd ever seen violence, he just seemed much too nice for the club business.

Oliver was talking but he could hear two of the men constantly whispering, as could Ben. Ben was about to say something when Oliver stopped talking and looked at the two men.

Everybody turned and eventually the two men looked up.

"Have you two got something you would like to share with us all?"

They shook their heads and again Ben was going to step in but before he could Oliver continued.

"Don't take me for a cunt, shut the fuck up when I'm talking, do you understand? And while we're at it, you're all to call me boss," he looked at the group. "That's simple, isn't it?"

The two men replied quickly in unison, "Yes Boss."

"Good, now as I was saying, we are going to buy back some of the clubs we sold before going to the states; there'll also be some new ones and we go from there."

Ben wanted to know more.

"Have the new owners agreed to sell back to you? I mean it's been a long time."

Oliver smiled, "Well, not exactly but we'll be making offers they will find very hard to refuse."

Ben wasn't convinced at all, he also didn't know that the reason the new group had been hired was that Oliver expected difficulties and it was always good to have some serious muscle on board.

"So, Boss, when are we starting?" asked Ben already knowing the answer.

Oliver smiled "Now Ben, right now," and he shook some more chilli vinegar onto his pie and tucked in.

CHAPTER 8

"It's so good to see you and you haven't changed at all."

Karen had spent hours trying to make herself look as good as possible, but the wine belly wasn't going away, and the facial lines were becoming more, and more difficult to hide. She wore a pair of tight blue jeans with a baggy beige top which covered a multitude of sins.

Karen laughed loudly. "Remember, I'm a copper, I can tell when someone's not telling me the truth."

Lexi laughed. "None of us are getting any younger but whatever it is, you've still got plenty of it."

They both laughed again. Karen had already noticed that Lexi looked fantastic. Lexi was wearing a white trouser suit that showed she was as thin as a rake but still looked gorgeous.

"Come on then Lexi, what's the secret, you really haven't changed."

Paul came through the door with a tray of champagne. "It's because I look after her so well."

"I do things in moderation Karen, always have and probably always will."

Karen nodded, "I smoke, I drink like a fish and lead a very stressful life at home and work, no wonder I look knackered."

Paul handed out the glasses of champagne.

"Well, if you'd come to work for me all those years ago, you would have had a much different life."

"No point having regrets, I've lived my life as I've wanted," she stopped and thought, "It's got me into a lot of trouble over the years but I've lived and have incredible memories."

Paul laughed, "And you're still young, for God's sake; you could still come and work for me Karen."

"I've a year to go for my pension, so thanks again but I think I'll see my time out. One thing is certain though, I will be looking for something to keep me busy when I eventually do leave."

"It's settled then in a years' time you'll come and work for the family."

Karen laughed, "You are so determined Paul, I've always liked that about you."

Paul grimaced.

"What is it?"

"Oh, Lexi has retired me, I'm not even allowed to go and buy the daily newspaper in case I fall over and crack my head."

They sipped at their champagne.

"Hmm, this is lovely Paul."

"Bloody well should be for the price, cost an arm and a leg."

"Nothing's cheap these days."

Lexi interrupted, "I hope you're hungry."

"Positively Starving, what are we having?" asked Karen.

"Poached Salmon with Salad and new potatoes, healthy eating, Karen."

Karen laughed, "If you worked at a nick you would be eating chips and pies! It's food for the boys, stodgy, filling and fattening."

Lexi excused herself to check on the lunch.

"You mentioned Traffickers, tell me more," said Paul with a frown.

"Can't say too much but that's my job at the moment; filthy scum from Romania trafficking in young girls to work as prostitutes, and most of them are fifteen and sixteen."

Paul shook his head, "Disgusting bastards! Should be shot, all of them. Everybody has to earn a living but that, it's the pits and the girls must go through hell."

"They take their passports, keep them penniless and if they become troublesome get them hooked on heroin."

"Jesus! These people are worse than animals! I hope you're dealing with the scum?"

"Takes time Paul; we know who they are but we have to make sure we have a solid case. There's no point arresting them only for the court to release them because there is insufficient evidence. It's a minefield, then of course there's the human rights laws which are always on the side of the criminals."

Paul had already formulated a plan but it would need Karen's cooperation to be put in place.

"Whenever I hear this human rights crap, it makes my blood boil; I feel as strongly as you about this, those kids need to be at home with their families. Anything you need or I can do to help, let me know."

There was a shout from the kitchen. "Lunch is ready!"

"Coming darling!"

Paul and Karen strolled through to the dining room. Paul was upset, he felt so strongly about the girls being trafficked and abused that he wanted to do something about it.

"Looks wonderful Lexi. Mmm, let's tuck in," said Karen, rubbing her hands.

The meal was finished, and they had solved the world's problems. Karen left promising she would return soon. Paul had decided he still wanted Karen to work for the family, and that she would be brilliant working with Oliver. He also couldn't get the thought of the young girls working as prostitutes out of his head, and thought perhaps that could be something to do with losing his young daughter Katie who had been murdered by the lunatic Callum. Lexi noticed Paul taking an unhealthy interest in the trafficked girls and wondered what he was up to. She had enjoyed seeing Karen and wanted to keep the friendship alive.

CHAPTER 9

Tony Bridge was utterly besotted with Sharon, in fact he had decided he couldn't live without her. It was Saturday morning and he was driving down Kentigern Drive towards the Hospital. He was dressed casually in blue jeans, a blue shirt and green jumper. He pulled into the staff car park and parked in the same bay that he always did. He turned the engine off, sat back and took a deep breath, then pushed the door open and stepped out into the bright warm June morning. He looked across the huge site and saw the new Hospital buildings that would open in a month's time; workmen were scurrying to and fro like ants building a new colony.

Broadmoor High Security Psychiatric Hospital opened its doors in 1863. It lies near the village of Crowthorne in South East Berkshire. It was a mixed Hospital up to 2007 but then the female patients were moved to Rampton, and other high security Hospitals.
The Hospital was used as a prisoner-of-war-camp during the first world war, with mentally ill German soldiers inhabiting one of the wings.

The buildings were old and falling to pieces; the new Hospital had taken two years of planning and was now nearing completion. The buildings were all up and the interiors were being decorated and fitted out with furniture. The buildings would be named after tube lines such as Jubilee, Central and Northern while the interior rooms would be named after Tube Stations like The Strand, Piccadilly, Bank, Kensington and many more. Another marked change would be colour usage - buildings would be recognisable by their colours of Red, Green, Blue, yellow and etc. New staff facilities were being introduced as well; security viewing rooms where one person could monitor a huge number of rooms and corridors through cameras. All in all, it was an exciting new beginning for the Hospital.

As Tony signed in with his plastic identity card, he noticed his hand was damp and shaking. He took a long, deep breath and the shaking stopped. He proceeded along the seemingly mile long white corridors to the guard changing rooms, his black steel capped shoes making a clicking noise as they connected with the hard-tiled floor. The smell of disinfectant seemed even stronger than usual. He changed into his thick white cotton trousers and white shirt, then sat on a bench to put on his white trainers. It was eight forty-five am. Other guards arrived and began to change; nobody spoke, there were hundreds of staff in the Hospital and he knew and mixed with very few of them.

Tony was working in the west wing which housed some of the most infamous patients. He had changed shifts with one of his few friends Richard Martin. Tony was on security surveillance and had control of all the doors, and he could move freely around the wing whenever and wherever he liked. He immediately located where Callum Bolton was and watched him as he chatted with several other patients. For just one second, he thought about not going ahead, then he thought of Sharon and Canada and a new start away from the disinfectant and the madness. He looked at the clock, it was 10 am.

The morning went like all the others before it, nothing happened. The patients went through their usual routines. Tony was far from calm and began sweating and getting nervous. He

Bermondsey Pie & Mash

glanced at the clock again, it was twenty-three minutes past ten. It was going to be a very long morning.

Eventually, lunch time approached, and Tony took a bunch of keys off the security board and calmly walked through two security doors into the main interior social room. There were twenty-seven patients in the room and they were getting restless as lunch time approached: five minutes away. Patients liked the routine of time. It was twelve twenty-five. Tony glanced around, he saw where Callum was and noted the guard at the other side of the room.

Tony grabbed one of the nearest patients, a serial killing madman called Andrew Denning and whispered in his ear."

"Andrew, there is no lunch today it has been cancelled."

Denning stood still, taking that in and then started flapping and demonstrating with no one in particular. Two seconds later, he rushed towards other patients, screaming they were not going to be fed and that they would all die of hunger. The shout was taken up by others and some started running to and fro, an within seconds, there was pandemonium. Tony very calmly, opened numerous doors leading out into the gardens, leaving them wide open; and of course, the screaming, very irate patients noticed and ran out of the building. He then found Callum and took his arm and led him to a side door, opened it, pushed Callum through and followed after him. Callum didn't understand what was happening.

"Your mummy," Sharon had told him he must use that expression as Callum would recognise it and know she had sent him. "sent me. Now do as I tell you and soon you will be free."

Callum understood the word free and smiled.

Tony again took him by the arm and walked him calmly without hurrying around the side of the building. They had gone forty feet when Tony stopped and bent down, and retrieved a white plastic carrier bag hidden in a flower bed. He shook the contents out and told Callum to undress, which he did very quickly. He then helped Callum into a pair of black trousers, a white shirt, blue tie, and a neon builders' jacket; the ensemble was finished off with a pair of black safety boots, an orange hard hat and a clipboard and pen. Callum now looked like hundreds of other builders who were scattered across the hospital building sites. Tony packed up the patient clothes and left them in the bag and pushed them back into the flower bed.

"Walk as though you are working here and without a care in the world." Callum nodded.

They set off and Tony's distraction was working: staff were flying in all directions collecting patients from every corner of the site.

They had gone one hundred yards and came close to the first security gate. Tony was then shocked as Callum launched into a performance worthy of the London Palladium.

Callum stopped and turned to look at the building, gesticulating wildy with his hands, then he turned back to Tony, pretending he was discussing some sort of building project. After a

Bermondsey Pie & Mash

minute, they moved on and soon they approached the gate where a guard where a guard was standing, looking worriedly towards the direction of the commotion. Tony's heart was in his mouth.

"Have you heard what's going on? Thirty odd patients running amok, apparently, they thought lunch had been cancelled!" he shook his head, laughing.

Callum said angrily, "Well, I shall be making some serious complaints; my life could have been in danger."

Tony almost laughed at Callum's cheek as he raised his eyebrows at the guard and said quietly out the corner of his mouth, "Fucking builders."

The guard let them through, pleased to get rid of them. The next security gate was even easier as the guard knew they had already passed through the first one.

They were on the outer limits of the new Hospital and Tony was looking but couldn't see her. Builders, carpenters, plumbers, and electricians were criss-crossing the site of ten newly built buildings. It was organised chaos on a grand scale. Then he spotted her, the slightly off yellow boots were the give-away.

"Follow me!" He hurried towards her.

Sharon was dressed as a carpenter with overalls, and tools were hanging out of numerous large pockets; her hair was tucked up into a hard hat.

"Mummy!" Callum went to hug and kiss her, but Tony pulled him back just in time.

"Let's all walk to the van. Follow me," and Sharon led the way.

They sauntered over to a van with "McConnell Builders" written on the side, of which there were several on site. Tony pushed Callum into the passenger seat and shut the door as Sharon got into the driver's side and started the engine and slowly pulled away, heading for the main gate. At the security gate, the young seventeen-year-old Irish lad smiled and waved them through; and seconds later, they were free, and driving down the road.

Tony headed back to the lunch chaos as quickly as he could without raising suspicion.

Sharon drove to nearby Foresters Way and pulled into a secluded space where they had hidden the Ford Focus. They got out of the van. Sharon was crying as she held Callum in her arms for the first time in years. She held him tight, unable, and not wanting to let go.

"Mummy, am I really free?"

"Yes, you are, and we must get moving very quickly!"

Sharon was disturbed by Callum's lack of excitement and put it down to the drugs he was taking. One of her first missions was to wean him off them and onto something less powerful.

CHAPTER 10

It had been a traumatic, first two weeks. Simona had started counting and the average number of men they both serviced a day was fourteen. Some were just blow jobs, many full sexual intercourse, and then the strange ones, men who wanted to be beaten, some who just wanted to talk, some who wanted to be spanked because they had been naughty; the list was endless, and Simona and Ana provided whatever the client wanted. They had also started getting some cash tips, they now knew if they performed to the client's satisfaction, or even went over and beyond what they expected, cash tips could be garnered. They pooled the tips and hid the notes, ten pounds and even some twenties. The notes all went underneath a corner of the carpet in their room. That would have been another mistake that they both would have paid for.

It happened before they started work on a Friday morning. The two girls were in pink dressing gowns in the tiny kitchen, making some warm buttered toast before starting work. The door opened and Albescu entered.

"You have not handed in your tips." And he held out his hand.

The two girls were shaken; they had agreed the money would be needed if they were ever to escape and they had vowed to keep it safe.

Simona answered for the two of them.

"What tips?"

"Don't play games with me, or it will be the worst for you." And he lifted his hand as if to strike her.

She didn't flinch, and stared into his hideous grey, evil eyes.

He laughed, scratching his greying stubble.

"You are a bit tough Simona but this one..." and he looked at Ana. "Come here."

Ana was terrified and was glued to the floor.

He screamed at her, spittle flying from his mouth. "I said come here! You stupid fucking bitch!"

Ana started shaking and took a step towards him. He grabbed her arm and dragged her next to him placing his hand around her throat and he squeezed.

"Do you want me to get my needle and give you injection, you bitch! have you still not understood? We own you, you do as you are told instantly, or we will cut you into pieces and send you back to your parents. Now where is the cash?"

"It's not much, we need it for make-up, for women's things!" shouted Simona.

Albescu was getting fed up. He dropped Ana and took a step towards Simona; he lifted his massive hand and gave her a resounding slap to her face, knocking her backwards.

"The money now, or I will inject into your eyes, blinding you!"

The girls were even more terrified and Ana blurted out quickly, "It is under the carpet, let me fetch it."

He nodded, and she rushed out the door. He held the door open and watched as she opened the bedroom door and lifted the corner of the carpet. A second later she returned and handed him the bundle of notes, it was fifty-five pounds. He counted it and pushed it into his front trouser pocket.

"Is that all of it?" Ana nodded

"Don't fuck with me next time you understand?"

"Yes boss," they chorused.

He left the kitchen and the girls waited a minute before speaking. Simona put her arms around Ana and hugged her.

She whispered, "We win this time," and they hugged even tighter.

The girls had known the thugs would know about tips and that one day they would ask for it. That was why they had split the money and hidden it in two locations. The escape fund was intact, and they planned to use every skill at their disposal to get as much money as possible out of clients to add to it.

They had their warm buttered toast and were soon told the first clients had arrived.

CHAPTER 11

"It's a fair price but as I've already told you, I'm not selling."

Oliver had booked a lunchtime table at E Pellicci on Bethnal Green Road. It didn't look much from the outside, but the food was pure Italian magic.

"Antonio, you are not getting any younger, you need to retire, play with your grandchildren, enjoy the money, travel; there are so many things you could do with twenty million pounds."

Antonio Conte was seventy-two, he coughed all the time probably due to his forty cigarettes a day habit. He was dressed in old baggie blue trousers, a white shirt and red jumper. Nobody would think of him as a multi-millionaire.

Antonio shrugged and lifted his hands, "My children are interested in the business and they must have the chance if they want to."

Oliver hadn't reckoned on Antonio's two daughters wanting to get involved in the business.

"Don't they run a restaurant in Pisa?"

"Yes, but they are thinking about coming over and helping me to run the clubs."

Oliver lifted a fork of the best cannelloni he had ever tasted into his mouth.

"The food is so good here, I must bring my family."

Antonio laughed. "Italian food is the best in the world!"

Oliver finished his food and placed the knife and fork on the white china plate.

"This country is not good for your daughters, it's dirty, there are mugger's and rapists everywhere, it is not safe for them; let them stay in Pisa, give them some money and let them build a restaurant chain at home."

"Oliver, do you not realise Italy is finished, the EU has fucked it so many times it can never recover. The girls are looking forward to coming over."

Oliver leaned forward and lowered his voice, "You owe my father a debt and he is calling it in."

Antonio looked sad, "Yes, it is true, your father let me pay him for the clubs over many years and all done on a simple handshake." He took a deep breath and looked thoughtful.

Oliver just looked at him, the next to speak would lose.

They just looked at each other not speaking.

"Maybe I talk to my daughters again and see what can be done."

Oliver smiled, "That's good Antonio, you know it makes sense for all your family."

There was no explicit threat, but Antonio understood, and his daughters meant the world to him.

"Now, Oliver, we must have some of your fathers favourite Italian dessert, Tiramisu."

Oliver did not want to let Antonio off the hook and he held his hand out.

Antonio looked at it, he clasped it tightly and then slowly shook it, not a word was spoken but the deal had been done; nothing could break the contract that had just been signed except death.

Antonio looked over to the waiter, "Tiramisu, and bring prosecco; we are celebrating."

Oliver smiled and had never been happier in his whole life.

***

"It is a good start and a fair price; what swung it for you?"

"He's old and loves his family, he has made a wise choice."

"How many clubs again?"

"Ten, it's more than I could have hoped for."

"When will it all happen?"

"The legal teams will meet next week, I've told them the deal must be done as quickly as possible, eight weeks if we're lucky."

"Just make sure the due diligence is done properly."

"It will be, don't worry."

"Let me know when you need the money."

"Thanks dad, I'll be in touch soon."

CHAPTER 12

The alarm had sounded an hour after the chaos at lunchtime. The grounds had been searched thoroughly until it was concluded Callum Bolton had taken advantage of the situation and escaped in the confusion.

"Do you want something to eat?"

"I'm not hungry, thanks mummy. I still can't believe I'm free."

"You are free and the first thing we must do is get you back to normal. They have been giving you so many drugs."

"What drugs?" Callum was annoyed.

"I'm guessing a mixture of Benzodiazepines and Antipsychotics."

Callum shook his head, "No wonder I feel like shit."

"When do they give you tablets?"

"In the afternoon, with tea and sponge cake."

Sharon glanced at her watch, it was eleven am.

Sharon had done exactly what Tony had told her, she sped down the M4, eventually turning off into a rural location and then arrived at the Travel Inn in Ramsbury, near Marlborough. Sharon had booked in and they felt safe for the time being.

"I've got to go out, you must stay here."

"No please, mummy, let me come with you."

"Do you want to go back to the hospital?"

Callum looked scared and backed away. "No!"

Sharon held his hand. "It's not safe for you to wander around now. I won't be long."

"Well, all right then, but hurry back."

Sharon was truly shocked at how ten years at the hospital and all the drugs had affected Callum. Where was the headstrong, tough boy she loved so much and whom she would willingly die for? She was determined to get her boy back, no matter what, or how long it took. There were two immediate concerns, one to get him off all the antipsychotic drugs and

secondly, to sort out how they were going to get back to Canada. Tony had said he could not visit for a couple of days as the police would be investigating the escape.
Tony eventually turned up on the Tuesday evening. It had been a fraught three days, lowering Callum's drug intake had been difficult but as far as Sharon was concerned, he was on the mend.

Tony was so happy to see Sharon he was all over her.

"Hey, Tony, not now please! I've got so much on my mind. What's happening in the outside world?"

He took a long deep breath.

"I don't think we have thought this through, there's no way of leaving the country now; every airport, ferry, and train station is being guarded. I kid you not, the whole country is looking for Callum."

Callum was sitting on the bed, listening to the conversation and then he spoke up.

"In that case, we will stay here for the time being as I have unfinished business here."

Tony just stared at him. There was something very different about him. His eyes were shining, and he seemed so much more confident. He was worried and turned to Sharon.

"What about his medication?"

"He's coming off it."

Tony was quiet. He turned to Callum who smiled at him, and again he noticed his eyes were shining like a beacon in the mist.

He turned back to Sharon. "Is that wise, Sharon?"

"Of course, it is, he's my son, I know him better than anybody."

Tony looked unconvinced.

"Don't worry Tony, it will all work out. Now, we need somewhere quiet, like in the country, somewhere we can lay low for a couple of months."

"Who's going to pay for that? I can't afford it."

Sharon smiled. "I'll pay for everything, but you must find the property."

"I'll go off sick and sort it."

"Good Tony, and don't worry, you'll get your reward very soon."

Tony smiled, but if he had looked across at Callum he would have noticed there was no smile on his face.

***

The house was found, a three-bedroom furnished detached property in Forest Lane, near the small village of Tadley, in Surrey. They were over a mile from their nearest neighbours which was perfect. Tony paid six months' rent in advance. It was all working out, Callum was coming off the drugs, they had a lovely house to live in and all was well.

"Mummy, how long are we going to be here?"

Callum and Sharon were sitting at the solid oak kitchen table, having a mid-morning coffee.

"Well, we'll have to see, but definitely for a few months."

Callum clenched his fists tightly.

"And what about him, is he going to be hanging around?"

Sharon gave him a quizzical look.

"I assume you are talking about Tony?"

Callum replied harshly, "Yes, I am"

"You wouldn't be free if it wasn't for him."

Callum didn't look impressed. "Have you paid him something?"

"I have but it hasn't been money; you don't need to know or understand that."

"So, it seems I must repeat myself, is he going to be hanging around?"

"Good you are getting better. Tony will be around until I… we have no more use for him, is that clear enough?"

Callum's face lit up in a big smile "That is just what I wanted to hear, I do love you mummy."

"And I love you too Callum."

CHAPTER 13

New girls had arrived at the flat. Three teenage girls also from Romania. They didn't have time to talk. The girls looked so young, fresh, and innocent; well they wouldn't be like that for long. Simona and Ana were told to pack and be ready to leave in five minutes. They were living out of suitcases anyway so didn't even take the five minutes. They trooped out and were soon in a car heading back to the original flat.

Simona followed Albescu into the hallway and was greeted by a hideous sight. She pushed herself against the wall as a huge man came towards her, dragging a girl by her arm along the floor. Simona could hear the girl moaning in pain and looked at her as she went past. Her face was covered in blood and her eyes were closing because of the bruises; Simona turned away. It would take weeks before the poor girl would be back to normal.

"You see what happens to cunt bitches who don't do as they are told," Albescu shouted at the two girls.

Neither girl spoke and just thanked God it wasn't them. They both headed to the bedroom they had always shared, to be met by another girl. Simona was surprised to see her.

"Who are you?"

"Anamaria. You?"

"I'm Simona, this is Ana."

The door opened and Dulca stuck his head in.

"Do you have nothing to do but talk? Clients will be here in one hour, make sure you are ready." He shut the door.

"How long have you been here?" Simona asked Anamaria.

Anamaria held her face in her hands and started to cry. "Three days. The things I have had to do!" and she cried even more.

Simona wrapped her arms around her and hugged her tight.

"Don't worry, it will not be for ever; you will have a new life again."

Anamaria pulled herself away. "Are you mad? they have my passport, I have no money, I have no idea where I am. What can I do except continue to do as I'm told. Did you see the other girl? She refused to work, she said she would rather die, and the bastard said that was the choice; do you understand that? The choice is work or die."
"We have a plan, all is not lost."

Anamaria laughed, "A plan, what plan?"

"Have you made any tips yet?"

"A few pounds."

"Good. Hide it in two places so when they ask for it, give them only one stash. We will need money when we make our escape."

"Escape!" she shook her head.

Simona was not going to give in.

"Be tough, give the men what they want and extra, get tips and save the money. We will one day get a chance and when we do, we must be ready to take it. Now we must all get ready for the clients."

CHAPTER 14

Oliver Bolton was more than annoyed. He was incensed. Margaret Fenner had cancelled, saying she had changed her mind and was not interested in meeting him and that they had nothing to discuss; she was not selling.

He was sitting with Ben in the CC Champagne Bar at the Hilton Hotel on Park Lane.

"Fuck it! Why has the stupid cunt cancelled at the last moment?" He was looking at Ben but knew he would not get an answer. Ben was there for one reason and one reason only: as muscle. This was not part of the plan; she had four clubs and he wanted them back.

He took a swig of Champagne. "Contact her again, offer her another million, money talks."

Ben didn't usually say anything but on this occasion decided to.

"Boss, she won't be swayed by money. We need to find her weak point."

"Maybe," Oliver was in a foul mood. "I want to know about her family. Get people working on it yesterday."

"Yes Boss. Now, the rest of the day?"

He looked at his gold watch, it was midday. "We're going to go and see a man called Caine." He lifted the Champagne bottle, it was still half full. He plonked it back on the table; eighty fucking quid that cost. Let's go"

They made their way down to the front main entrance and asked the concierge to get their car. They stood waiting and Oliver's mood was not getting any better.

The concierge informed them the car would be a minute, and they headed outside to Oliver's Range Rover.

Soon, they were heading west and were soon speeding down the Kings Road.

"Next left, Beaufort Street."

Ben swung the silver Range Rover left.

"Pull in here, we'll walk the rest."

Ben could tell there was something going on, he didn't like the sound of Oliver's voice or his blank expression.

Oliver set a brisk pace and one hundred yards later stopped outside a mews cottage. "The man's name is Caine and before you ask it's not **Michael Philip**, not that it matters. He's a gay and owns a club that I want back." Oliver pushed the black wooden gate and marched up the cobbled stone path. He pushed the white doorbell and heard the chimes echoing inside the cottage. The door opened to reveal a middle-aged man with long white hair swept back in a pony-tail.

"Well! Look what the fucking cat dragged in."

Ben was shocked, he had never heard anyone speak to Oliver Bolton like that.

"What do you want?"

"Talk," replied Oliver quickly.

"About what exactly?"

"I want the club back."

"Fuck you!" and he went to shut the door.

Oliver kicked it hard and the man flew back into the hall. Oliver walked in, closely followed by Ben.

Ben flew at the man, kicking him hard in the ribs. "Better have some respect Caine or it could get nasty."

"Respect for that wanker!" Caine laughed.

"I want the Twilight club back Philip. Name your price." Oliver said calmly.

"Twenty million!" and he laughed again loudly. "Didn't think you'd like that but that's the price, take it or leave it."

Oliver glanced around the room and then turned to Ben.

"Take him into the lounge and tie him up."

Ben didn't say anything he just gave Oliver a look that said, "Are you sure you know what you're doing"

"Do it!"

Ben grabbed the man, heaved him to his feet and dragged him into the lounge. He sat him in a straight backed heavy chair and tied his arms with a curtain pull.

Oliver came over smiled at him.

"So, what piece of filth are you living with now?"

Bermondsey Pie & Mash

"You bastard Bolton!"

"Find something to cut him with, try the kitchen."

Caine started whimpering and crying, "Please Oliver, I didn't mean it!"

"Who are you living with?"

"Spencer's his name."

"Where is he?"

"Gone to the local shop for milk and chocolates."

Ben reappeared carrying a long, sharp bread knife.

Caine started shaking. "Bastards! The two of you fucking bastards!"

Oliver turned towards the front door as he heard the key in the lock. He looked at Ben who moved close to Caine holding the knife to his throat.

The door opened, and someone stepped in.

A very effeminate voice rang out, "I'm back darling!"

Spencer entered the lounge and gasped as he took in the scene. He dropped the shopping bag and turned to run. Ben was on him in a second knocking him to the floor.

"Stay down gay boy or I'll cut you into pieces."

Oliver strolled over to look at the man.
"You make me puke, you arse loving faggot." And he gave Spencer a good kick in the leg.

He turned back to Caine. "So, the club?"

Caine spat, and it hit Oliver's trouser leg.

Oliver jumped forward raining blows down onto Caine's face and body.

He gasped for breath and stopped.

Caine looked up, "Shall I tell the hired help why you hate me so much?" And he laughed again.

Oliver just shook his head, "Be careful, I only have so much patience. Now, the club. I'll give you two million cash."

"A fair price if I was selling which I have already told you I'm not."

Oliver knew exactly what he was going to do. He looked at Ben and nodded at Spencer.

"No, you bastards!" Caine was spitting and screaming.

Ben moved menacingly toward Spencer who cowed with his hands in front of his face.

Spencer opened his mouth but could not make a sound he was frozen with terror. Ben bent down and pulled the knife across Spencer's thigh, ripping the trousers and cutting deep into the flesh. Spencer screamed, and Caine jumped up to attack Ben who proceeded to smash his fist into his stomach, doubling him up in agony.

"The club or it's going to get much worse," Oliver said in a calm menacing voice.

Ben held the knife up and was ready to strike again.

"Okay, okay! You win! I'll sell you the club! it's yours!"

Oliver smiled. "Now that's better. So, I want the papers drawn up and the deal done quickly. I don't have to tell you what will happen if you mess me about, do you understand?"

"Yes, I understand you bastard! Now, fuck off out of my house."

Ben wiped the knife handle clean and threw it on the floor.

"Remember what I said," and Oliver and Ben left the property.

Caine wrapped a bandage tightly around Spencer's thigh.

"We need to get you to the doctors for a few stitches, don't worry he's a friend of mine, there'll be no questions."

"How do you know that bastard?"

"I fucked him once darling. He thinks I took advantage of a teenager, but I can tell you he loved every minute of it. Now, we need to worry about you. Can you get up?"

CHAPTER 15

Life had settled down and become very mundane. Callum stalked around the house getting agitated at the smallest things, while Sharon did the shopping and kept Tony happy whenever he popped in. The house was large enough for Callum and Tony to avoid each other as they had grown to dislike each other intensely. Tony had insisted that Callum always remain inside the house as the hue and cry had not died down; and it had been weeks. Sharon had weaned him off the powerful drugs and he was getting more, and more like his old self every day.
Callum was sick and tired of the house, what he really needed was a woman, but under the strict regime of Tony, that was impossible. He made do with watching porn on a laptop Sharon had bought him, and jerking off three or four times a day. He had also taken to drinking whisky. He had had a massive argument with Sharon and she finally relented and bought him a bottle. Sharon was concerned that they might have to wait months before leaving the house. She wondered what she was going to do with Tony, but more importantly, what Callum was going to do. It was a difficult situation for all concerned but as Sharon kept pointing out to Callum, at least he was free from Broadmoor.

It was mid-July, Callum had taken to going for short walks in the forest surrounding the house. Sharon and Tony had at first objected but saw that he needed to get some fresh air and be outside. The forest was huge and the likelihood of meeting anyone, let alone the police, was doubtful. Callum used to have his lunch at one o'clock and then go out for a stroll. It was a Tuesday, Tony had left and gone back to his own house, so Sharon and Callum were alone. He finished his ham and tomato sandwich and took the stairs two at a time to fetch his jacket. He heard the shower in the bathroom and stopped on the landing. It was an old house and the bathroom door had not shut properly. He didn't want to, he tried so hard he wanted to move to his bedroom but couldn't; something was drawing him inextricably towards the bathroom. He took the first step and then the few more; then he touched the door and it opened enough. He saw his mummy in the shower, breasts hanging like ripe fruit to pluck off a tree, long legs and arse cheeks of such beauty, he couldn't take his eyes off the sight; it was too much for him. He slipped his hand down the front of his jeans. She suddenly turned, and he knew she had seen him. She held her hand up and motioned for him to enter. He was in another world as he pushed the door fully open; he took a step and nearly stumbled.

"Come to mummy Callum, it will be just like the old days, get undressed and I will wash and look after you."

***

Callum was running at speed, he was holding his hands up, pushing the twig like branches away from his face as he hurtled through the undergrowth. He was confused again, didn't know which way to turn. He ran on and on and on; and finally, he stopped. He could hear talking and laughing. He swept his hair back and walked deliberately towards the noise. He descended through the trees and then he saw it, a small country pub out here in the middle of nowhere. He saw a group in front of the entrance and then they split up, going in different directions. He moved down and stepped out into a small gravel car park, he walked to the front entrance of an old wooden door that looked a hundred years old with a small sign over it that read: The Foresters Arms. He pushed it open and went in and spoke to the man at the bar. "A pint of…" he stopped, he wasn't sure what they had or what to order.

"Why don't you try the real ale? it's on a special price," said a voice from behind him.

He turned to the voice and saw a young woman. She was in her late twenties, long black hair, pretty enough, and quite tall.

"Yes, okay I'll have that, thanks for the advice."

He rummaged in his pocket and drew out a crumpled five-pound note.

A pint of foul smelling watery real ale was placed in front of him on the bar.

"You from round here?"

"Yes, live about a mile away. I was investigating the area and accidently fell on the pub."

"We don't get many handsome young men coming in here."

He was confused again. Was she talking about him?

He smiled and pulled himself together. "Are you going to chat me up then?"

"I might, what do you think?"

"I think you're an attractive sexy woman who I'm definitely interested in."

She stood up and moved to stand next to him. He could smell her perfume, it was intoxicating.

"You better buy me a drink then."

"Be my pleasure," and he smiled at her warmly.

"I'm Rita Philips"

He nearly blurted out his real name, "Steve Cannon."

He suddenly remembered he had no money and the one pound fifty change wouldn't be enough.

"Oh God, I'm embarrassed to say I left my wallet at home."

"Don't worry," said the woman. "I'll get them, same again."

"Eh, not really. Would it be cheeky of me if I said I'd rather have a whisky."

Rita turned to the barman, "Large white wine and a double whisky please."

Callum pushed the pint of beer to one side and as soon as the whisky arrived and took a good gulp.

"You needed that then?" Rita asked, smiling.

"Yes, life's been a bit tough recently." If only she knew, he thought.

He studied her more closely. She was slim, with small breasts, he didn't mind that. His thought drifted back to his mother's breasts, full and ripe. He wanted this woman and he was going to have her. He took another sip of his whisky which had quickly gone to his head.

"So, you must be local," he asked.

"Yes, ten-minute walk."

"Well, shall we get going then?"

Rita half smiled, "I don't even know you, it's a bit quick, isn't it?"

Callum downed the rest of his whisky. "Up to you, believe me it would be good fun."

She looked at him, wondering if she should take the risk.

She knocked back the wine. "Let's go then."

She led the way out of the pub, then turned right and was soon strolling down a pathway back into the woods.

"What do you do for a living?"

Callum had to think quickly. "I'm a writer."

"Oh, really I'm impressed. What are you writing now?"

"Crime fiction. I live in London but had to getaway for some peace. It's so quiet here, it's perfect." He could smell her perfume, he wanted to touch her, to rip her clothes off, to stick his cock in all her holes.

"Why do you live out here?"

"Just got divorced, needed some time to recharge the batteries."

"How much further?"

"We're half way."

Callum looked around and listened, it was perfect and deathly quiet apart from the rustle of leaves on the trees."

"Stop a second." He took her in his arms and kissed her on the lips, he grabbed her arse with his hands and squeezed, she returned the kiss and then pulled away."

"Let's get to my place, it will be more comfortable."

She took another step and walked on.

"Don't you like the outdoors?" he was beyond waiting.

"I do but my bedroom is five minutes away. Be patient, it will be worth it; I promise."

"You have to understand, I can't wait."

She stopped and turned, he smiled as his eyes lit up.

"You'll have to. Let's go."

He was angry, she wasn't listening to him; mummy always listened. She had to be taught a lesson. he looked around and saw a hefty stick and he picked it up.

"You'll do as I fucking well say!" and he smashed the stick down onto the back of her head.

She howled with pain and stumbled, and he was on top of her in a flash, grabbing her by the arm and pulling her into the undergrowth. He pulled her twenty yards to a small clearing.

"You bastard stop it! Stop it! This has gone far enough!"

Callum laughed. "You bitch! We haven't even started yet."

He pushed her to the ground and started to yank and rip at her clothes.

"I'll scream!"

He laughed. "I don't think anyone will hear you!"

He lunged at her blue woollen jumper, yanking it up to pull it over her head, she fell back and kicked with her powerful legs; one caught him on the knee and he groaned in pain. He pulled his fist back and started pummelling her body, the kicks slowed down and she became limp. He pulled up her jumper and pushed up her black bra to reveal small pert breasts, he groped them, squeezing the nipples hard; she muttered in pain. Then he pulled her jeans down and the black knickers came away with them.

"That's better," he said as he stood back.

She was still groggy but managed to speak, "You're a sicko. If you touch me, it is rape, I will report you to the police. This is your last chance to go. Go now."

Police! Callum stopped. Yes, she would call the police! His mind was racing; he would end up back in Broadmoor! She would have to be silenced.

His eyes were shining even more brightly than usual as he undid his belt.

"Don't worry, you're going to love it."

He pushed her over and took her from behind, she didn't say anything or make a sound, she was waiting for it to finish and it didn't take him long. She curled up on the leaves and dirt and prayed he would leave. No one was listening. Then she felt his hands around her throat and then the pressure, it would soon be over, then it went dark.

***

The knock on the door was loud and made DI Karen Foster instantly look up from her desk.

"Yes!"

The door opened and Jeff Swan entered.

"Something's happened?" She put her pen down. Jeff looked as though he was going to tell her something dramatic. He got to right in front of the desk.

"An old friend of ours Callum Bolton…"

Karen was all ears, "Yes, go on"

"He's escaped from Broadmoor."

She was speechless for a few seconds.

"Correct me if I'm wrong, but didn't his father Tony do the same thing?" she shook her head "Was anybody hurt?"

"No."

"Well, I suppose that's something. I wonder if Paul Bolton has heard the bad news."

"He'll go after him, won't he?" asked Jeff.

"Maybe, who knows? He's obviously still sick, and remember, he's been in that nuthouse for years, so God knows what condition he's in."

"Good enough condition to get out, so that tells us something."

"Okay, thanks for letting me know. Anything else happening?"

"No, the Roman case is building up, they brought in more girls two days ago."

"I want those bastards behind bars for years, the misery they cause. I don't want any fuck ups Jeff."

"We should be ready to go in about a week."

"Good, we have surveillance on everybody around the clock?"

"Yes, it's a huge job but it's being done."

"I want those girls back with their parents, where they belong."

"We all do boss, and it's going to happen soon."

"Okay keep me updated." She picked up her pen, signifying the meeting was over and Jeff made for the door.

Karen sat back into the swivel chair and took a deep breath. She put the pen back down and reached for her phone.

"Hello Paul, it's Karen, how are you?"

"Great, Karen, and good to hear from you. What's up?"

"Bad news I'm afraid"

"It's never as bad as you think go on."

"Callum Bolton has escaped from Broadmoor."

There was silence.

"Paul!"

"Yes, I heard. That's bad, very bad news. Jeez! What is wrong with that place? They hold some of the most dangerous lunatics in the world and keep letting them escape. I could run it better myself."

"I thought you should know, he could come after you and Lexi again, and Oliver of course."

She could imagine how he was feeling.

"I know. Extra security's going to cost me a fortune; so be it. When are we going to see you?"

"Soon. If I get any more info, I'll call."

"Thanks Karen, I appreciate it."

"Love to Lexi and speak soon."

CHAPTER 16

Simona pulled the duvet cover up close around their necks. Ana was snuggled in close hugging her tightly.

Ana whispered, "It seems like we have been here for years and it has only been a few weeks."

"I know." Simona didn't know what else to say.

"What happens?"

Simona didn't understand. "What do you mean?"

"I'm talking about the future, what is going to happen?"

"We are going to escape," Simona answered firmly.

"What if we can't? is this our life for ever?"

Simona didn't answer.

Ana spoke again. "Because if it is, I would rather be dead."

Simona hugged her even tighter. "Don't say that, life is precious."

"Tell that to the animals who make us do this."

There was silence until Ana spoke up again, "I'm telling you, if we cannot escape, I will kill myself rather than live like this."

Simona had tears in her eyes and had to stop herself from crying loudly.

"You will do no such thing because you can't leave me on my own."

"I wonder how our families are?"

"Please Ana don't talk about them, you know we will both end up crying buckets."

"I know, but I miss them all so much," she sniffed as warm tears streamed down her face.

Simona wondered what was happening at home. Their parents would definitely have gone to the police; but what the outcome of that had been, she could not guess.

Simona kissed Ana on her forehead. "We must sleep now my sister."

"You called me sister?"

"We are more than even sisters. I would happily give my life if I was sure you could escape."

"Don't say that Simona, it's we both getting away or staying together, nothing else."

"Agreed, now goodnight."

"Goodnight Simona."

***

"Jeff, there is a development on the Roman case."

"Good or bad?"

"Without question good. I have heard from HQ: the Romanian police are sending someone over to liaise with us; apparently, they have a list of missing girls that they believe have been trafficked here."

"That's good news. When is he arriving?"

"Tomorrow morning. Can you pick him up from Heathrow?"

"Sure, what time?"

Karen laughed, "I'm glad you've already agreed; five am." She held her hands up, "Sorry, nothing to do with me."

Jeff shook his head. "No problem, but I'll be finishing early."

"You finish when you like, you know that."

"Where's he staying?"

"Holiday Inn."

Jeff took a deep breath, "It's alright for some."

"It's local so he can even walk there; it makes sense, we don't have to worry about driving him around."

"Yea suppose so. Maybe we can get a couple of five-star meals on his expenses."

Karen pointed her finger at him, "I like that thinking. So, anything else?"

"No, I'll take … what's his name, this Romanian copper?"

Karen looked down at her papers.

"Boian Lupei, not sure how you pronounce it but…" She raised her eyebrows.

"I'll take him to the hotel and we'll see you about nine am?"

"Yea, great, see you then." She watched him turn and walk out of the office.

CHAPTER 17

The mobile phone rang and Margaret Fenner pressed the green answer light.

"Hello Diana, is everything alright?" Diana was the nanny and it was school pick up time.

"There are two men following us, I'm scared. I've crossed the road twice and they keep trailing us, what should I do? I'm worried sick."

Margaret felt panic in her stomach but took a deep breath. "Where are you?"

"In the high street."

"I'll call the po... on second thoughts..."

Margaret had her suspicions what was going on.

"Go into the Costa, I'll be there in ten minutes." She grabbed her bag and rushed straight out through the door.

Diana was terrified for herself but even more for the children, eight-year-old George and seven-year-old Emma. She walked the thirty yards hurriedly and pushed open the Costa Coffee door. There were at least ten or fifteen people in the shop and she instantly felt more relaxed. She approached the counter and ordered a latte and two hot chocolates for the children. She turned just as the door opened and the two men walked in. They looked huge and terrifying. She stood wide eyed, not knowing what to do. The men came and stood next to her at the counter. The children were staring wide eyed at the men and Diana grabbed their shoulders to turn them round. Just as she did so, one of the men spoke quietly so no one else could hear.

"Lovely children Mrs, so well behaved."

Then the other one chimed in, "Got to keep them safe nowadays don't you agree Mrs?"

Diana couldn't speak, she was shaking.

"Lovely kids, be a terrible shame if anything were to happen to them, don't you agree Mrs?"

Diana burst out crying and that was the signal for the two men to walk back out through the door.

A few minutes later, the door flew open and Margaret rushed in; she saw them sitting at a corner table. Diana looked distressed and had obviously been crying.

"Are you all okay?" she touched the two children affectionately while looking at Diana. "Pull yourself together for Christ's sake!"

Diana wiped her face and sniffed loudly.

"They threatened the children," Diana blurted out.

"What did they say?"

"Said it would be awful if anything happened to them, said they had to be kept safe."

"I'm sorry Diana it must have been awful."

"The children are safe now, but shouldn't we call the police?"

Margaret was rattled, she knew who it was. It was that bastard Bolton; there were no witnesses and she knew they weren't afraid of the police.

"No police, I have an idea who it was and what they want."

Diana was lost. "Mrs Fenner, the children were terrified beyond belief. Please call the police."

"No. Wait here, I'll be a minute." She turned and went outside, and Diana saw her take her mobile out of her pocket.

"Hello Margaret, how are you?"

"You fucking bastard, Bolton! My children! You dared to threaten them! You fucking piece of shit!" Margaret was screaming down the phone. "You fucking coward! Threatening children is as low as you can get, and you are beneath that, you are scum, total scum!"

"Well now you've got that off your chest, can I assume we have a deal for the four clubs? it's an extra million for you."

Margaret went quiet; she didn't need the agro, the children were her life.

"You have a deal Bolton, but don't ever come near my children again or I'll come after you myself!"

"My lawyer will be in touch, you've made the right decision. Goodbye Margaret."

He heard her say bastard one more time before the line went dead.

He turned and smiled at Ben, "You see Ben, with a little creative thinking, things can improve very quickly. Now, how about a drink to celebrate our newly acquired four clubs?"

CHAPTER 18

"Go into London? Are you thinking straight?"

"I was better off in fucking Broadmoor, at least I had friends there."

"Calm down, shouting will get us nowhere at all," Sharon waded in placatingly. "Tony, is there anything Callum can do?"

"I've told you both a hundred times, go out if you like but you will eventually be seen, and you will be caught. It's up to you."

All three of them went quiet.

"I suppose we could do something creative with make-up and clothes."

"Change the colour and style of his hair, give him a tash or beard or even both," said

"I'll write a list. Can you get the stuff for me please, Tony?"

"Of cause, I'll bring it at the weekend, I'm off duty." He was waiting and expected Sharon to say something positive and be happy, but she said nothing.

He shook his head in anguish, thinking he'd got himself into a right mess.

Sharon got up from her chair and took Tony's hand.

"You're not looking happy and I have the perfect thing to cheer you up."

She led him to her room and as she pushed open the door she whispered in his ear, "I've been holding it back for a special occasion but I think it's time I gave you my arse. Are you happy?"

He'd always wanted to, but she'd always said no. He smiled happily.

"No talking. Get your clothes off and stick your beautiful arse up in the air." And he began ripping at his belt to remove his trousers.

Callum had immediately known what mummy meant when she said she was paying Tony, but it wasn't money. A minute later the grunting and familiar sounds of coupling emanated from the bedroom. He couldn't listen, he needed more sex. Fucking the woman in the woods had been exciting but he needed more. There was a loud gasp, it was mummy being fucked by that monster, Tony.

"That's it, push back, take it all in!" He heard the bastard Tony shout.

Callum jumped up and made for the back door. He was outside taking in deep breaths of the cool forest air. He relaxed and started thinking of what to do, and then he had an idea.

***

It was a lovely white painted cottage with ivy climbing up the walls next to the old wooden front door. He stopped to listen, there were no sounds. He walked slowl,y trying to avoid stepping on anything that could make a noise. He lifted the latch on the front door and pushed, he was surprised when it gave. He pushed it fully open.

"Hello! Anyone home?" Silence

He entered the low-ceilinged hallway and shut the door behind him. He stood still and listened again, there was silence apart from the chirping of birds outside in the woods. He noticed the staircase on his right but went left into the kitchen which had dark wood kitchen units with a backdrop of white and blue tiles; it was very clean. He opened the fridge which contained half jug of milk, butter, some leftover pasta in a bowl, a small loaf of brown medium sliced Hovis bread, Dijon mustard, a bottle of unfinished white chardonnay wine and a plastic container of sliced Ham. He pulled the wine out and unscrewed the top and put it to his mouth and gulped it down; soon it was finished, and he wiped his mouth with his jacked cuff. He turned and left the kitchen and entered a tiny lounge. There was a small television and not much else. He looked out of the French doors that led out onto a manicured lawn. Who cuts the grass? A gardener it must be. She wouldn't be here, maybe she didn't need to be. He wouldn't have to go into the house, but how would he be paid? He stopped thinking and listened, still silence.

For a second, he was scared. He pulled himself together and started climbing the stairs, he wanted to see her bedroom. There were two, he went in the first larger one which had to be hers. He scanned the room, taking in the pink walls, the white duvet covered double bed. Why had he killed her? It could have been regular sex in a lovely double bed. He shook his head, it had been a mistake. He noticed a bedside set of drawers; he pulled the top one open, inside were a collection of knickers and bras. He grabbed them and threw them onto the bed. He opened the second and was surprised to see a huge black dildo and a jar of some sort of lubricating cream. He took them out and threw them on the bed as well. The third drawer had tissues, socks and three neatly folded white t-shirts. He went to the small dressing table with lots of makeup. Mummy wanted make-up; he went to pick some up but stopped. If he took them, she would want to know where they came from. Instead, he picked up a red lipstick and threw it onto the other items on the bed.

Other items in the drawer were some cheap looking bracelets, rings and earrings. He fingered them for a second and then dropped them back down. He opened the tall large cupboard door to find a small selection of dresses, jeans, shirts, and jackets on old metal hangers. He shut the door and turned back to the bed. He sat on the side and started rummaging through the knickers and bras - red, blue, white cotton, lacey, all sorts of styles and sizes. He wanted to choose his favourite; he picked several up but couldn't take his eyes off the plain white cotton knickers and matching bra. He lifted them to his nose, they smelt fresh and clean. He put them back and lifted the dildo; it felt heavy. He pictured the woman lying on the bed masturbating with the dildo; he was becoming excited and could feel an erection growing.

Bermondsey Pie & Mash

He adjusted the high mirror and took a step away. He smiled, admiring the sight of the thickly applied bright red lipstick on his lips, and he was wearing the white cotton knickers and bra set. He had tucked his semi erect cock under his arse and was moving his hips from side to side. The underwear felt wonderful against his skin and he decided to keep them on. Next, he picked up the dildo; it must have been eight inches long and thick. He put it down and picked up the jar of lube. He turned the top, took it off and scooped out a dollop and rubbed it all over the dildo. He climbed on the bed, resting his back on the headboard. He pulled the white knickers down and opened his legs lifting them back towards himself. He then moved his right arm down and gasped as he pushed the dildo…

He pushed open the back door to see mummy and Tony sitting at the breakfast room table drinking coffee.

"Hello mummy. Any coffee?"

"Where have you been? We've been worried sick."

"Just getting a bit of fresh air. I haven't been that long."

Sharon looked at her watch, "Three hours. What the hell have you been doing?"

"Nothing mummy, just strolling around; there is nothing to do here."

Sharon knew him so well and knew he hadn't just been wandering around.

"Have you cut your lip?" She got up to look more closely.

"Don't worry, it was a branch. I didn't see it." And he quickly wiped his lip with his sleeve.

Sharon sat back down as the red mark disappeared.

"Kettle's boiled. Can you make it yourself?"

"Of course, mummy. I know how to make coffee."

Sharon smiled, and Tony wanted to throw up.

Callum moved towards the kettle, enjoying the sensation of the cotton knickers and bra rubbing against his skin.

CHAPTER 19

Jeff felt like a right prat. He was holding a piece of card in the air with Boian Lupei written across it in biro. It would be a miracle if the Romanian copper saw it, let alone read it. The flight from Bucharest was twenty minutes late landing and Jeff was getting very cheesed off. He had arrived at British Airways Terminal five at four thirty am, just in case the flight landed early. He should have known better. He glanced up at the flight information board and ran his eye down the list; good he had landed, so now, hopefully, Boian was going through luggage collection and passport control. He wondered if Romania was in the European Union, if it was he would be out very quickly, if not, he might have to even go through channels to confirm the officer was on Government business. The doors from arrivals kept swinging open as passengers from all over the world walked through. Jeff hadn't a clue what Romanians looked like but kept studying the people as they poured through the doors. He hoped his copper's instinct would help in identifying Boian Lupei, a fellow police officer. He saw several scruffy CID types but none of them turned out to be Lupei. It had been forty minutes and Jeff thought he might have missed him. The doors opened again and a continuous flow of passengers pushing trolleys entered the cavernous arrivals area. Jeff pushed to the front of the rails and held the placard up high. Young women with children, old men and women, smartly dressed business people, scruffy student types, they all poured through and no sign of Lupei.

"Fuck!" he whispered to himself as a hand suddenly touched his shoulder. He spun around to be confronted by a very smartly dressed, tall handsome man.

"I am Boian Lupei from Romania. You must be a metropolitan police officer, no?"

Jeff smiled and didn't remember the man coming through the doors. He looked at Boian and his first thought was that Romanian coppers dressed much better than their counterparts in the Met. He thought Lupei's suit was handmade and he had a purple silk tie and a very expensive looking lighter shade of purple shirt. Lastly, Jeff sneaked a look at the shoes which were pure, dark, brown leather.

Jeff held out his hand, "Jeff Swan."

Lupei shook it warmly. "Boian Lupei, very pleased to meet you and thank you for picking me up."

Jeff laughed. "Someone had to, and I drew the short straw."

Lupei looked confused, because although he spoke good English he didn't understand the comment.

Jeff grabbed one of Lupei's bags. "Let's go. A good flight?"

"Alright, packed in like..." he hesitated. "Sardines," Jeff added.

Lupei laughed loudly, "Yes, like sardines!" and he laughed again.

Jeff smiled, thinking it wasn't that funny but happy that the Romanian seemed like a reasonable sort of bloke.

"Where are we going?"

"Holiday Inn," Jeff smiled. "It's a nice hotel; you'll be very comfortable."

"Good, and when do I get to visit the police office?"

"We call it a station, police station."

"The police office is in a train station?"

Jeff burst out laughing. "I can see we're going to have some fun! No, not in a train station!"

They were striding across the vast expanse of Terminal five when suddenly they both heard screaming and shouting about a hundred yards away near to the shops and restaurants. Jeff dropped the bag, turned quickly, and started jogging towards the commotion.

***

Ted Morris had known Paul Bolton for years. They went back to the old Bermondsey days when Ted use to deal in smuggled cigarettes. He had heard the word and rang to see what was what; they had then met in secret at night in a car park in Brentwood Essex. Paul explained the situation to Ted and a couple of days later Ted confirmed that he would do it.

The man had come through arrivals a minute after Boian Lupei. The man was accompanied by his wife and to anybody looking at them, they were typical Americans: tall, overweight, and dressed in gaudy white shorts and multi-coloured shirts and jackets. Ted had been watching for an hour, he checked the photograph again, and again, so he would not miss them. The man had finally arrived, and Ted nonchalantly followed them as they made their way to the Italian restaurant Carluccios. He quickened his pace and caught up with them just in front of the restaurant door.

"Ethan Babich?"

The man stopped and turned around, opened his mouth to speak but nothing came out as he felt a sharp pain in his stomach; it was a searing pain and getting worse. Ted pushed the heavy sharp hunting knife deep into the man's stomach and started cutting in an upwards motion. The man's wife was screaming.

He leaned into the man's face and whispered, "Welcome to London. Compliments of Paul Bolton," and he smiled widely.

The huge man's blood and pink guts were beginning to spill onto the concourse as other passengers started screaming and running in every direction. Ted continued to hack away until the man fell forwards and landed with a crash onto the hard concourse floor. Ted was in no rush; he calmly plunged the knife into the fat man's back, stabbing in and out and then carving through flesh as hard and as deep as he could. There was a loud rush of air followed by the noise of the man shitting himself; the stench was disgusting. At last Ted pulled away as the man became still, dead. Ted's hand was covered in mottled intestines and thick dark blood. He dropped the knife and calmly started walking back across the concourse towards the exit. He had taken ten paces when he heard a voice behind him.

"I'm an armed police officer! Stop where you are and get on the floor!"

Ted continued walking.

"Stop and lie down on the floor or I will shoot!"

Ted continued walking.

"This is my last warning, stop where you are and lie down on the floor!"

The armed police officer was standing aiming directly at Ted's back.

Ted stopped and turned around, paused, and then calmly slipped his hand into his jacket and started to withdraw something.

The high velocity shell exploded in his heart throwing him backwards onto the floor killing him instantly.

Jeff heard the shot and saw the man hit the floor. He grabbed his badge and waved it in the air shouting.

"Police officer! Don't shoot!"

There was pandemonium as people rushed away from the scene. Mrs Babich, her hands smeared with her husband's blood, was still screaming loudly as she knelt beside her butchered husband's body, until a waiter from the restaurant grabbed her by the arm and dragged her inside the door.

Jeff reached Ted first; he took one look and knew he was gone. Blood was pouring out of the bullet wound in his back. He turned and looked at the fat American man on the floor, blood and guts were running in a river across the concourse.

Boian Lupei arrived panting and wide eyed.

Paramedics and what seemed like hundreds of armed police officers arrived to seal off the concourse. Terminal five was closed and then the forensics team arrived to begin the painstaking work on the crime scene.

Jeff had been asked to provide a statement; he and Lupei didn't leave Heathrow until 11.30am.

CHAPTER 20

"Ana, what's wrong?"

It was ten am, Simona had woken to find Ana roasting hot and sweating profusely beside her.

"I feel terrible. God, I think I'm going to die," Ana said weakly.

Simona felt her forehead, it was so hot she couldn't believe it.

"You have a fever. I must tell someone."

She jumped up from the bed and quickly left the bedroom. She heard talking in the kitchen and pushed the door open. Ciprian Albescu was drinking coffee with another man she didn't recognise. Before she could speak Albescu barked at her.

"What do you want?"

"Ana is very ill, she needs a doctor."

"Give her some aspirin, work starts soon." And he turned away.

"Listen, she cannot work, she is very ill, come and see for yourself."

"I'll come when I have finished my coffee. Now get out!"

Simona shut the door and hurried back, muttering bastard as she went.

Ana was still very hot to the touch, so Simona rushed to the bathroom and soaked a flannel in cold water and quickly applied it to Ana's forehead and the shock of it made her open her eyes.

"That's nice, thank you, Simona."

"If you're trying to get a day off, you have succeeded, there is no way you can work like this."

The door opened and Albescu entered. He looked at Ana and his expression changed briefly. He put the back of his hand on her forehead and then spoke.

"The quack will be here in a couple of hours, meanwhile give her aspirins and keep the cold compresses going until he arrives. Neither of you work today but you will make the time up and the money you are going to lose us."

Simona just looked at him and Albescu knew exactly what she wanted to say to him.

He lifted his fist as if to punch her. "Say it then if you're brave enough!"

Simona smiled, "I must wet the flannel." she stood up and waited in front of him. He turned and left the room. Simona went to the bathroom, muttering all the way, "bastard, bastard, bastard."

The doctor arrived at two pm. He was dressed in jeans and a black leather jacket; he did however carry a black bag that looked like one that a doctor would carry. Ana's condition had not improved. The doctor pulled back the single sheet and lifted her nightie. He examined her thoroughly; he pressed all over her abdomen and when he pressed a certain area she winced in pain.

"Tidy up," he said to Simona and walked out.

He was also a Romanian and his name was Florin. He had been struck off in Romania for corruption and negligence. He opened the kitchen door and shut it behind him.

"The girl has acute appendicitis, if she does not have an operation very soon she will die."

"Shit!" blasted Albescu. "You are sure?"

"Without question. What do you want to do?"

"Can you do the operation?"

Florin thought he was completely mad. "No! She needs expert care. This is serious, she should be in a hospital."

"It is not you're concern." He took out a wad of notes from his pocket. "How much?"

"Two hundred."

Albescu peeled off ten twenty-pound notes and handed them to him.

"Thanks, see you again."

"What are you going to do?" Florin asked as he pocked the cash.

Albescu raised his voice. "It is not you're concern, you have been paid goodbye."

Florin opened the door and left the flat.

Simona had crept to the kitchen door, she could not hear every word, but she did hear something like Appendix; she knew what that meant, and that Ana needed urgent help. She sat mopping Ana's brow and waited for Albescu to come and see them. It had been half an hour and he still hadn't come. Simona had waited long enough. She stormed to the kitchen and slammed the door open. Albescu jumped to his feet.

"You fucking bitch! What do you want?"

"What is happening with Ana? She needs to go to hospital."

"Yes, she is going to hospital in..." he looked at his watch. "about ten minutes, don't worry, a nurse we know will take her to the local hospital; he is on his way."

Simona looked at him steadily. "Good, because if anything should happen...," she didn't finish.

"Get the fuck out of here now before I lose my temper! Go on, fuck off!" He shouted.

About twenty minutes later, another man arrived at the flat. He had an old rickety wheelchair with him and seemed like a nicer man. They loaded Ana into the chair, strapped her in and wheeled her out of the flat and into the lift. Simona watched from her window as they loaded her onto the back of some sort of medical-van and drove off.

Simona went to the kitchen again.

"I want to visit her in hospital"

"No."

"I give my word I will behave."

"No."

"How long will she be away?"

"A week to get over the operation and a month to convalesce."

"And then she will come back here?"

"I expect so, a new girl will arrive later today to cover."

***

The van pulled off the makeshift road and drove deep into Epping forest. The two men stopped near a newly dug six-foot hole in the ground. They opened the back door of the van and pulled the wheelchair onto the lift. Ana was slumped to the side and then she managed to speak.

"Am I at the hospital?" she was delirious.

"Yes."

"Are my mama and papa coming to visit me?"

"Yes, they will be here tomorrow, rest now child."

They turned the wheelchair so it was facing the hole in the ground and then pushed. The chair fell crashing to the bottom of the hole and landed heavily in six inches of water. The two men picked up shovels and started to refill the hole with earth.

"Doing anything tonight?"

"No."

"Fancy a couple of pints and a curry then?"

"Sure, sounds good, maybe we get lucky and meet some horny bitches."

"Now you're talking."

CHAPTER 21

It was nine am. Sharon had been working on him for an hour.

She laughed out loudly. "Even I wouldn't recognise you!"

Callum was standing in front of the mirror and couldn't believe it was him either.

Sharon had given him a dark brown long-haired wig. He had also not shaved for days and had a very healthy tash and beard stubble. An earring had been added and the overall effect was startling. He was wearing beige corduroy trousers with a sixty's flower patterned blue shirt. The final piece was a light blue linen jacket. He adjusted the lapels and couldn't take his eyes from the mirror. He was very pleased he knew he could go out and no one could possibly recognise him.

"Mummy, it's wonderful! You've done a very good job! It's incredible." And he couldn't stop shaking his head in disbelief.

"Perhaps I should become a film star dresser or something similar. It looks marvellous!"

Callum flexed his muscles and felt his strength had returned. The copious amounts of good food mummy had plied him with had added bulk to his muscles and he was back to his pre-hospital weight. He was also taking a very small dose of an anti-psychotic drug, he felt back in total control of his nerves and sanity.

"I'm going out," declared Callum in a loud voice.

"Are you sure you're ready?"

"Look at me mummy, I'm like a new person! Nobody would have a clue I was an escapee from Broadmoor nut house!"

"Please don't talk like that darling, you know I don't like it."

"Sorry mummy. So can I go?"

"Well, yes, suppose so. But where exactly are you going?"

"Up to the local pub for a start."

"Is there a local pub around here?" asked Sharon with a frown.

"In fact, why don't we go together?" Replied Callum.

Sharon liked that idea as she would be able to keep an eye on him **and at the same time, judge the reaction to the disguise.**

"That's a great idea but they will only be serving coffee, it's too early for alcohol. I'll just quickly change. Oh, by the way do you know where the local pub is?"

Callum knew it was a trick question. "How would I know? I've been a virtual prisoner here for weeks. We'll just drive up the road until we come to one."

Sharon was thinking and didn't move.

"Go and get ready then."

"Okay, I'll be down in a minute."

Sharon disappeared up-stairs and Callum continued to stare at himself in the mirror.

They'd driven about a mile when Callum spotted the Foresters Arms. "Do you think they serve coffee in the mornings?"

"I'd guarantee it, stuck out here in the middle of nowhere. They need to take every penny they can get."

Sharon pulled into the car park and they jumped out.

Callum pushed the wooden door open, expecting to find it empty but immediately heard chatter and laughing. Sharon was surprised too, she did a quick count - there were seven people in the bar, and it wasn't only coffee they were serving; huge plates piled high with sausages, eggs, bacon and fried potatoes sat in front of hungry customers.

"Good morning," said the cheerful young girl behind the bar. "What's your pleasure?"

Sharon turned to Callum. "Well I don't know about you but I'm having the works."

"Me too," Callum couldn't resist a full English.

"So, two full English then. Tea or coffee?"

"Coffee for both of us please," said Sharon.

"That's twelve pounds please. Take a seat and I'll bring it over as soon as it's ready."

Sharon paid with a twenty-pound note. "Thank you."

They went and sat in the corner and no one paid them any attention at all.

The large breakfast was devoured with gusto and it was time to leave the pub.

"Mummy, can you drop me at the station please, and I need some cash."

Sharon looked worried. "Station, where are you going?"

"Just local, you know I love trains."

"When will you be back?"

"Mummy, I'm an adult not a child. I'll be back when I'm ready."

"Well, okay." she rummaged in her bag and took out her wallet. "Is twenty enough?" He smiled and raised his eyebrows. "Okay then, forty," and she gave him two twenties.

"So, shall I cook dinner for you?"

"Of course, I'll be starving by tonight."

The nearest station was a few miles away at Silchester. They arrived at midday to find a tiny ghostlike station with no office and just a ticket machine.

"I wonder how long you'll have to wait for a train."

"Doesn't matter. I have nothing else to do. Thanks mummy, see you later."

Sharon drove off, reminding Callum to phone when he got back. He walked towards the large board with a plan of the rail network. He could get a train to Reading or Basingstoke depending on which turned up first. From those two stations, he could be in London within an hour. He was excited and bought a travelcard day ticket from the machine for twelve pounds. He sat on the platform for thirty-five minutes, and it was a very long, quiet thirty-five minutes. He knew a train was coming as three men and two women turned up practically all at the same time, obviously knowing a train was due. And it turned out just so.

It was Reading and then a fast train to London Paddington and then he could go wherever took his fancy on the tube. Two pm found him on the Bakerloo line, and five stops later, he alighted at Oxford Circus. He climbed the steps and came out into Regent Street amidst a bright sunny July day. He stood for a moment and surveyed the area. He loved London, there was just something about it. He was on automatic pilot. He started walking down Regent Street. He passed the Apple store, H &M and on past Hamlet's and Levi's. He took the next left, and first left and he was there. He looked up the street and there it was, the Den nightclub, home of Paul Bolton and his evil offspring Oliver. He thought back to the moment he strangled Katie Bolton; she was a beautiful young woman. Then he thought of the nymphomaniac Mandy. He wondered where she was. He strolled slowly towards the entrance, nothing had changed, two heavies outside the door and he could see more inside, Paul Bolton never took chances.

As he became level with the entrance, the doors opened, and four well-dressed men left the club. They looked like business men who had had a very good expense account lunch. He stopped again and pretended to look in the shop window; expensive cars pulled up and

Bermondsey Pie & Mash

spewed out well dressed patrons even in the middle of the afternoon. Then it happened, a silver Mercedes pulled up and the customary door-man opened the rear door, and an older man got out and Callum recognised him instantly. It was him, the devil himself, Bolton. He wanted to rush across the road and attack him. If he'd had a gun, he would have taken a shot; it was all he could do to stop himself calling out. He walked across the road to get a closer look. It was him and he was surrounded by four body guards as he chatted to the door-man, then he disappeared inside. Callum ambled to the entrance and looked inside, he felt an arm on his shoulder.

"Move on!" was the command from one of Bolton's gorillas.

"Take your fucking hand off me or you'll be sorry," spat Callum.

The man laughed. "You and who's army mate? Go on, clear off!"

Callum strolled on and then came to the realisation he wasn't fit enough to tangle with bodyguards or anyone else for that matter. It was something he would have to remedy very quickly. Ten years in the nut house had turned him soft and he needed to re-hone his martial arts skills; it was something he would start immediately and enjoy. He stopped and glanced back at the club with shining eyes; he would love to have taught them all a lesson, the bodyguards, Paul Bolton, Oliver and of course not forgetting the delectable Lexi. He had time, it would make the reckoning even more enjoyable when it came.

Callum strolled around Soho, enjoying the sights and sounds, none more so than the gorgeous looking tourists and Chinatown oriental woman. It got to six pm and he was exhausted. He made his way back to the tube and headed to Paddington. It was rush hour and he was cursing as he was jostled to and fro by the large crowds getting on the trains. He had to stand on the Basingstoke train which annoyed him even more, but it was a fast train and before long he was getting out to connect with a local one to Silchester. He waited another fifty minutes for the local train and finally got off at Silchester at nine fifteen pm. He was exhausted. He glanced at his mobile, it was black, he had not charged it for at least two days and it had gone dead.

"Shit!" he muttered. He checked his pockets, he had plenty of money.

The cab pulled up outside the Foresters Arms and he paid the driver. A minute later he was standing at the small bar with a whisky in his hand. There was a different barmaid on and he couldn't stop admiring her huge breasts. He finished his drink and beckoned to the girl.

"What's your fancy?" She asked quietly.

He couldn't help himself and replied whilst looking directly at her heaving chest, "Asking that could get a beautiful young lady in a lot of trouble"

"So, what did you have in mind then?"

"You name it, I'm up for it."

"Why don't you take your eyes off my tits for a second and actually look up at me?"

"Sorry," and he looked up and smiled. "What's your name?"

"Abigail, you?"

"Cyrus."

"That's an unusual name."

"I'm unusual, you should try me."

"Well, I know you'd like to get your hands on my tits, but what else are you going to do to me?"

Callum was in his element, talking about sex was a great starter before the main course.

"Tongues are not just for talking, there's so much more you can do with them."

"Now you're getting my attention."

Callum was more than surprised that he'd been in the pub twice and looked like he could be making it two out of two.

"So, what time do you finish?"

"Closing time is eleven."

"Where do you live?"

Abigail smiled and laughed, "This is my pub, I live upstairs."

"Really?"

"I knew you'd like that, not far to go for a good shag, eh?"

"Well, I wouldn't want to presume."

"You can presume. How about a top up?"

Callum held out his glass. "Don't mind if I do, thanks."

Abigail disappeared to serve a punter and Callum decided to sit at one of the empty tables. He sipped at his whisky, trying to fathom out what was happening and then it hit him. They were in the middle of nowhere, most of the pub customers were couples, so what was a full-blooded young, sexy woman with big tits meant to do. The night dragged on but at least he had a free continuous supply of whiskies. Finally, it got to eleven pm and the pub closed with an old-fashioned ring of a bell. The last punter left and in seconds, Abigail was standing in front of him.

"Let's go then."

"What about the clearing up?"

"You can help in the morning, that's if you have any strength left," and she laughed loudly.

He was climbing the stairs, watching her nice sized arse swaying from side to side when he had a terrible thought. The wig! What the hell was he going to do? He couldn't bear the thought of it coming off in a moment of passion. Shit! What to do?

Then he said casually, "I'm wearing a wig at the moment."

Abigail stopped and didn't speak for seconds.

"Does your cock get up alright?"

"Of course."

She started climbing again. "Thank God for that, I need a good fuck and I hope you're big."

"I don't get any complaints."

She laughed. "That's what I like to hear."

CHAPTER 22

"So where is the girl now?"

"We haven't established…, well, we're trying to get more information…"

Karen exploded. "Just answer the fucking question! Where is she?"

The officer rubbed his face with his hands. "We have no idea."

Karen was either going to scream or cry but refrained from either.

"Why wasn't the van followed?"

"Steve called in sick, we got the photos, that's all."

Karen shut her eyes and heard a knock at the door.

She didn't mean to, but she shouted, "Yes come in!"

Jeff and somebody who could only be the Romanian Police officer entered the meeting room.

She said in a raised voice, "Sit down and listen to this shit."

She picked up the photos and studied them again.

"This young girl is sick, you see the way her head is lolling to the side? She looks like shit, she looks seriously ill."

"Yes Ma'am."

"She is strapped in a fucking wheelchair and cannot move…" Karen stood up and took a deep breath. "We have failed, we have let two Romanian thugs take this young girl who we believe to have been trafficked here to work as a prostitute, and we have no idea where they have taken her!" She turned to the surveillance officer, check the hospitals…"

"It's not my job I'm a…" the officer began to say but Karen was almost screaming at him. "You'll do as your fucking well told" she stopped and sat back down. "We are all under pressure! Forget it, go back to your surveillance."

She turned to Boian Lupei. "Officer Lupei, perhaps you would be good enough to check through these photographs and see if you can help with any identifications." She handed him a file.

Lupei took the file and placed it on the table. He lifted his colossal black case and opened the zip. He took out a folder with clear plastic sleeves which were chock-full of hundreds of images of girls. He opened Karen's file and started looking.

Karen turned to Jeff. "What a shit morning! Any update on the murder at Heathrow?"

"I spoke to the investigating officer; apparently, the victim was a casino owner name of Ethan Babich who had just arrived from Las Vegas. The killer was an elderly man who has no record and it all seems a bit strange. The man looked as though he was going for a weapon in his jacket but there was nothing; it was as though he wanted to be shot. A madman I reckon.

Karen shook her head. "Good job it's nothing to do with us then, sounds like a tricky one."

"Could be."

"I have a match," shouted Lupei excitedly.

"Her name is Ana Funar, sixteen years old, comes from a small village called Ploiesti, reported missing in June. She was on a flight to London on June 10th, because we are in the EU there is no need for visas, so you just get on a plane and next you are here in London."

"Sooner we leave the EU the fucking better," spat Karen.

Lupei looked at her but kept his mouth shut. There were no senior female police officers in Romania, it was a very male dominated force, and he could see she was in a very bad mood.

"We got a window photo of another girl in the same flat; the photo next to her; check it please."

Fifteen minutes later, they knew that the girl left in the flat was sixteen-year-old Simona Dumitrescu.

Boian Lupei looked Karen in the eye, "Officer Foster we want our girls back and we want the bastards responsible to be extradited so we can deal with them in Romania."

Karen looked thoughtful then said, "Nothing is more important than releasing all the girls from their living hell, and I give you my word we will not rest until they are back with their families, and those responsible are locked up for a very long time. The bad news is that they will almost certainly have to serve their sentences here because of the EU human rights laws."

"That's a pity because we know how to treat scum like these bastards, maybe we'll be lucky, and we can shoot them dead."

"Do you have a weapon with you?"

"No, you know I am not allowed to carry a weapon in a foreign country."

"Just checking," and she smiled at him. She took a closer look at Lupei. He was handsome, well dressed and maybe a couple of years younger than her; she knew the signs, she was interested, but was he?

CHAPTER 23

"So, it's going well?"

"Better than I could have hoped for. What's the financial situation?"

"We're okay, don't worry about the money, that's my job."

Oliver and Paul Bolton were sat in the lounge of the Virginia Water house. Lexi was out shopping so they had the house to themselves.

Paul looked thoughtful. "So much for the big move to the States. But you know, sometimes, things just don't work out. I can't believe we're back in the club business and with so many of the old ones."

"Why don't you come and visit some, we could do a grand tour together."

Paul nodded. "I'd like that, maybe even see some faces from the old days."

Oliver laughed. "There are still a few around."

"Three other things, how are Mandy and James doing?"

"They've been at the Den long enough, they're both exceptional and will have their own clubs very soon."

"I want to see them; do they look like Duke at all?"

"James is the spitting image, tall, built like a brick shit house, Mandy is much more like Carole."

"He was the best." Paul was flooded with memories of his closest advisor and best friend, Duke.

"I know."

Paul was day dreaming. "He was hit with twenty-one bullets, imagine that! Twenty-one, nearly cut him in half, died instantly which I suppose was a blessing."

"You said three other things."

Paul said thoughtfully, "Oh yes, payments for Ted Morris's grandchildren?"

"All done; a hundred grand each. How did you know?"

"I put the word out I needed a job doing, Ted came to me, he got a lot extra because of the cancer."

"How long did he have left?"

"Two or three months, he wanted them to shoot him, much better than dying in prison."

"Babich was a fool coming over so soon."

"He didn't think he was in any danger, he never understood me and especially that I would not forget."

"He got what he deserved, cheating bastard. Carter won't be so easy?"

"Well, one thing's for sure, he won't be coming over here, so maybe we'll have to pay him a visit."

"Now, that is going to be tricky"

"I've told you a thousand times, with money you can do anything, hit men in the States are two a penny."

Oliver nodded. "So, I guess you've saved the best till last?"

"You could say that. Callum has escaped from Broadmoor."

Oliver was silent because he knew how serious that piece of news was.

"I know it's unbelievable, like father like son." Paul shook his head. "I've got two armed guards at the house and Lexi cannot go out without one of them. You need to think about your own security and more importantly Becca and the kids."

"Shit! Fuck! It's just, you know, we have enough going on without that lunatic causing trouble."

"He'll come after us, I'm sure of it; it may take him some time but it's going to happen, and we have to be ready."

"I'll sort it."

"Good, and sooner than later."

CHAPTER 24

Tatiana Negrescu had arrived at the flat twenty minutes after Ana had left. Simona wondered at the seemingly inexhaustible supply of girls and wondered how many naïve young Romanian girls had been as stupid as her and Ana. They had got on well immediately. Tati, which was how she liked to be called, had been in the UK for six months; she was a seasoned campaigner and knew all the tricks of the trade. She had been in four flats and knew they were all in North London, aside from that, she did her job and kept herself to herself. Simona was worried sick about Ana and couldn't wait for her to return. She repeatedly asked how she was recuperating and was always told she was making good progress. Life went on, the endless stream of male customers continued; the degradation became the norm and it took something unusual to arouse feelings of discontent. Such an act occurred one day, and it was also interesting because Simona realised she did not know what day it was; she vowed then to always know what day of the week it was and what the date was. A client was shown into the working bedroom, Simona was dressed in white matching knickers and bra and a flimsy see through white lace nighty.

She opened the door to join him. "Good afternoon sir"

The man was quite tall and slim. She thought he was about forty and looked slightly different to the usual punters that came in. He was dressed in a shirt and jeans, was clean shaven and quite handsome. But the real surprise was that he looked slightly Romanian.

He was sitting on the bed, looking thoughtful and didn't reply.

She tried again, "Good afternoon sir." She was standing in front of him.

He looked up at her and whispered, shocking her beyond belief. "Hello Simona."

She stepped back as her hands went to her mouth in shock. Then she realised he must be one of them. Then she thought again, her real name was never used, all the girls were known as princess.

She pulled herself together, thinking someone must have told him her real name.

"So, what have you come for today? Do you want me to tell you what is available and how much it would cost?"

"No, I am here to help you and all the other girls."

She was shocked even more; her immediate reaction was to think he was a plant come to find out information.

"Help?" She gave him a quizzical look.

"I am a Romanian police officer, my name is Boian Lupei, I am working with the UK police to shut down the traffickers. I shouldn't be here, but I had to come and tell you your nightmare will soon be over."

Simona's face went through a transformation of shock, disbelief, and shock. She stared for a long moment then said, "How do I know you're tell me the truth? Prove it to me"

"I spoke with your parents in Ploiesti, oh, and Ana's."

Simona couldn't take it in any longer and she burst into tears.

Through sobs she asked, "How is Ana?"

"I must tell you the truth, we don't know. You probably know she was taken in a van from here but where she was taken, the local police do not know."

"She must be in hospital."

"She is not in any hospital, I'm sorry."

"So, where is she?" tears ran down her cheeks.

"We don't know."

"What are you doing here? Why do you not rescue us now?"

"You have three more days until Saturday; that is the day we will rescue you and arrest all the men. I know it is hard, but you must be brave, and be patient. I will see you Saturday."

"I wish Ana was here," Simona sobbed uncontrollably, as more tears poured down her face

"We will find her, we know who the two men are that took her. So, we have an hour and I want to ask you many questions, come sit and relax."

The questioning finally came to an end and Lupei left, and Simona went to her room to await the next client and to try and take in everything that had been said. She could survive easily till Saturday and then it would be all over. "Thank God," she said to herself.

***

"Where is Lupei?" asked Karen.

"Apparently, he's not feeling too well and is in bed!"

"Jesus! He's only been here a couple of days. Is everything ready for Saturday?"

"Yes, I'm so looking forward to it, I'm hoping they put up a fight so we can smack them around a bit."

Karen just looked at him.

"Well, they deserve it."

"That may be the case, but we do it by the book, and hope to hell it doesn't turn out to be a gunfight at the OK corral. I don't want anyone getting injured."

"Couldn't agree more boss, but we better go tooled up just in case."

Karen gave Jeff another long look and wondered if he was becoming a bit too gung ho.

"I want all the locations hit at the same time, no cock ups and I'll be personally arresting our two friends Alexandru Dalca and Ciprian Albescu."

"I could do that if you want?" said Jeff hopefully.

"I just said I was going to do it, one of the perks of being the boss."

Jeff gave in. "Okay, I'll take one of the other sites, I'll enjoy that just as much."

"I want a full briefing with everyone on Friday at ten am."

"It will be done boss."

Bermondsey Pie & Mash

CHAPTER 25

Sharon had been worried sick, she couldn't get Callum on his mobile and in the end, gave up and went to bed at midnight. She woke early at six and immediately rushed to his room; he had not come home. She felt a sickening feeling grip her whole body; thoughts of him having been arrested flashed through her mind. She stumbled to her room and lay back down on her bed. She thought she wouldn't be able to get back to sleep but woke with a start at the sound of loud noises from the back of the house. She leaned over to her bedside drawers and picked up her mobile. She pressed the button to light up the screen, it was nine thirty; she couldn't believe she had slept so long. There it was again, a wooden hacking noise. She jumped up and almost ran to the bathroom; she opened the window and looked out to see Callum chopping at a huge tree trunk with an axe.

He caught the movement and looked up.

"Good morning Mummy! Sorry if I woke you up!"

Sharon was about to berate him but instead shut the window and rushed for the stairs. She was soon pushing the old rickety wooden back door open.

"You are in big trouble Callum! Where the hell have you been? And why in God's name did you not phone me? I've been worried sick!"

Callum stopped chopping. He had removed his shirt and his torso was glistening with sweat. He wiped his forehead with his hand.

"Sorry mummy, my phone ran out of battery so I couldn't call."

She just looked at him.

"That may be the case but where the hell have you been all night?"

Callum thought for a couple of seconds, wondering whether to tell the truth or not.

"I met someone and stayed at their place."

Sharon could hardly comprehend what she had just heard.

"Are you..." she was about to say "mad" and stopped herself. "Seriously? Who did you meet and where did you stay? I want to know and no lies."

"I met a lady mummy, a very nice lady and I stayed at her place, I have needs like anyone else."

Sharon shut her eyes and looked to the heavens.

"Do you have any idea of the risk you have taken? My God! I can hardly believe what I'm hearing!"

"I was testing the disguise, it worked a treat and I had a great time."

"I bet you did. So who is this woman?"

"She owns the pub down the road."

Sharon was aghast. "The local pub! The one we had breakfast in?"

"That's correct."

Sharon shook her head, she was lost for words.

"Did you tell her about this house?"

Callum's demeanour changed instantly, and Sharon knew he had.

"You bloody fool!"

"I only told her I lived locally not the exact address."

"You are not to go near the pub again, do you understand?"

"But mummy! I'm seeing her tonight!"

"No, you are not! You'll stay in the house until I say so."

Callum had to think quickly. "But it would be strange for me not to see her." And then he had a brainwave. "She could even come looking for me."

Sharon was wide eyed in horror and needed time to think.

"You carry on chopping and I'll make some breakfast."

"Not for me, I've already had a massive full English." And he smiled at her.

"Payment for services rendered no doubt?"

"We are both adults and both enjoyed the experience."

"Yes, I'm sure." She turned to go, "And what the hell are you doing all this wood-chopping for?"

"I need to get fit mummy, very fit."

She shook her head again and headed for the kitchen to make coffee.

Sharon told Tony most of what had happened, and he was as horrified as she had been. He was adamant that he should be confined to the house, and he made sure Sharon understood they would both go to prison for years if Callum was caught. Sharon was unsure what to do and felt the situation was almost getting out of control. She looked at all the options and then decided on the one she had initially thought: madness.

***

"I was born here but I've lived most of my life in Chicago, it's a great city. Have you been to the states?" Sharon was lying.

Abigail was sitting next to Callum at the dining room table.

"Yes, a couple of times. I've done the East coast and my favourite place of all is California."

"So, you're well-travelled? It broadens the mind and is fun at the same time."

Abigail turned to Callum, "You must have been to the states lots of times?"

"Actually, no, never."

Abigail looked confused. "You haven't been out to visit your mother?"

"Oh dear," Sharon said quickly. "I'll have to tell you one of Callum's secrets." Abigail was all ears. "He's terrified of flying, won't go near a plane for love nor money."

"There are a lot of people who suffer from that, how awful," agreed Abigail.

"I know, and there's nothing I can do, I've tried everything."

There was a two second silence before Sharon spoke again.

"So, you have family?"

"Not really. Mum and dad were killed in a car crash ten years ago, I've got an Uncle up North somewhere but haven't seen him in years."

"You poor thing, losing both parents, I'm so sorry."

"I came out here to get over it and ended up buying the pub, I love the quietness…" she laughed. "Not that I get much time to enjoy it."

"Of course, you don't; a pub's a full-time job and more. Do you have many staff?"

"No, I do as much as I can myself, running a pub is a very expensive business."

"Well, Callum can always help out, can't you darling?"

That surprised Callum. "Eh yes, of course I can, anything at all."

Abigail laughed and smiled at Callum. "Minimum wage mind you."

"I'll work for free, don't worry about paying me."

Abigail knew exactly how she would pay him, which wasn't just with huge breakfasts.

She looked at her watch.

"I have to get going, there's work to be done before opening time."

Callum stood up, "I'll get my coat and walk you back."

"Thanks for the tea Sharon."

"It's been a pleasure. I'm sure we'll see a lot more of each other."

"That would be nice; bye for now." Sharon heard the front door bang as they left.

CHAPTER 26

The noise was deafening as the swat team stormed through the front door.

"Police! Police! stand where you are and do not move!"

Eight officers armed with Glock semi-automatic machine rifles in full swat team body armour charged into the hall and then into the rest of the rooms one by one. There were five men sitting around the kitchen table drinking coffee; they were immediately thrown to the floor and their hands secured behind their backs with plastic tapes. Another man was discovered blindfolded and naked, tied to a bed with a naked young girl in another room; he was a customer and he was told to dress before being interviewed. The young girl was covered with a bedsheet and told also to dress and pack. Another scantily dressed girl was discovered in the second bedroom; she was also told to dress and pack her belongings, and to prepare to move out immediately. It was Saturday afternoon and the raid was one of six simultaneous brothel swoops in the North London area.

Simona Dumitrescu and Tatiana Negrescu were huddled together on the bed. The door opened and a man entered. Simona leapt off the bed and threw her arms around the man and started to cry loudly.

"Thank you Boian, thank you!"

"Everything is OK now, don't worry." He gently pushed her and held her at arms-length.

"I told you it would soon be over." He turned towards Tatiana.

"What is your name please?"

She told him.

"So, from here you will be taken to a property which is a police safe house, there will be other girls from other locations. You will go through a debrief with the local police who will take statements from you. These will be used in the courts to help convict the pimps of running brothels and trafficking. You may well be required to attend court to confirm the identity of the traffickers. You will be able to speak to your parents later this afternoon."

Both girls were crying tears of happiness.

"Officer Lupei, what about Ana?" Simona asked hopefully.

"The pimps and the two men who took her away will be interrogated, and we go from there."

"Do you think she..." Simona couldn't say it, but had to. "Do you think she is still alive?"

"I hope so, Simona. Our other priority is to find her. Now, I must go. I will come to visit you either later today or tomorrow. Any questions?"

"Will we be safe?" asked Tatiana.

Boian smiled, "You will be in a secure police property with local police officer protection; yes, you will be very safe. I'll see you soon." And he left the room.

The five men were still on the floor as Detective Inspector Karen Foster strode into the flat. She conferred with the lead firearms officer and was directed to the kitchen. On the way, she saw the two girls being escorted out of the flat by women police officers and social workers. She stood looking down at the men and recognised the two who had driven Ana Funar away from the flat, she also recognised Dalca and Albescu. She was handed five pink EU passports, she flicked through them looking at their names.

"I am Detective Inspector Karen Foster and I am arresting all five of you on suspicion of trafficking young women into the United Kingdom for the purposes of working in the sex industry. There could well be other charges which will be established in the coming days. You will now be taken into a police custody where you will remain for the immediate future."

Karen spoke to an officer who left and then more officers returned and took away Dalca, Albescu and Gavril Sala. The two drivers were left on the floor.

Karen, two officers and Boian were present in the kitchen. She had the two men lifted onto hard backed chairs.

"Do you speak English?"

They looked at her and muttered something in a foreign language.

Karen turned to Boian. "What did they say?"

"They said they don't understand English. They are probably lying."

Boian looked at the two men and spoke rapidly to them in Romanian.

"Where is the girl you took from this flat in the wheelchair?"

The two men did not answer.

Boian turned to Karen.

"I have asked where they took Ana Funar; no answer."

"Let's take them to the station."

"Sure, whatever you say."

"I'll see you back at Tottenham nick," and Karen made to leave.

The crime scene team had arrived and were in the bedrooms collecting samples. One officer had been left with Boian, while others were outside the flat waiting to take them to the police station. Boian asked the officer to wait outside the kitchen door.

He started to question the two men once again.

"You two scum are very lucky you are not back home, if you had been you would have been near death already. Taking our young girls out of the country to be used as prostitutes is unforgivable, you will rot in prison for years but there is one thing you can do to get a much shorter sentence. I want to know where the girl in the wheelchair is; by the way her, name is Ana Funar from Ploiesti. So where is she?"

No answer.

"The girl was ill. What exactly is wrong with her?"

One of the men finally spoke.

"The girl was fine, we took her to the train station and left her there; she wanted to go to London."

"You are a fucking lying, you bastard!" Boian jumped at the man and smashed his fist into the man's nose. There was a sound of breaking bone and blood poured from the wound.

"Now I'm going to ask again. Where is Ana Funar?"

"You fucking Romanian coppers don't know shit." It was the other man.

Boian clenched his fists and smashed the man twice in the face, his eyes started to close almost immediately as the bruising swelled up.

"Where is the girl?"

No answer.

He punched the man with the broken nose repeatedly to the face around the eyes. In seconds his eyes were also closed and beginning to swell; the rings on Boian's fingers had cut into the skin around the eyes and blood poured down his face.

He turned back to the other man.

"Where is she?"

The man laughed loudly, mocking him.

Boian was incensed; he took a small hardwood baton out of his pocked and commenced to smash the man's face into a pulp. Both men were still sitting, with their heads lolling on their chests.

The door opened and the police officer waiting outside the kitchen door stuck his head in. He looked at the two men and stepped in.

"You bloody fool! Do you realise what you've done? Get out!"

An ambulance was called, and the two men were taken to Whittington Hospital in Archway.

Karen Foster was informed, and she went ballistic, assigning a liaison officer to accompany Boian Lupei at all times.

The operation had been a major success. Twelve young Romanian girls had been rescued and taken to a safe house in Hampstead. Social services and police liaison officers had moved into the property to look after the girls and to take lengthy statements. The girls were ecstatic at having been released from hell and spent hours crying in happiness. Those that hadn't cried certainly did so when they spoke on the phone to their parents and relations back home in Romania. It was very exciting as they watched the successful police operation broadcast on the BBC News. Although Simona was overjoyed at having been saved, her happiness was tempered by not knowing what had happened to Ana. She was desperate for news and the officers at the house told her they were trying to find out what had happened and as soon as they had, they would let her know.

***

Karen, Jeff and Boian were sitting on one side of the table; facing them was Alexandru Dalca, a Romanian speaking lawyer and a Romanian translator. Karen made them aware that the interview was being taped and the time was noted at exactly two pm.

"Mr Dalca, I am reliably informed that your English is very good so we propose to hold the interview in English. Can please you confirm you are happy to proceed?"

Dalca spoke to his Lawyer in Romanian which Boian translated word for word to Karen. He had asked his lawyer if it made any difference whether the interview was in English or Romanian. The Lawyer had replied it made no difference, but if the English confused him or he wanted to reply to something specific in Romanian, he was free to do so.

Karen looked at Dalca. "What is your country of birth?"

"Romania."

"And whereabouts exactly?"

"Bucharest."

"And your address please?"

"No address, I stay in Hotels."

"You realise that the charges against you are extremely serious and if found guilty, you will almost certainly spend several years in prison. I tell you this because if you answer questions honestly and help us with our enquiries, then you could get a reduced sentence."

"I have nothing to hide; ask your questions."

The prosecution service had decided to charge all the Romanians with crimes against one individual as a test case. When that case had been proven, a further set off charges would be made and a new prosecution commenced. The test case was Simona Dumitrescu who the police and prosecution service had decided would be a very good witness.

"You met Simona Dumitrescu at the Gara de Nord mainline railway station in Bucharest?"

"No."

"I have CCTV footage from the station showing you sat drinking coffee, you then followed a young girl as she gets off a local train; that girl has been identified as Simona Dumitrescu."

"Pure coincidence, I left the station and went for a walk."

Boian interrupted in Romanian, "You're a fucking lying bastard!"

The lawyer jumped to his feet. "The Romanian police officer is swearing at my client! This is totally unacceptable."

Karen told him to sit down and told Boian that one more interruption and he would be chucked out.

"Where did you meet her then?"

"I went in a coffee shop, two girls asked me to join them which I did."

"And what happened then?"

"They found out I was a model scout and asked me if they could have some work."

"I told them almost jokingly that the only work available was as prostitutes in London."

"Carry on please."

"They said they would do it for two years to save money to buy a property in Romania, that's it."

"The truth is, is it not that you tricked them into travelling to London, stole their passports and made them perform sex acts with numerous men for financial gain."

"They were willing and enjoyed their work."

"But you didn't even pay them?"

"The money was kept safe for them so they would not spend it all on clothes," He laughed. "You know what teenagers are like."

"Apparently, a doctor came to the flat to see Ana Funar. Is that correct?

"Yes, she had a bad cold and we take no chances with the girls."

"I have reliable information that Ana had severe appendicitis; is that true?"

He laughed, "That is not true."

"She was taken from the flat in a wheel-chair, so she must have had more than a cold."

"As I said, we take no chances with the health of the girls."

"Where is Ana Funar now Mr Dalca?"

"I have no idea; she asked to be taken to the railway station which is what happened."

"I put it to you Mr Dalca that you are lying, and I warn you that if anything has happened to Ana Funar, you will be held accountable."

Dalca smiled at her and Karen could easily have lost control and smashed his face, she didn't and decided a break was needed.

"Ten minutes break. Thank you, gentleman."

Karen, Jeff and Boian were in her office drinking coffee. The phone rang and Karen picked it up.

She listened quietly, her face slowly turning a grey colour.

"Yes sir. Yes sir, I understand fully."

"Yes sir, I take full responsibility."

"Yes, I know sir."

"Thank you, sir."

She put the phone down and almost collapsed back into her black swivel chair.

She was silent for several seconds. The tension was unbearable.

Jeff broke the ice. "What the fuck has happened?"

"The Director of Public Prosecutions has dropped the case against all the Romanians. It's over before it's even begun."

Boian was beside himself. "This is madness! What sort of crazy country is this?"

Karen just stared at him. "This is a country that has standards and the rule of law, and part of that is you are innocent until proven guilty. You stupid man, you are responsible, beating up the two men in the flat; and now, the case cannot continue because of police brutality." She stood up, kicked the desk leg and swore loudly, "Fuck!"

Boian couldn't take it in. "They are going free, is that what you are saying?"

"Yes, exactly what I am saying."

"This could never happen in Romania! This is wrong..." he was raising his voice shouting, "They are all guilty and I believe they have murdered Ana Funar. What are we going to do?"

There was silence. Jeff decided to answer for Karen.

"Nothing, I'm sorry Boian. but there is nothing we can do."

"I will kill them all myself, and if I spend the rest of my life in prison it would have been worth it. My God they are going to walk free it is unbelievable."

"Jeff, go and tell the lawyer; I can't face it and I don't want to see those Romanians. Kick them out the station as soon as possible."

Later that day Boian visited the safe house and spoke to the girls. They were free to go home and the Government were paying for their air fares. The girls again cried for hours and wanted to leave as soon as possible. Only one girl was unhappy and that was Simona.

"Simona, you can go home, I will be here for some time and rest assured I will not give up until I find her." Boian could not bear to tell her all the traffickers had been released.

"She is dead, they killed her, and nobody cares." She broke down again in floods of tears.

"She was more to me than a sister; I promised I would look out for her, that we would both live or..." she didn't finish the sentence.

Boian put his arms around her. "Life is sometimes a bastard. You have the chance to start again, you are young go back to your family; live your life to the full. I will hound these bastards to the ends of the earth to make them pay for what they have done. Trust me they will get no sleep."

"Whatever you say, Boian. You have tried your best, thank you. Now I must go and lie down."

"Of course, I will drop by tomorrow to say goodbye. Sleep well."

"I will sleep very well this night. Goodbye Boian."

CHAPTER 27

"So, to recap, we now have sixteen clubs."

Oliver was sitting with Ben in Manze, eating pie and mash.

"What's the plan on staff?"

"Simple, we keep everybody on for a month and then decide who we want to get rid of. We will definitely be replacing some of the managers and security teams."

Ben was keen to find out what was to become of him.

"Eh what about me boss?" He gave Oliver a smile and rubbed his hands together.

Oliver went all serious. "You will continue as my right arm, with a big pay rise."

"Hmm."

"What's wrong with that?"

"I was hoping to have one of those fancy titles, it would impress the wife."

Oliver shook his head and laughed. "So how about Head of Security?"

"Hmm not bad. I was thinking of maybe Vice President of Security Operations."

Oliver shook his head again. "Jesus that's a mouthful! Look, get some cards printed with whatever you want but you are Head of Security."

"Thanks Boss, the wife's going to be very happy with the pay rise. How much is it?"

"How much are you on now?"

"Fifty k and a car."

"So, we'll make it seventy-five plus a yearly bonus; say, another twenty-five; how's that?"

Ben had difficulty keeping calm. "It's eh, more than I could have hoped for." He held out his hand, "Thank you, Boss."

Oliver shook his hand warmly. "In a couple of years' time we'll talk share options; you're doing a great job."

They both tucked into their pie and mash.

"I want you to visit all the clubs except the Den, check out the security, see who's on the fiddle, get a feeling for what's going on and make recommendations."

"Recommendations about what exactly?"

"Ben, use your instincts; look listen and learn and then recommend to me who stays, who goes, who should be promoted, who gets a pay rise, all simple stuff."

"I thought I oversaw door security and was a bit of muscle?"

"Do you want to earn a hundred grand a year?"

"Okay I get the picture, it's a big job."

"Big pay equals big job equals big responsibility; you alright with that?"

"Now I fully understand. Yes, I'm more than alright with it."

They talked about Callum Bolton being on the loose and the need for vigilance.

"So, the last matter at hand is George Cauldron," said Ben between mouthfuls.

"He has four clubs I want, I will then have the twenty I wanted to end up with."

"Sounds like another problem needs solving?"

"Of course, there's always a problem that needs solving," Oliver laughed out loudly.

"So, what are we up against this time?"

"Couple of well to do Londoners, shouldn't be too difficult. The wife could well be the problem. Her name's Charlotte Imogen. Can you imagine?"

Ben laughed. "When are we going to see them?"

"I'm not; you are."

"Why's that then?"

"They dislike me intensely, so we'll start off by you making them an offer; hopefully, they can't refuse, and if they do well, we'll have to become imaginative as usual. So, offer them..., no, on second thoughts, let's set you a challenge. I'll pay ten million but everyone hundred grand less than that figure, you get ten percent of. What do you think?"

"So, if I get them for nine million I get a bonus of a hundred-grand simple, but I'm sure the deal won't be."

Bermondsey Pie & Mash

"I'm sure your right," Oliver agreed.

"Have you set up a meet?"

"Yes, you're going to Weybridge tomorrow for dinner at eight-thirty pm."

***

Ben pulled up outside the gated mansion that he thought was probably worth at least four million or more. He announced himself on the intercom and the electric gates slid silently open. He felt out of place already and prayed they didn't see his company car blue Ford Mondeo. He parked up well away from the huge double sided front door and slowly emerged from the car. It was very quiet; he looked around, everything was immaculate, the beautiful bright green grass looked like it had been cut with scissors. He was wearing smart casuals, cream chino trousers with a white shirt and blue cashmere pullover, and he hoped he wouldn't be out of place. He pulled the front door bell and waited. A minute later the door opened, and a butler appeared.

"Good evening sir."

"Ben Jones."

"You are expected." And he opened the door and stood to the side. Ben stepped into the massive hall and couldn't take his eyes off the massive staircase right in front of him.

"This way please sir."

The butler led Ben down a long, blue, thickly carpeted corridor and finally opened a door and stepped in. He stopped by the door and then announced in a loud voice.

"Mr Benjamin Jones!"

Ben stepped into the room, eagerly looking to see who was there. There were two couples, all mid- fifties; they were in dinner suits. "Fuck," he whispered to himself. All four turned to see him and he felt them laughing at his clothes. One of the men broke away from the group.

"Mr Jones, or may we call you Ben."

"Ben is fine, thank you Mr Cauldron. I'm sorry, I didn't realise it was dinner suits."

"Don't worry, and please call me George. Come and meet the others."

The rich blue carpet felt like it was a foot thick. He glanced at the beautiful pictures hanging on the walls.

"This is my wife Charlotte, and friends of ours, Harry and Elizabeth."

He looked closely at the two women, both in their forties, attractive and dressed in flimsy evening dresses, he wondered what they would look like naked.

He shook hands with them all, hoping the evening wasn't going to be as bad as he thought it might be.

"Harry's my business partner in the clubs," he paused. "Oliver Bolton said it was important that we meet up and then sends you," he paused again. "Sorry, I didn't mean to offend."

"Don't worry, I don't take offence easily. Seems we're getting straight down to it then?"

"Well, why not? We know he's been buying up his old clubs so he wants to make us an offer?"

"That's the sum of it. How much do you want?"

"Well, we have discussed it and thought twelve million was a good starting point."

Ben was slightly taken aback but then rallied.

"That's a ridiculous price. I'll be on my way then."

He turned to leave and took two paces.

"Ben, we haven't eaten for goodness sakes! You can't come all this way and not eat with us."

Charlotte and Elizabeth both rushed to Ben and grabbed an arm each.

Charlotte whispered in his ear. "Ben, we want you to stay; have dinner, some drinks, and then who knows what could happen later."

He was now more interested, and it was obvious twelve had been a hopeful starting point.

"Of course, I'll stay, and I have a big appetite." He looked at Charlotte and smiled, she smiled back, he thought it could turn into a very interesting evening.

They all trooped into the dining room which was spectacular, a long mahogany dining table with beautiful cutlery, glasses and flowers adorning the table. He looked a up and admired the incredible chandelier. He was sat next to Charlotte and opposite Elizabeth.

The butler reappeared and served champagne. He was back a minute later with a lobster salad starter which Ben thoroughly enjoyed. The plates were cleared, and a white wine was poured.

"Ben, we have made our opening statement; so how much does Bolton want to pay?"

"Eight million seven hundred thousand."

Both men laughed, and Harry asked, "You're not serious?"

"Deadly serious old chum, I don't mess about when it comes to money."

Suddenly Ben felt something on his leg, it was a foot; it slid up his leg and into his inner thigh. He looked over at Glynis who gave him a cheeky smile. He could feel movement in his boxer shorts as Glynis massaged his balls with her toes. And then it got even more interesting as a hand ran down the top of his trousers and started massaging his now erect cock. He was finding it hard to concentrate and made a sideways movement which caused Glynis and Charlotte to move their hands and feet away. He was back in control.

Delicious dover sole was served with a mussel and cockle white wine sauce.

"Look, the simple fact is that the clubs made two million pounds profit last year, we want six times the profit which is where we got the twelve million figure from. It's not an unreasonable equation."

Ben sipped at his wine. "There are of course other factors to consider."

George and Harry looked at each other and then George replied, "And what might they be?"

"George, your other businesses are not doing well, you're even behind on your huge mortgage payments; and you Harry, lost a fortune on the stock exchange last year."

"You are well informed Ben," George said, not looking very happy.

"So, I'll raise the offer to nine million, but that's my final offer."

The butler interrupted and brought in a huge platter of cheese and a decanter of vintage port.

The hand was back in his lap searching for his cock.

"We'll think about it and let you know, there are other parties who may well pay more."

"I'll hold this offer for an hour and then I walk away."

"My God this is more like blackmail," Harry spluttered.

George looked at him and laughed. "For God's sake Harry! Stop being so dramatic!"

He turned back to Ben. "You will have your answer within the hour. Now let us go through to the lounge."

The two couples sat on small sofas while Ben was ensconced in a very comfortable single easy chair. The butler was summoned and told to leave some bottles of wine and told his services were no longer required for the rest of the evening. Music burst into life and everybody relaxed and sipped at their drinks.

"My wife is a very special person, Ben."

"I already know that George."

"I'm sure you do." He turned to Charlotte, "Some entertainment darling, if you please."

"As it happens, it does please me thank you George."

She stood and moved to the middle of the room and she started to sway to the music. She then slipped the straps of her yellow dress off her shoulders and it fell softly to the floor. She was in black stockings, knickers, and bra; she looked fantastic and Ben's erection returned. She was dancing to the music and then sashayed towards Ben; she held her hands out and took his and pulled him up. She placed her arms around his neck and started gyrating against his groin, then she pulled away and slipped her knickers down to reveal a smooth pussy. Ben was in heaven but suddenly turned and sat down.

"You don't like the entertainment Ben?" asked George

"I love the entertainment and I'm looking forward to Elizabeth joining Charlotte, but I can't concentrate until we have concluded business."

"I see. Well, in that case, Harry and I will leave you for ten minutes to discuss your proposal." They stood and left the room.

Elizabeth stood and moved to the right in front of Ben. She undressed to reveal a superbly toned sun-tanned body. Charlotte moved to join her and they both sat on the carpet next to the chair. Elizabeth then grabbed his trousers, removing the black belt and releasing the huge erection which Charlotte was soon sucking as though her life depended on it. Within seconds, Elizabeth had straddled him on the chair and was kissing him ferociously. The door opened, and George and Harry strode in.

"I see you really are enjoying the entertainment Ben."

"I hope it's…"

"Good God old boy, get stuck in. Now, as to your offer, it is unacceptable but we will accept nine and a quarter million. Take it or leave it."

Ben held out his hand, "It's a deal."

Both George and Harry shook hands with Ben and then they both started to undress.

"Now let's party!" George said loudly as he flung his tie across the carpet.

CHAPTER 28

"I have to stay for another two months at least; the Metropolitan Police are building their case and need my Romanian expertise to help." He lied through his teeth; he had to stay in the United Kingdom.

"Okay, I'll pay for the bloody hotel myself!" Boian had visions of a cheap nasty bed and breakfast.

"Yes, well thank you for that!" He slammed the phone down and turned to Jeff.

"I can stay as long as I want but I've got to pay my own way, can you fucking believe that Jeff?"

"Seems to me police forces are the same the world over. Don't worry, we'll sort something. There must be a safe house somewhere you can stay."

"What about the one where the girls are? They'll all be leaving today and tomorrow."

"Could work. I'll speak to the boss and see what she says."

"Thank you. Jeff, you're a true comrade."

"You could say friend Boian; comrade, well it smacks of Russia and the cold war and communism."

Boian shook his head. "Jeff, it means fellow officer, that's all. My God, I need a holiday."

Jeff looked at him and they both smiled and then laughed at the same time.

Jeff spoke to Karen and she agreed that as soon as the last Romanian teenager had left the safe house, Boian could move in, but he would have to look after himself. She also arranged for him to have whatever meals he wanted at the Sutton nick staff canteen, free of charge.

***

Tatiana was up early; she looked at her watch, it was seven am. She thought Simona would still be asleep but couldn't resist the urge, and a few seconds later she was tip toeing down the corridor towards Simona's room. She got to the door and listened, there was no sound and then she sniffed, there was a smell and it was revolting. A chill ran down her spine as she took hold of the handle and turned; she pushed and the smell hit her nostrils and she recoiled in horror. She put her hand over her mouth and pushed the door fully open with her foot. The scream erupted from her throat like a fiery volcano. she stumbled backwards screaming, as she fell to the floor. She was floating, she could hear voices and then more screaming...

It wasn't until one of the police liaison officers arrived at the room that the door was shut. Several of the girls had seen the cataclysmic sight. Simona was dangling from the light socket by a rope around her neck. Her face was a red and grey colour, her eyes were bulging and almost popping out of their sockets, her black tongue was protruding and lolling out of her mouth, her trousers were sodden with urine and excrement that had dripped down the trousers and formed a puddle on the floor. The window had been left slightly open and the wind was making her swing from side to side. It was a terrifying sight and the girls that had seen it were back in their own rooms lying in bed crying. A met police doctor was called to pronounce Simona was dead and after that, a crime scene team turned up to establish the facts. Ten minutes after Simona had been discovered Karen was informed. She immediately called Jeff and explained what had happened. Both were shocked and disturbed by the apparent suicide.

"I know Boian will be so upset. God what a mess, and those bastards are walking the streets."

"Karen, I'm picking Boian up; let me tell him, we are good mates now."

"Of course, Jeff…" Karen was relieved she didn't have to do it.

"We'll be in later."

"Thank you, Jeff."

Jeff left home a bit earlier than usual, he was upset by the suicide and wanted to take his time driving to pick Boian up. He wasn't looking forward to telling him but it had to be done. He arrived at the Holiday Inn and parked; he sat there for five minutes, unable to move but eventually opened the door and made for the entrance. He was caught off guard as he entered reception and Boian was there waiting for him.

"I am becoming very fond of the… urm… full English breakfast, I think is how you say it."

"Let's go and sit in the corner," Jeff said quietly.

Boian knew immediately something was seriously wrong.

"What's happened? Not more bad news?"

Jeff could hardly speak. "I… I don't know how to say this, so look, we're both coppers; I'll just tell it as it is. Simona was found dead this morning, suicide. I'm so sorry I know, she, like them, all meant the world to you; they were your people."

Boian wasn't ashamed and he didn't care who saw, he burst into tears.

"More deaths and those bastards are strolling around North London enjoying coffees and women. How did she…"

"Hung herself with a rope she took from the garage. It's terrible Boian, I'm so sorry."

"You can be sorry Jeff but what are we going to do about it? Those bastards might as well have hanged her, they are responsible, and they will pay; one way or the other they will all pay."

Jeff rested his arm on Boian's shoulder, knowing nothing he could say would make things better.

"Was there a note, anything?"

"Yes, they found a note, she said she was going to see Ana. We are not one hundred per cent sure Ana is dead, until we find the body there is always a…"

Boian interrupted, "She is dead Jeff, those bastards murdered her when she was ill." Rather than seek medical care for her, they killed her." He thought for a moment. "Yes, that is where I am going to start, we need to find out what happened to Ana."

Jeff was worried. "The case has been dropped Boian, there is nothing you can do."

"I can make my own investigation and that's exactly what I intend to do."

"Remember, you may be a police officer in Romania but you have no power here, none. I'm not going to say anything to the boss but don't break the law because if you do, she will come down on you like a ton of bricks."

Boian laughed. "What is this ton of bricks used for? I will never understand some of your sayings."

"If you need my help, you know where I am."

"Thanks Jeff. Maybe one day, you could visit Romania?"

"Yes, I'd like that."

***

Boian looked at the number and did not recognise it.

"Boian Lupei."

"Yes, I understand."

Boian couldn't believe what the man was saying to him.

"Yes, I would be happy to meet with you. That's fine, I look forward to seeing you. Goodbye."

Boian just sat on a chair in his room, taking in what the call had meant Now, he could move quickly, and he closed his eyes and clenched his fists in satisfaction.

CHAPTER 29

Callum was sweating profusely; it was a hot sunny day and the heat had sapped his strength. He slowed down and finally stopped. He placed his hands on his knees and took deep breaths of the fresh country air. Cars and lorries roared past as he took a well-earned five-minute rest. He had already finished his water but was determined to finish the ten-mile run. He had put in place a strict fitness regime which included a daily ten-mile run, an hour of weights and two hours of martial arts training. He took one final deep breath and set off once again.

He pushed the back-door open and almost collapsed into the kitchen.

"Whatever you do, don't shake like that dog advert on telly."

He laughed, picturing his sweat flicking all over the kitchen.

"Fancy a sweaty one then?"

"No! I bloody well don't, thank you very much. Have a shower while I'll knock up some food. You must be starving?"

"Yes, but I need a drink first, my water ran out."

Callum turned the cold tap on and stuck his head underneath, letting the water cascade over his head; then he turned and opened his mouth, sucking in huge mouthfuls of the delicious cold water.

"I'll shower then. See you in a minute."

He practically lived at the pub and all the regulars now knew him as Abigail's partner. It was a brilliant cover, and he was very pleased with the arrangement as he now had food, drinks and because of Abigail's voracious appetite, as much sex as he wanted. Tony was now the happiest he had ever been; Callum was out of the way most of the time which meant he could fuck Sharon for hours without interruption.

"How long are you planning to stay?" Abigail asked as she prepared breakfast for him

Callum thought for a second. "Good question. I'm not sure, there are some things I need to take care of; some people who I owe, maybe another month or two."

That calmed Abigail's nerves, he wasn't leaving in a day or two. She had got used to having him around and his huge cock was a bonus, and the fact that he liked to use it on a regular basis.

"Do you owe people money?"

"No, not money, something else."

Abigail replied with earnest, "If you need my help, I'm here for you; doesn't matter what it is, I can be right by your side."

Callum almost said something then thought better of it; but he did not discount her helping him in the future.

"I'll bear that in mind and thank you for the offer. Now where's the food and then maybe we could…"

"That's a wonderful idea but there is a lot to do before we open, and I have a list of jobs for you."

"I had a funny feeling that's what you were going to say." Callum had quickly grasped that running a pub was a twenty-four seven job.

The jobs had been done and they had half an hour before opening for lunch. Callum and Abigail were sitting in the small kitchen sipping at hot coffees.

"So, you want to help and stand by my side no matter what it involves?"

She thought for a second but had already decided.

"Yes, whatever it is."

"Someone murdered my father, I am going to re-visit the same on them."

She couldn't speak, her mind was confused and then it became clear to her.

"I'll do whatever it takes, we are a partnership now in life and death," She smiled.

He moved close to her and kissed her. "Together."

She smiled again. "But only if you call me Abi, agreed."

He laughed, "Agreed, I wanted to do that ages ago. So, we'll do lunch and then I'll tell you more."

"I can't wait," she said, glad that they were now like one.

CHAPTER 30

Boian Lupei was watching the block of council flats. He was sitting in the front passenger seat of a black Range Rover opposite the main entrance. The driver was smoking and blowing thick clouds of smoke out of the wound down window. He had gotten the address from the man he had been to see. The flat was on the third floor; the three big men climbed the stinking dirty stairs and arrived on the long landing. They walked along it, looking for flat 4 which they soon came to. The first man knocked on the door and the three of them got ready. The door opened and before the man could even open his mouth one of the men had jumped forward and smashed a steel baton into his nose. The man shouted as blood spurted from his smashed nose into the air as he fell backwards, desperately trying to stay on his feet. The three men stormed into the flat, trampling over the man, kicking him as they rushed into the small flat. There was second man who had been sitting in the lounge; and on hearing a commotion, he sprang up to see what was happening. He opened the lounge door to be met by two of the men pushing him back in and telling him to lie face down on the thin worn beige carpet. He knew it was over before it had begun and lay down on the floor. The man with the smashed nose was dragged into the lounge and both men were then tied to hard backed wooden chairs.

Boian looked across at the man in the driving seat, "I wish I was in there."

"You are not needed and can't get into trouble for sitting in a car; relax, they will do a good job."

The three men lit up Marlboro cigarettes and soon the room was engulfed in smoke. One of the three men took a deep drag and spoke.

"I see you have already suffered some attention to your faces, that is nothing to what awaits you if you do not answer my questions. So, we start, I know your English is not perfect, but you will understand me; I speak very simply and all you must do is tell me what I want to know. What are your names?"

Neither of them answered and the only noise was the one with the broken nose moaning in pain.

"Names, what are your names?"

The unhurt one answered, "Andrei Vasile."

"Cezar Albert," the other man spluttered.

"Good." He turned to one of the other men, "Write all this down, don't worry about spelling, write it how it sounds. Andrei and Ceza,r nice names for a couple of murdering Romanian gypsy scum."

The man thought everybody who came from Romania was a gypsy.

"We want to know what happened to the girl Ana Funar?"

There was silence.

"Last chance. What happened to the young girl, name of Ana Funar?"

Silence.

"You two heroes picked her up from the flat, she was strapped into a wheelchair and you took her away. Where did you take her?"

Andrei answered, "We took her to the station."

"That's what they said you would say. Which station?"

"The local one."

"Where?"

"I don't know; we were given directions and dropped her off, that's all I know."

The man asking the questions took something shiny out of his pocket and attached it to his fingers. It was a set of steel knuckle dusters. "I don't believe you," he said as he pulled his fist back and crashed it into the man's nose. There was a crunching noise of bone and flesh as blood flew in every direction. The man screamed and gasped for air.

"Where did you take her?"

"The station!" the screaming man spluttered.

Smash, the man's clenched fist crashed into Andrei's eye, and it immediately began to swell and turn a deeper purple, yellow, and black.

The interrogator turned his attention back to Cezar.

"Your face is a fucking mess, it's going to get much worse if you don't answer the questions correctly. What happened to the girl?"

"Took her to the station, she was going to London."

"Liar!" and he smashed both fists into his face. The man's head crashed back and forwards.

"What happened to Ana Funar?"

Neither answered.

The man nodded at his companion.

The companion took a pair of plyers from his pocket and handed them to him.

"This is going to get much worse and if needs be, we will be here for days. Now, tell me the truth or you are dead men."

They both mumbled "Station" yet again.

The man used the plyers and forced open Andrei's mouth and clamped the plyers onto a large front tooth and pulled for all he was worth. Andrei shook as the man pulled and pulled and finally a spout of blood shot onto the carpet as the tooth came free. Andrei howled and gurgled with the searing pain as he swallowed some of his own blood.

"Please no more, no more!" he moaned.

"What happened to the girl?"

The man pulled out three more teeth and Andrei collapsed, unconscious.

He turned his attention back to Cezar.

"Do you want to lose all your teeth, Cezar?"

"I know nothing, I only did as I was told."

"And what were you told, Cezar?"

"To take her to the station; honestly, I'm telling the truth."

Blows rained in on his body and then it started: the man tore out six teeth and still Cezar would not speak the truth.

"You think you are winning; we will be here for hours and we have not even started to give you pain."

He turned back once again to Andrei and then changed his mind. He left the room and entered the kitchen and took out his mobile.

The three men made coffee and sat chatting in the kitchen. It took a full twenty minutes for the mobile to ring in return.

The three men finished their coffees and ambled back into the lounge.

"So, we have exciting news; your families are well back home. Andrei, your wife and son send hello to you, Cezar your wife and twin daughters are healthy. Both men shook in their seats at the mention of their families.

"You bastards! Don't touch my family," Andrei managed to shout through his bloodied swollen mouth.

The man laughed as he moved closer and shouted in their ears, "I don't think you're in a position to be issuing threats." He added menacingly, "If you want to protect your families, tell me what I want to know, or I swear, we will maim and disfigure all your children."

Andrei spat blood onto the carpet. "You will have to kill us! I'm not talking! Fuck you, bastards!"

The man said to Cezar, "Do you want your pretty daughters to be butchered? I promise you, that is what will happen. Tell me what happened to Ana Funar."

"He did it, it was his idea; I just did as I was told."

Andrei spat at Cezar, "Shut up, you fool!"

"Carry on, Cezar."

"He pushed her, it was him."

"Pushed her where, Cezar?"

"Into the hole."

"What hole?"

"A hole in the ground."

"Was she dead Cezar?"

"She was in the wheelchair, I wanted to shoot her before... he said it would be a waste of a bullet. He pushed her in the hole; she was still alive."

Andrei was screaming at Cezar to shut up; the man couldn't take it anymore and brought the gun butt down on his head, knocking him out.

There was silence and finally the man spoke again to Cezar.

"There is one more thing to do before it's over; tell us where the body is."

"Woods, in Epping Forest, buried; can't tell you where exactly it is."

"In that case Cezar, there is only one thing you can do and that is to take us there."

"Yes, if you promise, promise I can live."

"I promise you will live."

CHAPTER 31

"Bad news, Oliver."

"What's happened?"

"I just got a call from my solicitor; that wanker Cauldron has backed out."

"Bastard! He shook hands with Ben on the deal; is he after more money?"

"Yea, the slimy bastard has asked for another million. What do you think?"

Oliver was incensed and knew Ben would go crazy when he told him.

"He shook hands on the deal. There's no more money."

"I was hoping you'd say that; we can't get a reputation for being soft, after all a handshake is a handshake."

"Leave it with me."

"Sort it Oliver." And the phone went dead.

Oliver pressed speed dial 4 and Ben's familiar voice answered.

"Yes, Boss."

Oliver hated swearing but he couldn't stop himself. "That cunt Cauldron has backed out, unless we pay him another million."

"We shook hands on the deal, nine and a quarter million. Bastard! What are we going to do?"

"We're going to pay him an unannounced visit and then he's going to change his mind. And don't forget, if it does go tits up, you'll have to give back that huge bonus I've already paid you."

"Don't worry, it's not going to happen, we shook hands on the deal and that toe rag will honour it," Ben said evenly.

"My sentiments exactly, and the old man agreed as well. We're going tomorrow evening, pick me up at six."

***

Ben had changed his car and now had a five series BMW, the embarrassment of driving the Mondeo into Cauldron's mansion had necessitated a very quick change.

"New car, Ben?"

"Yea; well needed some decent wheels, especially when I'm representing the family."

Oliver got in and immediately handed Ben a small heavy bag.

"Put this somewhere safe."

Ben took it and knew immediately what it was.

"Is this what I think it is?"

"Probably."

"What make?"

"Smith and Weston; old, but one of the best."

Ben placed it under his seat and they set off to visit Cauldron and Charlotte.

It was still light when they arrived. They pulled up to the gate and announced themselves. The gate whirred open and they drove in. Ben parked right in front of the doors, picked up his new weapon and jumped out. He pushed the pistol into his trouser belt and covered it with his jacket. They rang the door-bell and Jeeves opened the door.

"Mr Cauldron will welcome you in the drawing room. Follow me, please."

They were announced and entered the room; Cauldron was on his own.

"Oliver, you came yourself this time. Do we have an agreement?"

"No, we fucking well don't, you cunt."

Oliver took three quick steps and punched Cauldron in the stomach. Cauldron doubled up and fell forward onto the rich thick, blue carpet.

"You cunt! Who do you think you're dealing with?" And Oliver gave him a heavy kick into his groin area. Cauldron howled with pain.

"Now listen to me, cunt! You shook hands with Ben on the deal, and you will honour that or suffer the consequences. So, what have you got to say for yourself?"

"Ben, we're friends; tell him to go easy, please."

"I may have fucked your wife but believe me, we are not friends; you'll honour the deal, or it will be me that dishes out the consequences."

Cauldron laughed. "You going to kill me then? What about the butler, people have seen you drive in, there's the CCTV; you're not going to kill me."

Ben looked at him and made the biggest decision of his life. He lifted the heavy pistol as Cauldron watched intently with frightened eyes. Ben rotated the chamber and then clicked it open, he turned the gun up and six shells fell into his hand. He looked at Cauldron to make sure he could see, he then placed one bullet back in the chamber and rolled the chamber.

"We're going to play a game. Have you seen the film, the Deer Hunter? Well, if not, the game is called Roulette, Russian Roulette."

Cauldron looked very worried. "Don't be ridiculous Ben, this has gone far enough."

Ben took a step towards him and placed the gun barrel to his temple.

"Don't worry if you're unlucky, at least, you'll die instantly."

Cauldron was now sweating and terrified. "Ben, don't do it...!"

Ben pulled the trigger there was a loud click but no explosion. He spun the chamber again and replaced the barrel this time to Cauldron's forehead.

"Start praying, you bastard."

Cauldron was shaking and sweat was pouring off his face.

Cauldron let out a near demonic scream. "Stop it, for God's sake stop! I'll agree, I'll agree to anything!"

"Are you fucking sure, you cunt?"

"I swear it Ben, on my life!"

Ben pushed the barrel hard onto his forehead.

"Good, but it's not only your life, it will be your wife's and your kids and even the fucking butler..." he shouted, spittle hitting Cauldron in the face. "I will come for you if you fuck me around. Make no mistake, you will be fucking dead meat!" He lowered the barrel from off his face and took a step back.

Ben took a deep breath and turned to Oliver.

"Boss?"

"Good." He turned to Cauldron who was lying on the floor exhausted and frightened.

"Remember what Ben has said and I'll be right next to him. We'll be off and no more fucking around, eh?"

Cauldron was still shaking. "Yes Oliver, I agree; anything you say."

Ben looked at him one more time and said just one word to him, "Cunt."

As soon as they were back in the car Oliver was on his mobile.

"Cauldron is sorted."

"That was quick, well done."

Oliver turned to Ben, "And the old man's happy; a very successful evening. I think a light refreshment is in order; the Lord Nelson I think, and step on it."

CHAPTER 32

"Are you completely crackers? Perhaps you should be in Broadmoor. Jeez! I can't believe you said that!"

"Think about it Sharon. Callum's got lucky, the girl loves him; God knows why but she thinks the sun shines out of his arse hole."

"I don't care; ten years Tony, ten fucking long years I've been without my son, do you have any idea what that is like? No, it's not going to happen, never! It's impossible."

"Nothing's impossible Sharon, you can visit him whenever you like. He's made, he's got a home, a business and a good-looking woman all in the same place; it's like heaven!"

"You'll never understand! You have no children."

"All I'm saying is, think about it; we could leave for the states in a month's time and then drive up into Canada."

"Tony, I will not think about it and the answer again is no."

Tony was beginning to lose his temper.

"It's always about you Sharon, you and your fucking precious little boy; he's over thirty, for God's sake. Let him take responsibility for his own life for once!"

"You still don't get it, do you? He is my flesh and blood. I carried him in my womb for nine months, and then went through more pain than you'll ever know to bring him into this world. I am responsible for him and remember, he has been sick for years…" she raised her voice, "Now listen to me you fuck! I am not leaving! End of story!"

"You are an imbecile, throwing your life away on that no good useless fucking twat Callum. Face up to it Sharon, he'll be free for months, maybe years, but one day they'll get him, and he'll be back in the nuthouse where he belongs."

The slightly open door crashed into the room and a maniacal Callum sprang at Tony, smashing him on the back of the head with a claw hammer. Tony crashed to the floor, moaning in agony. Abi, who had been right behind him, kicked his head twice as if it was a football before Callum held her arm and she stopped.

"Stop it, stop it," screamed Sharon.

"The cunt deserved it," said Callum as he kicked Tony's head just above the ear.

"He deserved it Sharon, bastard talking about my Callum like that."

Sharon couldn't believe it, she didn't know whether she was more shocked by the violence or Abi saying my Callum.

Tony was moaning and there was blood seeping out of the head wound onto the kitchen tiles.

Sharon had almost lost her composure. "What the hell are we going to do now?"

Callum had gone quiet, but Abi hadn't.

"Can't get help for him; we'll have to finish him off and lose the body."

Sharon gasped. "He should go to hospital! Maybe he can be saved!"

Callum rotated his head, stretching his neck. "No, it's too dangerous; if he recovered he would give us away. Abi's right, we need to get rid of him."

Sharon was crying. "I can't, I can't do anything like that, you'll have to do what you think is best. I'm going upstairs." She hobbled out of the room and they heard her climb the stairs.

Callum looked at Abi "So now we really are a team."

"I told you I have your back. What are we going to do with that?" she said looking down at the body.

Callum took an almighty swing with the hammer and brought it down on Tony's head, there was a loud crack as his skull caved in and then a last exhaled breath and he was gone.

"That's sorted that then, now all we have to do is get rid of the body."

"Callum, I just love it when you're so decisive." Abi grabbed him and started kissing him passionately. Within seconds they were ripping at each other's clothes and he fucked her over the wooden table from behind. All the time he was thrusting into her she was smiling and staring at Tony's lifeless face which was looking up at her.

Callum chopped the body into hundreds of pieces and left it for the wild animals to eat. He checked back the next day and couldn't even find a single tooth. Sharon moved to the pub for a few days which pleased Abi even more, now they were a real family.

CHAPTER 33

There were two cars, the black range rover in front with the Driver and Boian Lupei in the passenger seat, Cezar was sat in the back, giving directions, the second a green land rover with blacked out rear windows followed with two bodyguards, a driver and Andrei Vasile cuffed and strapped into the back. A barrage of plasters had been stuck on both Romanians to stop the bleeding and the guards had had to cut the swelling around their eyes so they could see. The drive to Epping Forest took half an hour; they turned off the Epping New Road and disappeared into the vast interior. They traversed several dirt tracks eventually coming to a stop in a small clearing. Boian jumped out the car; he wasn't looking forward to the next hour or two. Andrei Vasile was dragged out of the Land Rover and thrust forward.

"So, here we are. Now, where is the grave?"

Cezar started to walk, not completely sure of his bearings.

"You will regret this Cezar, you piece of shit!"

One of the men smacked Vasile around the face. "Shut it!"

Cezar had found what he was after; he stopped and pointed to a spot in the shrubs, "It's here."

The group walked to a relatively fresh-looking mound of earth.

One of the men went back to the Land Rover, opened the boot, and took out two brand new expensive spades and re-joined the group. He threw the spades onto the ground next to the Romanians.

Boian spoke for the first time, "Dig you bastards, and don't take too long about it."

Vasile said defiantly, "I'm not digging! fuck off!"

One of the men rushed at him and smashed him to the ground and started to kick him angrily.

Boian had had enough. He picked up one of the spades and brought it crashing down sideways onto Vasile's leg; the crack was audible as the leg bone snapped.

One of the three guards said, "Well, he can't fucking dig now, can he."

"I'm going to do it myself in respect of Ana." He took off his jacket and rolled his sleeves up and started digging.

The ground was still a little soft and made for easier digging. About forty-five minutes later they were getting close. Boian was in the hole digging with Cezar Albert.

"Time for you to get out," said Boian to Cezar.

Cezar scrambled up the steps they had dug into the side of the hole.

Boian started to dig slowly looking for the wheelchair, he didn't have to wait long as he struck something very hard, it was the arm of the wheelchair. He dug around it even deeper. Soon, he felt something very soft, he was very careful when he touched the body which was still in reasonably good condition. It took a further hour before they could attach a rope to the wheelchair and haul it out of the pit. She was a pitiful sight, maggots had eaten half her face and the smell was disgusting. Boian tried hard to stop the tears but he couldn't as they ran down his cheeks. He thought of Simona swinging from the bedroom ceiling; he wiped the tears away and turned to face the two men.

"You are Romanians; how could you do this to a young girl from your own country? She was sick, you didn't just murder her, you betrayed her and buried her alive. You are both going to burn in hell for all eternity."

Cezar shouted pleadingly, "Not me! You promised I could live! Please! I only did as I was told!"

Andrei Vasile laughed. "You fool! did you really think they would let you live? Act like a man and die respecting yourself."

The guards were eager to get the job done as quickly as possible.

"Let's get on with it."

Two of the men picked up Andrei Vasile; he held his breath trying not to scream. They took him to the hole and threw him down where he landed with a thud and the men heard a moan of pain and anguish. They turned around and made towards Cezar, he turned to run but didn't get two steps as the third man had already positioned himself behind him, ready and waiting for such a move. Cezar dropped to the ground and scrabbled amidst the grass and dirt trying to get away. The guard kicked him under the chin, nearly taking his head off. One of the other men helped lift him and they moved towards the hole, Cezar hadn't given up, he bucked and manged to get loose, he ran again towards the trees, a shot rang out and he fell somersaulting to the ground. Boian had shot him in the leg, he wouldn't be running anywhere else.

They didn't lift him, instead one of the men dragged him along the ground. He was screaming in terror as they got closer and closer to the pit, soon they were on the edge and the man dropped his arm and started kicking him over and down into the pit on top of Vasile. The screams were terrible as two of the guards began filling in the hole with earth. As the pit filled up with earth, the screams got quieter and quieter. Boian was glad it was over as the pit filled up with more dirt; and then suddenly and frighteningly, a face appeared above the pit top, it was Cezar. His face was black with earth and his white eyes were popping out of their sockets. He put his hands over the top and readied to pull himself out but Boian lifted his pistol, aimed it at his forehead and fired; the bullet entered his head which exploded into a rain of blood and brains and what was left of Cezar fell back into the hole.

Boian went to the boot of the land rover and took out a body bag and two pairs of extra strong, long gardening gloves and handed one pair to a guard. He unstrapped Ana from the wheelchair and let her drop to the ground. He placed the body bag next to her and they rolled her into it and sealed it tightly.

***

Karen and Jeff looked down on the black body bag.

Jeff was upset. "It's been confirmed it is Ana Funar, at least she will get a proper funeral."

A phone call had come in saying the body of Ana Funar was in a body bag at an old industrial estate in Ponders end. The police had retrieved it and were arranging for Ana's body to be flown to Romania so her parents could give her a proper funeral.

Karen, for some reason, didn't look that surprised. "I feel for her so much, but life goes on."

"How the hell did she get here?"

"Who cares? Let's go, we have work to do."

***

"What are we going to do?"

"What do you think? Shall we get jobs in a sandwich factory paying two hundred pounds a week?"

"We could go home?"

"Go home?" shouted Alexandru Dalca. "What the fuck are we going to do there?"

"Open a club, make some easy money for a change, drink beer, fuck bitches and do coke."

Ciprian Albescu and Alexandru Dalca were sitting in the Euro Café on Tottenham Court Road, drinking coffee.

"We need money, I haven't paid for the studio this month; Gavril, Diona, they all have to be paid."

Ciprian couldn't understand it. "What's happened to the money?"

"We spend money without any thought. Do you know how much we have spent in restaurants, the rent on the flats..." he shook his head. "We are broke and it will get much worse if we sit here drinking coffee all day."

"So, we need to make some money, we have always got out of the shit before."

Alexandru was the brains and the leader. "Yes, but the police will be watching us. Maybe we should try those factory jobs," they both laughed.

"Imagine them sending a fucking copper from home! Unbelievable."

"I haven't heard from Andrei or Cezar. I wonder what they're up to?" Alexandru looked slightly worried. Strange that I keep ringing their mobiles but they're just dead."

The two men sat quietly sipping their coffees and then the door opened.

They were stopped in their tracks as they stared at the man as he sat at the next table and ordered a bacon roll and black coffee.

The man stared at them and said, "Well look who it is the two tough guy Romanians who like pushing woman around, scum of the earth."

Alexandru had recognised him straight away. "What do you want Lupei?"

"Good you remember my name from the interviews. Remember also, I will be with you until you are in prison. When you look over your shoulder you will see me, when you drive down the road and look in the mirror you will see me, when you pop in the coffee shop you will see me, when you go to the supermarket to buy your cigarettes you will see me." He raised his voice, not caring about the other people in the café. "When you are on the fucking toilet, think of me because that's all I do at the moment, I think of you two gypsy scum every waking second of my life."

Alexandru replied in a menacing tone, "You are good at speeches, I give you that, but you should be careful; I think the British refer to this as harassment and I may have to report you."

Boian Lupei laughed. "Do that whenever you like; I am a private citizen on holiday, it is pure coincidence that I come in here for a coffee and you two gypsy scums are here."

"You don't annoy us by calling us Gypsies, you're wasting your time."

Lupei just smiled at them. "One day..." he learnt forward nodding his head. "One day soon, you will be taken care of, just like..." he paused and whispered, "your two friends."

Cezar spoke for the first time, "Our two friends?"

Lupei smiled. "Andrei Vasile and Cezar Albert; didn't you hear they have both suffered a terrible accident? You will never hear from them again."

Alexandru wasn't about to be intimidated.

"You fucking wank-off coppers! You should all be shot! Fuck off back to Romania where you amateurs belong. I feel sick just looking at you."

Lupei lifted his bacon sandwich and took a bite.

"We found the girl Ana Funar, she'd been buried alive. Was that your orders to those other scum?"

Ciprian was shocked but Alexandru didn't bat an eyelid.

"It makes no difference now; so, the girls have all gone back to Romania?"

"Yes, they are out of your clutches now."

"Shame we could have done a deal and all made some money."

Lupei jumped to his feet. "You bastard! You think I could be involved in something like this?"

"Most of the coppers I know back home are all bent; you're saying you don't take money?"

"I do not and that is one more mistake you will pay for. God, I could kill you right here, right now and be happy for the rest of my life."

"Do it then, you piece of shit!" Alexandru went on the offensive. "I Don't want to see you again; next time I will not be so accommodating to your threats."

Lupei stared hard into Alexandru's eyes and whispered again, "The hole that Ana Funar was in has two new occupants, buried alive like she was; the maggots will be eating their faces as we speak and that will be the outcome for you two, and when it happens, oh, I will be the happiest Romanian on the planet."

Lupei relaxed and tucked into his roll and slurped at his coffee. "Now be good boys and fuck off."

Ciprian stood up, he looked in shock.

Alexandru stood slowly. "You have signed your death warrant today; you will pay for Cezar and Andrei."

He turned and strode to the entrance followed, closely by Ciprian.

Lupei sat and took a deep breath; he was thinking of Ana and Simona.

Alexandru and Ciprian came out of the café and stopped on the pavement. Alexandru thought for a second where to go, he then noticed the black BMW five series car across the road. There was a man taking photos of the two of them. He quickly turned right and made for their car.

"Buried alive, fucking hell! I want to go home, Alex."

"Go home? Lupei will arrange an accident, or more likely you'll be arrested for some trumped up charge and spend the rest of your life in Gheria Maximum Security Prison, and you know what that would be like."

"What are we going to do?"

"I'm not sure but first is to find somewhere we can stay in safety."

CHAPTER 34

"I'm very happy at the moment, thank you Foster, and I thank you for asking."

Boian Lupei, Karen Foster and Jeff Swan were in the Green Man pub on the outskirts of Sutton that police officers from the nick favoured. The landlord was a friend of one of the coppers so they got well looked after, and the pub never had any trouble. It was six thirty pm and they were having drinks and then a meal in the restaurant.

"Boian stop calling me Foster; I keep telling you Karen is fine, we are off duty so relax."

Karen was drinking Ginger wine with lemonade in a long glass with lots of ice, Jeff and Boian were on Budweiser.

"I love Friday's start of the weekend and all that. Boian, tell us all about Romania," Karen said, taking a sip at her drink.

"Where to start…" he laughed. "Well, we do not have many women police officers and certainly none at the level of Detective Inspector."

"Shame on the Romanian Police, I say," said Karen, pointing a finger and laughing.

Jeff was watching her and could tell straight away she was making a play for Boian.

Karen finished her drink and called to the barman for two bottles of house red.

"I have to tell you Karen, I am not a big drinker."

"What!" she almost screamed. "And we're celebrating, remember."

Jeff wanted to know more.

"What exactly are we celebrating, Boss?"

"Never you mind, but let's make a night of it!"

Jeff could see trouble ahead. Karen was knocking it back and that usually led to trouble of some sort.

"Romania is a beautiful country, I look forward to going home."

"Why are you not married, you're not gay are you? Not that it would matter if you were; I just wondered."

Boian went all quiet, "You have found out my secret."

Karen stopped as she lifted her glass to her mouth and there was silence.

"Only joking Karen!" and Boian laughed out loud, and then Jeff and Karen joined in.

"Ha! Ha! You had me then, Boian."

"So, why are you not married then, handsome man like you?"

"I have been working too much and my career has come before marriage and family. That doesn't mean I have been a saint though; I love women."

They all laughed. "Drink up and then we will have dinner. And it's all on the Met. So, as they say, fill ya boots!"

Boian looked mystified. "Fill what?"

"It would take hours to explain it." She looked at Jeff. "Jeff, you're a bit quiet."

"I'm tired and hungry."

"You can have a huge steak that will…" she was momentarily lost for words. "It will un-tire you; is that even English?"

"No idea but I get the jist of what you were saying."

Karen looked at Boian, "Boian, what are you going to eat?"

He thought for a second.

"I am placing myself in your hands Karen, whatever you suggest I will be happy with."

Jeff swore he was now flirting with Karen; he couldn't wait to get away. He didn't like gooseberries and didn't want to be one for the evening.

"Let's go in and order then I could eat a horse."

Boian made a funny face. "Jeff, you are going to eat a horse? I am surprised it is on the menu."

Jeff shook his head, thinking it was going to be one of those nights.

The three officers ambled into the restaurant and found a table tucked away in the corner.

"So, Karen, you are married with a family?"

Jeff and Karen looked at each other and then at Boian.

"Urm, well not exactly," replied Karen uncertainly.

"What does this mean then?"

Karen laughed and slurped at her wine.

"It means we talk about something else, in fact anything else…" she couldn't think of anything to say so repeated "You were saying Romania is a beautiful country"

Boian felt he was being side tracked away from something but…

"A very beautiful country Karen. Have you been to Bucharest?"

"No, should I have?"

"It is like London, parks, museums, coffee shops, so many attractions."

"And lots of handsome men like you, Boian."

Jeff ate even quicker, it was going to get embarrassing.

"You think so Karen?" he was beginning to slur his words a little.

"You're young, good looking; so, a great catch for someone."

"Catch, what is this catch?"

Jeff didn't have a mouthful of food so spoke. "Like a football, catch it, you know."

Boian was confused, and the wine wasn't helping.

Karen ordered another two bottles of red, and as it was placed on the table Boian, looked at it and then at Karen.

"You are not serious?"

"Of course, you must always be serious about wine, and especially red wine."

Boian laughed, "Someone will have to carry me out of here."

Karen was losing it. "Don't worry just relax enjoy yourself, we'll have some shots after dinner."

"Shots, we are going shooting later? This cannot be."

Even Karen was confused, "Shooting, what are you talking about, Boian?"

"Never mind. I must go to the men's room." He got up and stumbled away from the table.

"Karen, don't you think you've had enough?"

"I know but it's a night off and I'm trying to relax."

Jeff finished his food and placed the knife and fork on the plate. "I'm off"

"What! You can't go, it's early! The night is young!"

He stood up. "Say goodnight to Boian for me. See you on Monday."

"Jeff I..." he was already on his way out.

Karen took a long pull on her glass of red. "Fuck it! Who cares."

"What did you say Karen?"

She looked up, Boian had returned.

"Now, are we going to do some serious drinking or not?"

"I must slow down, or I will be on the floor," Boian laughed.

"You look even more handsome when when you laugh."

"I must laugh all the time then." Then he suddenly remembered Jeff.

"Where has Jeff gone?"

"Had to rush home, family emergency."

"Oh no, not serious, I hope"

"No, nothing too serious." She poured him another glass of wine and lifted her glass.

"Bottoms up!"

Boian thought it was another strange English saying and couldn't be bothered to ask what it meant."

Karen had a picture in her mind of being on all fours as Boian rammed his cock into her from behind.

The two of them talked rubbish, solved the problems of the world, and talked some more rubbish, it was ten pm and then it happened.

Boian noticed the elegant, very attractive dark-skinned woman heading straight to their table. The woman was slim, and really gorgeous. She got closer and closer and he wondered who the hell she could be.

The woman stopped right next to Karen, leaned down and kissed her full on the lips.

Boian was shocked and then laughed, "Who are you, beautiful Lady?"

"I am Nina."

Karen was quiet and raised her eyebrows at Boian, she knew what was coming."

"And?"

"Oh, I'm Karen's other half, and most say, much better half." She looked down at Karen.

"Are you misbehaving darling?"

"Does it look like it? This is Boian, he's the Romanian copper I told you about."

"Yes, you told me, but you didn't tell me he was so damn good looking."

She turned to Boian and nodded at him, "Pleased to meet you."

"Likewise, Likewise," and he couldn't stop laughing.

Nina sat between them. "So, this is very cosy. Are you both having an affair?"

Boian understood for a change. "Don't be crazy' if Karen's with you, she obviously likes women, and boy, you are a beautiful woman."

"For your information young man, Karen likes pussy and dicks, don't you darling?"

Karen made a face and reached for her glass.

Nina looked at all the bottles.

"Had one or two glasses, have we?"

Boian spluttered, "Few bottles Nina, Karen drinks like a... what is that word?"

Nina took a deep breath, "Fish darling, drinks like a fucking fish."

"Are you ready?" asked Nina.

"No, I'm not ready, and how the hell did you know I was here? Oh, I see my friend Jeff called you. Wait till I see him."

"I'm going to the loo, be ready to leave when I get back."

"Better do what your wife says, Karen."

"Don't you fucking start!" Karen took another great slurp of wine. "Do you want to come back with us for a drink?" She leaned forward. "And you never know what else could happen!"

Boian did a shock horror face. "Maybe, Karen; but what about Nina?"

"Ask her, she won't mind, I promise."

Five minutes later Nina returned, Karen was stuck to her chair and did not give the impression she was ready to leave."

Nina sat down.

Boian was drunk and slurred her name.

"Ni... Ni...na I'll come back to your place if you promise we can have a threesome; what do you say?"

Karen laughed and knew exactly what was going to happen next.

Nina picked up a glass of wine and threw it in Boian's face.

"Not my idea of fun, you pervert, although I know Karen would be very up for that!" She turned to her, "Wouldn't you darling?"

Karen was finding it hard to string a sentence together.

"Variety is the spice of life, as they say."

"Well it's certainly what you say. Anyway, Boian, you are drunk and no good to woman or beast."

"My dear Nina..." he slurred. "You do not understand. I am a Romanian police officer, we are re... known for our strength and fortitude which, translated, means we have big dicks and can fuck all day."

"Not with me darling." She looked at Karen again. "Are you coming or are you going back with him."

"Let's all go back to our place for a drink or two."

Nina leaned across and whispered in Karen's ear, "You are embarrassing yourself, let's go home and go to bed."

"Now you're talking but..." Karen looked at Nina pleadingly. "Can Boian come as well? He's good company and it's not as though he's the first."

Nina spoke quietly so Boian could not hear, "He may not be the first but I have a say and on this occasion, I'm saying no."

"Why exactly?"

"Because you're getting old and he's very young, and he works with you and most importantly, you'll really regret it tomorrow morning."

Karen rubbed her mouth. "Yea well, you're always right, aren't you? Fucking annoying that is, you know; always fucking right."

"Are we going?"

"Yes, we're going, would you organise a cab for Boian, please."

Nina leaned over, kissed her, and squeezed her thigh. "We'll have a good time later darling, that is if you can stay awake long enough."

CHAPTER 35

Abi was in her usual blue jeans and blue sweater. She had climbed the stairs and walked along the small landing to their bedroom; she got to the door and pushed it open. Callum was standing in front of the long mirror in some of her sexy red underwear; he had bright red lipstick on and a red hair wig.

"Honestly, I don't know what I'm going to do with you?" She said shaking her head.

Callum didn't bat an eyelid. "What do you think?"

"Well, it's umm, certainly interesting." And she chuckled.

"Come here then, sexy."

"In for a penny…" and she got close to him. He pushed his erection against her thigh.

"You're pleased to see me then."

"Always, and I do get very horny when I dress up a bit."

"Yes, I can feel that." She slipped her hand down and pulled the red knickers down at the front to release his massive erection. She started to stroke him.

"That's good." He closed his eyes, enjoying the sensation.

"But," she pulled away from him. "That will have to wait, we open in five minutes."

"Quick hand job would only take a minute the mood I'm in."

"Well, seeing as you asked so nicely."

Abi got on her knees and started a ferocious stroking, she wasn't going to mess about."

It was all over very quickly but Abi was annoyed with herself as she would now have to scrub the carpet clean.

"Here's your list of jobs."

I'll get on the case then." He went to leave the room.

She held his arm out to stop him leaving.

"Might be a good idea if you took the wig and lipstick off before going downstairs. We don't want to frighten the customers too much"

He looked at her and then down at her red knickers and bra.

"Yes, alright; you can keep them on if you must."

He smiled. "Great! They're so lovely and comfortable."

Abi went back downstairs, laughing to herself at how Callum had changed her life. She now had meaning to it, someone to fuss over and fuck all the time. She opened the front door and went back behind the bar to put some peanuts out. Two customers walked straight in.

"Good day gentlemen. What'll it be?"

"The first man replied, "You look like the cat that got the cream."

"Really? well yes, I guess so, life's pretty good." And she gave them both a beaming smile.

The lunch service was reasonably busy, so the time went quite quickly. Abi and Callum always had a cup of tea after closing; it had become a daily ritual.

"Abi, I wanted us to go out for the day, can you get some cover?"

"You want to take me out? How sweet; and yes I can. Where are we going?"

Callum twiddled his fingers. "Day out in London and then Virginia Water."

Abi didn't say anything straight away and then said quietly, "So, this isn't really a day out for me then?"

Callum blew his cheeks out and then took a deep breath.

"Well not exactly but it's a very important day and I promise you'll enjoy it."

"So, what exactly are we doing?"

"We're doing what in the army is called reconnaissance."

"I haven't been in the army but so we're going to sus something out."

"I couldn't have put it better myself and while we're doing that, I'll buy you some nice grub and we'll have a good time."

"What are we going to look at?"

Callum went all serious. "We're going to see the devil's lair."

"So, you're going to show me the Den club in London and then the house in Virginia Water?"

"I knew I made a good choice, you are so in tune with things. Yes, right on both counts. I want you to see the two properties and with a bit of luck we could even see one of them."

"I'm excited already; if he's out we could visit the bitch in the house?"

"I want to see what security improvements they've made, I'm sure they will have extra guards; we need to know how many and where they are."

"Of course, we do; we can't just turn up we need a plan, and then we can do the bitch."

"All of them Abi, they all have to pay and by God, they will wish they hadn't been born when I've finished with them."

"We Callum, when we have finished with them."

He smiled at her, "Yes we, thank you Abi."

"It's my pleasure. Now, talking of pleasure, I, eh, am feeling decidedly randy so how do you feel about getting that nice cock of yours out?"

"Delighted to be of service ma'am."

***

"Come on Abi run!"

"If I'd known I would be running I would have worn trainers!" gasped Abi as she hurtled as fast as she could down the platform to the waiting train. The guard lifted his flag just as Callum opened the door and held it so Abi could jump in. He pulled her in and she collapsed onto the seat in an empty carriage as the train started to move.

"Bloody hell! I can hardly breath!"

"You're out of condition, don't worry I'll get a fitness program set up for you."

"No, you bloody well won't, thank you very much."

"It's a good job we got in, we would have had to wait an hour."

They were sat opposite each other. Abi learned across and adjusted his wig.

"This is cosy."

"It's a train"

Abi was back in control. "Have you ever, you know, on a train?"

"Urm, don't think I have."

Abi raised her eyebrows and smiled. "What do you think then?"

"Sounds like a very interesting proposition."

"I thought you'd say that so…"

The door at the end of the carriage opened and the inspector shouted, "Tickets please!" There was no need to shout they were the only ones in the carriage.

They showed their tickets and then the train pulled into the next local station. Two families got on, so any naughty escapade was out of the question.

The train pulled into Paddington mainline London station and the contents spewed out onto the platform. The train had filled gradually with what seemed like hundreds of stops at tiny rural and local stations. Callum told Abi to remain seated as they were in no rush and He didn't like being in the rough and tumble as commuters jostled and sped towards the ticket barriers. The carriage emptied and then Callum and Abi dropped onto the platform.

Callum looked around, the crowd had gone.

"This is nice lots of room for us." And he started casually strolling across the concourse towards the battery of barriers.

Abi slipped her arm into Callum's and they looked like any other couple in love. They got to the barrier and Callum put his hand in his pocket to retrieve the tickets.

"Shit! Where are the tickets?" He pulled his hand out and started searching his other pockets, two minutes later he held his hand up.

"I must have dropped them. Bloody hell! That's really pissed me off."

"Don't worry, it's only a couple of rail tickets."

"Can I help you?"

Callum turned to see a large fat Railway guard standing next to him.

"Lost the bloody tickets," and he shook his head in exasperation.

"Maybe you dropped them on the train, you could check."

Callum turned and looked, the train was still on the platform, but it was a good walk.

"We bought two day passes at Silchester station, can't we get new tickets?"

"Yes of course, but you'll have to pay for them."

"I just told you we bought two tickets at Silchester; I'm not buying any more tickets."

Callum started rummaging in his jeans and jacket again and felt something in his back jeans pocket.

"I think I've found them." He pulled the paper out it was a receipt and he studied it.

"Great! This is the receipt for the two tickets dated today, so now can I get two more free tickets."

"I'm afraid not sir, someone could have given you the receipt while they used the tickets."

It took Callum a second to understand that and he was not happy at all.

"You're a fucking jobsworth, aren't you, wanker!"

The station guard put his hand up.

"I understand you're not happy, but I am just following the rules."

"Cunt, you're a fucking right jobsworth!" He was losing control.

Abi pulled him around by the arm and whispered in his ear. "He will call the police. Shut it."

Callum took that in and tried to calm down.

Abi turned to the guard and then noticed an armed policeman walking towards them.

"He's been under a lot of stress recently. We'll just buy two new tickets please."

"Okay madam. If you go to that ticket office over there," and he pointed. "They will issue you with two new tickets."

"Thank you so much."

She pulled Callum with her and they walked off towards a small ticket kiosk twenty yards away. They got to the kiosk and Abi explained what had happened, the ticket man charged them for two new tickets and this time Abi put them in her handbag. They headed back to the barrier, noticing that the policeman was watching them as he chatted to the railway guard.

Abi gave Callum his ticket and they went through the automatic barrier, once through, she took the ticket back for safe keeping. They then headed towards the underground entrance.

"Cunt! I'm going to have him, if he's here when we come back, I swear, he'll regret being born."

Abi said quietly, "You hold him while I stab the cunt, I'll cut his fucking bollocks off. Are you carrying a knife?"

"Yea, a flick knife, you never know when you might need one. He doesn't know how fucking lucky he was. It would have been worth going back inside just to cut him and see his blood and guts spilling all over the ground, fucking fat bastard."

"Try to forget him, he's just a fucking Railway jobsworth."

"I'm trying, but it's difficult. Fucking cunt."

They followed the endless tunnels and by the time they stepped onto the platform, Callum had stopped swearing and had pulled himself together.

They alighted at Oxford Circus and Abi surprised him.

"There's somewhere I want to pop in."

"I've got a list of things to do. Where are we going?"

"Brook street, just around the corner."

"To visit...?"

"Victoria's Secret"

"Who the hell is Victoria?" he laughed

"You've been away too long. Women's sexy lingerie."

Callum's eyes lit up. "Ah, well, that's urm, definitely well worth a quick visit. Let's go then."

Abi laughed, and they skipped off up Regent street and turned right into Brook Street. They were soon at the entrance pushing the door open.

Callum stopped and did a quick scan of the store. There was row after row of beautiful, sexy underwear; then he noticed the manikins dressed up in black stockings and underwear. He stared intently, thinking he would like to try on the knickers and bra and even take the manikin home for some fun.

"Stop staring and come with me."

Abi pulled him along until she stopped at the leather section.

"What do you think?"

He looked at another manikin that had shiny black leather from top to bottom.

"It looks tight, would take ages to get it off."

"Crutchless, I think."

He looked but couldn't see.

"So, you fuck with it on; well, we could try it,"

"It's very expensive do you want me to get it?" asked Abi.

"God, yes! We could try it tonight."

Abi smiled, "I love it and can't wait to try it on; you're in for a treat tonight."

"Can't wait. So, let's move along we're visiting the Den club."

She stopped for a second. "The enemy camp, good job you're disguised then, but are you sure?"

"Yes, but do you really think they would expect Callum Bolton to stroll into the Den club? No fucking way, safe as houses."

"I did wonder why you put on a decent pair of trousers and a jacket."

"Go and get on with it then," he said, giving her a gentle push. "I'll just have a wander.

"I bet you will. See you in a minute."

***

Callum felt slightly nervous as they approached the club.

"Don't worry, we'll have a drink and then disappear."

"Yea, it's just that if I see them, I could lose it."

"You lose it and you could lose your life, or even worse, go back to you know where."

"You're right as usual."

They walked confidently past the door guards and into the club. Callum was a bundle of nerves but did not show it. They went through the interior doors and past more security. At last they entered the club proper. It hadn't changed much, the same long bars, thick carpets, chandeliers, and chrome everywhere, the huge fancy staircase going up to the VIP and executive facilities.

"Let's get a drink."

Callum noticed a young gorgeous woman approaching them.

"Hello, how are you?"

Abi took the lead. "Fine thank you."

"I'm Emma, one of the club's hostesses. Are you having lunch today?"

"No, just a drink at the bar, thank you."

Callum couldn't take his eyes of her ample breasts.

"If you make your way to the bar, the hostess will be pleased to serve you. The restaurant is

Bermondsey Pie & Mash

open upstairs and bar snacks are available. if you require any further assistance, do please call me over I am always in the bar area."

"Thank you, Emma."

She went off to chat to other guests.

Callum and Abi ordered two glasses of white wine which came to twenty-eight pounds. They went and sat in a corner where they had a good view of the whole downstairs area.

"Fucking hell, I charge twelve quid for the same wine in the pub."

"That's how come they make so much money, it's a goldmine."

They sipped at their drinks as more, and more customers arrived for drinks and lunch.

Abi raised her eyebrows. "I wonder how much lunch would be?"

"We should have lunch and then do a runner."

"I assume that means we would not be paying for said lunch?"

"You assume right but we'd have to get from the restaurant and out the front door before the guards were informed and they stopped us."

"We'll have the drink and then disappear. It's a really nice club."

"Yes, makes a fortune."

"Why don't you have some fun and close it down?"

"What did you have in mind?"

"Introduce a colony of rats and tell health and safety or whoever it is."

"Environmental health actually. It's an interesting thought; could be fun."

"It would be some fun before you…" she waved her hand. "finish the job."

His face turned very serious. "Don't worry, the job will be finished this time."

Callum kept glancing around, remembering Katie Bolton. She'd been in a blue mini skirt, and then sex maniac Mandy; it had been good while it lasted.

"Penny for them?"

"This is where I met Uncle Paul, Oliver and Katie for the first time."

"Lots of memories then?"

Callum nodded, "So many." He could hardly remember strangling Katie to death as he thrust into her, but he had. He'd be happy to see Mandy again and wondered where she was. He wouldn't mind some sex with her again and he laughed as he thought he could strangle her as well.

"Shall we get going then?" Abi asked.

"Pity we didn't see anyone."

Bermondsey Pie & Mash

"Maybe not." Abi finished her drink and stood.

Callum did the same and they headed for the doors.

"Thank you, we look forward to seeing you again," said the hostess with the mostest.

Abi smiled but thought to herself, not at these prices, luv.

***

They were soon climbing the stairs up to Paddington mainline station.

Callum was acting relaxed for Abi's benefit, but he was taut and looking for Jobsworth. They strolled over the concourse and then stood viewing the huge automatic timetable to look for Virginia Water trains.

"Platform 8 but we've a fair wait of urm…" she glanced up at the large clock "About twenty minutes."

And then it happened. The fat jobsworth came into Callum's view. He was on the other side of the ticket barriers walking with a purpose. Callum looked ahead to see where he could be going. He started following him, oblivious to Abi who suddenly noticed him gone and sped after him. He moved quickly, making sure to keep Jobsworth in view and avoiding the fast-moving commuters. Callum was determined not to lose him. Suddenly, jobsworth opened a gate and walked through over to Callum's side. He was headed somewhere, and Callum kept back a little so as not to alert him. He went into W H Smith and came out a minute later holding a daily mail newspaper. He turned to go back the way he had come and then stopped. Callum stopped and turned around and glanced back and then he was on the move again. Callum surveyed ahead and saw a sign to the toilets.

"What the hell are you doing?" shouted Abi as she grabbed his arm.

"Wait over by the shops I'll be back in a minute."

He moved off again and put his hand in his pocket to feel for the comfort of the knife.

Jobsworth stuck twenty pence in the machine and entered the toilets. Callum thought that there must be Staff toilets, why was he here? Perhaps he had been caught short and needed to go urgently. Callum followed him in, taking it slowly and quietly. There were two people at the urinals and one of the cubicles was locked, so it had to be him. He stood at the urinal and peed; the two men finished, one walked straight out and the other washed his hands before he too left. Callum was on his own and didn't care if anyone came in or not. He walked to the front of the cubicle door and closed his eyes; when he reopened them they were shining brightly and he was ready. He took the knife out of his pocket and flicked the catch, the six-inch razor-sharp blade leapt out and he gripped the handle tightly; it was time. He smashed the door with his foot almost taking it off its hinges; the door flew open to reveal the fat jobsworth sitting on the seat with his pants and trousers around his ankles. There was a foul smell of shit; he opened his mouth to speak and then a spark of recognition came into his eyes and he went to lift his trousers up, Callum lunged forward and buried the knife blade deep into the fat man's neck. He pulled it out and plunged it back in again, blood was flowing down the man in rivers, then he heard a vaguely familiar voice behind him.

"Give me the knife."

He turned ready to fight and then saw it was Abi.

"What the…" before he could finish she had grabbed the knife.

"Disrespect my man, you cunt!" and she thrust the knife into his chest and ripped with all her might.

It was over, the man was dead and slumped on the seat. Callum and Abi stepped out of the cubicle and shut the door. They made for the entrance.

"Slow down and relax." Said Abi as she took his arm.

They headed straight across the concourse and went through the ticket barrier towards platform eight. They walked to the furthest point of the platform and sat down on a bench.

"Shit!" said Callum as he took a massive deep breath.

"That fucking fat jobsworth won't bother anyone else, eh!"

"Fuck, you surprised me."

"I saw him and couldn't let you have all the fun."

"Where the hell did you get the hat?"

She was a wearing a man's flat cap with her hair tied up.

"It was on a bench, I nicked it."

"That's theft Abi, you could get arrested for that."

They looked at each other and then burst out laughing.

The train pulled into the station and they jumped on, sat down and started discussing the Rat idea.

Numerous men had gone into the toilets. Most of the blood had been soaked up by the fat man's clothes, but eventually it started running out of the cubicle. A young teenage boy went in and noticed the blood, he ran back out to where his mum was waiting; he told her there was blood on the floor coming out from a toilet. She started shouting at a railway worker nearby who hurried over to see what the fuss was about. The fat jobsworth was found a minute later, and the alarm raised.

Bermondsey Pie & Mash

CHAPTER 36

"We have to assume we are being followed at all times, can they trace our mobile phones?"

Alexandru Dalca and Ciprian Albescu were sitting at their kitchen table sipping noisily at scolding hot instant coffees.

Ciprian thought for a second, "They can locate where we are but not listen into the calls. Well, the truth is, I'm not positive about that."

He got up and went to the side of the window. He looked through the dirty white net curtains down at the road below.

"Bastards are there still. Fuck! What are we going to do?"

Dalca was the brains and he laughed, "Perhaps we should make a complaint that we are being harassed."

"How the fuck you can laugh at a time like this, I don't know."

"Ciprian, listen, we have lived by the sword all our lives, we have survived, and we are still here drinking coffee as free men. Even if we were arrested for our so-called crimes, we would only do some time; we haven't killed anyone, the British legal system is shit, we would get a few years and be out half way through for good behaviour." He slurped at his coffee and reached for another cigarette from the packet on the table. "You need to relax more."

Albescu shook his head and looked back down at the road.

"They are outside the car, two of them, come and see."

Dalca lit his cigarette and stood. "Let me see the bastards."

He looked down and saw two well-built middle-aged men in dark suits stretching their legs.

"They look experienced." He took a deep breath. "We could always kill them."

Ciprian was shocked. "Kill two coppers, are you crazy? We would get life."

Dalca moved away from the window. "I was joking. I've told you, don't worry so much."

***

The two men had been sitting in the car for hours and decided to get out and stretch their legs.

"I wish someone would tell us what the fuck is going on. We've been following these two for days and they never go anywhere or do anything, it's a fucking boring job."

"You can say that again, no, don't, I couldn't agree more. if they're criminals then the old bill should be on the case, not us. I don't get it at all."

"Look, as usual, we do as we're told; we're getting well paid so can't really complain."

"How about I go to the café for coffee and bacon rolls?"

"Now you're talking great idea. You got cash?"

"Yea no problem, and he strode off up the road."

***

"Look, maybe the best thing we can do is just open up somewhere else"

Albescu just looked at him in horror. "You're not serious?"

Dalca hunched his shoulders. "What else do we know? We get a couple of girls and run a very small tight operation. We still have the Hatton Crescent flat, no one knows about that, so we don't have to look for premises; why not?"

"What about the cops? You really think they're going to go away?"

Dalca looked thoughtful.

"I guarantee they will, might take a bit of time but they will be gone in the not too distant future."

Albescu was intrigued. "What makes you say that? How do you know?"

Dalca became animated, throwing his hands in the air. "It stands to reason, read the papers, the Met Police are under immense pressure and having two coppers sat watching people in a flat drinking coffee all day; no, it's not going to last."

"You know what, you could be right."

"You know I am always right," Dalca said smugly.

"Nearly Alex, nearly always right. So, what do we do?"

"We sit tight and as they say, smell the coffee, and enjoy it."

***

The man left in the car pressed a speed dial on his mobile, it was answered instantly.

"I think we're wasting our time, all they do is sit at home and do nothing. The most exciting thing they do is go to the corner shop to buy fags, papers, ready meals and jars of fucking coffee."

"Yes, I know it's easy work but it's so fucking boring."

"Yes, but how long are we going to keep watching them?"

"Okay well that sounds reasonable, yea, speak soon."

Fifteen minutes later the car door opened. "Rolls and coffee"

"Bout fucking time as well; did you have to cook the bacon yourself?"

"Very funny. What's the news?" He knew he would have phoned the contact.

"Three more days and we can fuck off."

"Nice one, that'll do me."

***

Four days later, Albescu woke at his normal time of eight thirty and immediately went to the lounge and looked down at the road. He checked up and down, looking closely at the cars. He smiled to himself, Alex had been right, they were gone. He turned, wanting to give Alex the good news and then decided to wait; Alex usually slept till at least ten. He went to the kitchen and put the kettle on for coffee.

CHAPTER 37

As usual it was a blistering hot day, the sky was bright blue without a single speck of cloud. Las Vegas was its usual self and the Caesars Palace Hotel was alive and buzzing as it was open twenty-four hours a day, three hundred and sixty-five days a year. Dick Francis woke at nine am having had a good night's sleep. He didn't gamble and hadn't been enticed onto the thousands of fruit machines, or into the world-famous casino. He was working and had his professional reputation to maintain. He had flown into McCarran International airport from New York the night before and was scheduled to leave this afternoon at five pm. He stretched and pressed a control button on his consul and the curtains swished as they parted, and the sunlight flooded the room. He was happy; a good well-paid contract for a change with no bickering about the price. The two hundred and fifty thousand dollars was already in his account and he had told his wife she could go shopping with her card and spend twenty-five thousand of it on whatever she wanted. He got out of bed and looked in the full-length mirror.

He was forty-six but looked younger. He was fit, there wasn't an ounce of fat on his body that was rippled from top to bottom with muscle. He ambled into the bathroom, took off his black boxers and got in the shower. He luxuriated in the cascading hot water longer than usual and then washed with the provided Coconut shower gel. Thirty minutes later he was sitting in the Payard Patisserie Bistro restaurant drinking coffee and tucking into Brioche and maple syrup pancakes. Thirty minutes later, he went back up to his room and packed; that took all of five minutes and then he went and stood looking out the window. He took out his mobile and pressed a speed dial.

"It's Book Mark. You have the parcel for me?"

"Yes, it's ready for collection."

"Good, I'll be there at exactly eleven thirty. How long will it take me from Caesars Palace?"

"Fifteen minutes by cab."

"Good, see you then."

He placed the phone on the beautiful mahogany writing desk. He picked up the hotel phone and called reception and booked a cab for ten minutes past eleven. He then went to his holdall and pulled out his latest book, moved to the soft easy chair, sat down, and opened "The Vineyards of France" and started to read.

He checked out later, paying the three hundred and fifty dollars in cash. He had used false Identification so there would be no record of his staying at the hotel. The cab was waiting for him and he jumped into the back and told the driver where to go.

The cab pulled out, turning left onto the Las Vegas freeway. Dick looked at his watch, he was on time. He didn't like Vegas much, in his opinion it was just a group of hotels built in the desert to rob people of money. He looked out of the cab window as they passed the Vdara Hotel and Spa, and next was the strangely named New York New York Hotel and Casino, then the Excalibur Hotel, then the Luxor, the Mandalay, and then there was nothing. They had left the Vegas strip and were as good as in the desert. They turned left at the next major junction onto the Bruce Woodbury Beltway. They kept on the Beltway for eight minutes and then turned off into pebble Road and then turned sharply into a small industrial estate. There were eight units and Dick told the driver to stop just inside the entrance. Dick took every tiny

Bermondsey Pie & Mash

security positive he could, the driver would not know which unit he had visited. He paid, and the cab roared off, kicking up a storm of orange dust. Dick looked for number six and walked quickly towards it. He heard noises round the back and strolled to the back. There were two men messing about with the open hood of an old red Cadillac.

"Good Morning."

The two men looked up and didn't look friendly.

"I'm Book Mark, I've come for my eleven thirty parcel."

Another security was them not knowing his name.

A smile appeared on the older of the two.

"Welcome," and he held out his hand.

Dick took a thick envelope out of his inside pocket stepped forward and handed it to the man. He took it and passed it to the younger man.

"Count it."

Dick was annoyed but kept stony faced. "The parcel"

The older man walked into the unit and reappeared a minute later carrying a long box. He looked at the other man who had finished counting the money and nodded. He handed the box to Dick who took it and sat down on an old chair.

"It's a beauty."

"Should be for the price."

Dick opened the box and slid the rifle out, he knew straight away the man was right, it was beautiful. The Barret 8250 calibre recoil-operated, semi-automatic sniper rifle was state of the art. Also, in the box was a full magazine, a tripod and telescopic sights.

"I'm very happy with the parcel. The car?"

The man threw him a key. "Silver Ford parked out front, it's got a full tank."

"Two forty-five pm here this afternoon and I'll need dropping at McCarran."

"Fine, see you then."

Dick walked slowly back around to the front of the unit. He clicked on the key, the lights flashed on the car and he heard the click as the locks opened. He had driven hundreds of different cars over the years. He got in and started to adjust the seat. He messed around with the position of the seat for a good five minutes, there was nothing worse than driving in an uncomfortable position. At last he was ready, and he pulled out of the estate, heading back to the strip.

He drove back down the strip passing Caesars Palace, the Mirage and Treasure Island Hotels; it wasn't far, now. He turned right at Charleston Boulevard and headed down to the art district. Five minutes later he pulled into Paradise Road and drove half way down, then he saw the parking sign and pulled into the multi-story car park. He stopped at the barrier and took the token, the barrier lifted and he drove in and straight up the first ramp; he kept going until he reached the twelfth floor which was the last. He was the only car on the floor; he slowed down and found what he was looking for. He parked next to the staircase door and turned the engine off. He pulled a plastic folder out of his inside pocket, pulled a piece of paper from it and began to read and study the picture. The picture of the man was a target, nothing more nothing less. He didn't care about the what or why, it was a job and he would fulfil his part without asking any question. He studied the face, he didn't like making mistakes; he looked into the man's soul, he knew him and would recognise him at any distance.

He put the paper back in the folder and into his pocket. He pushed the door open and pulled himself out holding onto the door rim. He shut the door and went to the trunk, took out the box, rested it on the ground and locked the car. He lifted the box and made for the stairs door, he pushed it open and instead of going down turned right and went up. He took the two flights easily and then saw the roof door with the sign, No Admittance. He put the box down again and took a small bag out of his jacket pocket; he took a tiny metal pole out of it and inserted it into the lock. He fiddled for about two minutes and then the lock opened; it had been easier than he thought. He pushed the door open and stepped onto the roof.

The sunlight was blinding and he immediately worried that it could affect the shot. He walked to the edge of the roof, keeping back so no one could see him from below. He had a perfect view and had chosen well. He opened the box and took out the deadly black rifle and laid it on the concrete ground. Then he pulled out the tripod, set the rifle onto the tripod and fitted the telescopic sight. He looked through and adjusted the focus with his right hand. The blur turned to clarity and then he had the perfect black line sight he could have wanted. He moved the rifle round and stopped and refocussed the sight minutely. He was pleased with himself as he left the rifle and consulted another piece of paper he withdrew from his pocket.

He studied that for a moment and went back to the rifle sight. He moved the rifle slowly, counting the floors and he was soon at eight, he then counted the windows across from East to West, he stopped at fifteen, all was set. He checked once again to make sure the sight was perfectly focussed, it was. He looked at his watch, he had to wait two hours. He thought he could have timed it better but liked to have plenty of time in case of an emergency. He sat down on the concrete and rested his back against the wall. He took out his mobile phone and checked the battery and the signal. All was well, and he relaxed.

The phone alarm went off loudly and he woke with a start. He turned it off and rubbed his eyes and then looked at his watch. It was two pm and time to get to work. He stood up, brushing his suit down to get rid of the dust. He checked the rifle sight, it was perfectly zoomed in on the target. He brushed his hair back and spat on the ground. He rotated his neck, hearing a succession of clicks. He stretched his arms and was totally focussed. He looked at his watch again, two-eight; it was very nearly time. He picked up the mobile phone and got ready, he looked through the telescopic sight and held the view. It was time. He pressed the speed dial and heard the mobile ring.

"Steven Carter."

"Mr Carter, I have a message for you from Paul Bolton."

"What?"

It all happened so quickly Carter looked up and then at the window, then he knew but it was too late. The bullet, travelling at one thousand three hundred and fifty feet per second hurtled through the glass and smashed into his forehead. The high velocity shell penetrated his skull which exploded; the brain, tissue and head erupted in every direction, showering his naked mistress who was standing behind him in thick dark blood and pink brains. Dick Francis saw the woman lift her arms and could imagine the scream as he saw her open her mouth. The job was done. He undid the tripod, took off the sight and with the sniper rifle packed them away back into the box.

He walked calmly down the stairs, got in his car, and drove down the seemingly never-ending twisting exit ramps. He reached the barrier, inserted his token, and paid by card. It had taken seconds and he was back on the Freeway, heading back to the industrial estate. He didn't give the dead man or the blood covered woman a second's thought. The job had been a success and all he had to do now was remain calm and be on his way home. He pulled into the industrial estate and parked in front of the unit. He got the box out of the trunk and carried it around the back. The two men were still there. He handed the younger of the two the car key and the box; he checked the contents of the box and nodded at the other man. He took an envelope out of his side pocked and handed it to Francis. He felt the weight, it was a lot lighter and of course he had expected that, but it was as he expected.

"Thank you for the service, the weapon was excellent."

The two men just stared at him and then the younger one moved towards the car.

"McCarran," Francis said as he strode back towards the car.

Francis looked out of the window as the man drove him back down the famous Vegas strip. It had been an easy job. He glanced at the driver, he liked the two men; they said only what needed to be said, there was no small talk. Twenty minutes later they pulled into McCarran International Airport where he was dropped out side departures and the man muttered before driving off.

"You know where we are."

Francis nodded and got out of the car. He strode into the airport and straight towards the check in desk. It took a couple of minutes and he was done. He looked for and saw the multiple phone booths and headed to the first one. He picked up the phone.

"Job done, it's been a pleasure."

"Thank you."

And they both hung up.

Francis headed to the upmarket Airport Bistro, he was starving and intended on eating a first-class steak and to have some good whisky.

***

"Oliver, some good news."

"I love good news, dad."

"Seems Carter had an accident in Vegas."

"Oh dear, that's shocking news! Terminal, I hope."

"Very, tell you about it soon." And he clicked off.

CHAPTER 38

Tatiana Negrescu had decided to stay in London. She was a tall attractive dark haired, mature nineteen-year-old and had been in the UK for six months. She had spoken to her parents to tell them she was well, but she didn't really get on with them and had no job to go back to. She had been given some money by social services and been put in touch with a local charity that arranged a hostel for her to stay in. She was happy, she had gotten her life back, the Romanian animals were in prison and would be there for a very long time. The next issue was to find work. She had been a dental assistant in Romania, but she would have to retrain to do that in the UK. She spoke quite good English and decided to look for work in Pubs or restaurants; everybody working in the catering and hospitality industry seemed to be from the EU.

Two days later Tatiana was starting a shift as a catering assistant at Pret-a-Manger in Tottenham Court Road, North London. Her responsibilities would include making sandwiches, clearing tables, and filling in wherever she was needed. The hostel was in Green Lane, Tottenham and she had been told she could stay there indefinitely. There were other young teenage girls in the hostel from Poland, Bulgaria, Spain, Portugal, Latvia and Lithuania, a real melting pot of cultures and she began to make some good new friends. Her life was well and truly back on track although it would take some time for her to get over the horrific six months she had endured, and particularly the death of her friend Simona Dumitrescu.

Tatiana worked six days a week either on an early or late shift. The sandwich shop was shut on Sundays. It was a Wednesday morning, she was on late and had nipped out to buy some new makeup. The local convenience store didn't have what she wanted so she strolled down towards Boots and Superdrug on the high street. It was ten am and quiet, she was relaxed and thought she would buy some Cadburys milk chocolate as a special treat. She was daydreaming a little and wondered if she would ever meet a nice boy who she could settle down with.

The silver Mercedes car had been crawling along the kerb on the other side of the road for half a mile. The driver and the man in the passenger seat were looking, checking, waiting for the right moment, it was early, there were not many people about. A police car sped by and they nearly abandoned the idea but kept going. Whenever the girl slowed down they did the same; they thought it was time, there were so few people and none near her. The driver increased speed, slowly moving the car across the road, hugging the kerb once again. Suddenly he sped up and they pulled up a few feet ahead of Tatiana and the passenger seat man jumped out and in a second, he had Tatiana in a head lock and was dragging her to the back of the car, pushed her in and followed in after her. He pushed her to the floor and grabbed her tightly around the throat. Tatiana was terrified and then she saw who it was and couldn't believe her eyes.

The two men were laughing loudly.

The man in the back looked down at Tatiana.

"It is good to see you again Tatiana Negrescu."

She looked up in terror and still couldn't understand; these two bastards are in prison, or had they already escaped?

"She's wondering how come we are not in Prison."

The driver laughed.

"Tatiana, I know you can hear me, you start work lunchtime; I hope you haven't forgotten how to fuck" and he laughed loudly. "But don't worry, we will all have some fun when we get back to our new home, so we can make sure you are well oiled."

Tati was in shock and couldn't speak, what she did know was that soon she would be servicing disgusting filthy men again; she started to cry and the tears flowed endlessly.

Dalca and Albescu were so happy they couldn't believe their luck. They had been driving around looking for an off licence when Ciprian had nearly jumped out of his seat. He had spotted Tatiana and they couldn't believe she was still in the UK. They immediately hatched a plot to take her for their new enterprise.

They arrived back at the new flat in Hatton Crescent. Ciprian squeezed her neck with his hand, stopping the airflow.

"We are walking to the flat, if you do anything stupid I will kill you on the spot, do you understand?"

She couldn't speak, darkness was enveloping her; she thought she was near to death. She nodded and felt the pressure on her neck relax. They got out of the car, Ciprian had hold of her arm and led her stumbling towards a front door. They went in and then climbed a single flight of stairs and were soon in the hallway of a two-bedroomed flat. The familiar smell hit her nostrils, stale sweat, toilets; the smell of hopelessness and degradation.

"Take the smaller bedroom, you will work in the other one. Get ready, we have not had a woman for a long time, you are going to be fucked hard for hours."

She cried pitifully.

"Shut up, you fucking bitch! He lifted his hand and took a step towards her menacingly. She ran to the bedroom pushed open the door, went in and shut it behind her. She collapsed onto the bed and asked God why? Why had he punished her like this? What had she done to deserve this living hell all over again? She heard a shout from along the hall.

"Be ready in ten minutes!"

She sat up and wiped her face with her hands. She knew what she had to do, and she knew what was coming. She closed her eyes and changed to someone else, someone who only cared about surviving, someone who could and would do anything to live. She stood and left the bedroom, looking for the bathroom, it was close by. She washed her face and pulled herself together, she applied some very quick makeup and went back to her new prison. She undressed, put on the white knickers, bra and see through negligee that had been lying on the bed.

"Come to the other room!" A voice shouted out to her again.

She was ready and left her room. She pushed the door open of the other bedroom, the two animals were ready for her, both naked; they stood with massive erections.

"So, bitch get on your knees and suck." She was good and would make sure they had a good time, it would mean decent food and treats. She knelt in front of them and hell started again.

CHAPTER 39

Sharon had spent three days in bed in the pub following the gruesome killing of Tony. She knew Callum had violent tendencies that needed to be controlled by strong drugs. The trouble was she wanted him to be like his old self, tough, reliable, strong, and thoughtful but he couldn't be that if he was drugged up to the eyeballs. She wouldn't change anything and now there was a new dynamic, with Abi on the scene. She liked her, she loved her devotion to Callum, she was one of those women you could rely on in peace and in war. Sharon knew Abi would gladly give her life for Callum; that was who she was, and she loved her for it.

Sharon was back in the real world; she had showered and taken time to shave her underarms, legs and pubic hair. She dabbed perfume on all over her body and dressed smartly for a change. Callum and Abi had gone to London, so she was on her own and she made the most of it. She took her time eating a lovely pain au chocolate breakfast with lots of strong filter coffee. A bar maid was coming in to do the lunch shift and they were only offering microwave-ready meals, albeit expensive ones, as the food on offer.

She wanted to get back to Canada and work. Perhaps Tony had been right, Callum and Abi were a fixture, he could live comfortably in the pub, and if he really wanted to, even start a family. She smiled to herself, her little boy being a dad, and she'd be a grandma; she would give it serious thought later in the day. She went downstairs to open the front door. There were no breakfasts today, so they weren't opening until eleven o'clock.

She called Abi.

"Hello Abi, I can't get Callum, is everything alright?"

"Hi Sharon, everything's fine. I expect he hasn't charged it as usual!"

"So, what are you up to?"

"Just been to London, sightseeing, had a lovely time."

"Is he behaving?"

A picture of the fat jobsworth blood gushing out his neck flashed before her.

She regained her composure.

"He's been an absolute angel." She looked across the seat at Callum and smiled at him.

"Oh good, I'm so pleased, I worry about him so much."

"Sharon, no need to worry; he's a big boy..." she had to stop herself laughing and Callum was holding his cock suggestively. "So, don't worry and you know I wouldn't let anything happen to him."

"Yes, I know. I'm so pleased he met you, Abi."

"Same for me Sharon, he's a right little cherub."

"Well I'm not sure... anyway, what time will you be back? I'll cook."

"That's nice Sharon but don't worry, we'll get something out."

"Okay, so see you later then, love to Callum."

"Bye Sharon," and she cut off quickly.

"Your mom loves you, you're a very lucky boy."

He didn't answer straight away because he detected something in Abi's voice he didn't like.

"You don't like mummy then?"

"Callum, I love your mum very much."

"Good, because I was worried for…"

Abi interrupted him. "You must never worry, I love you and I love your mum; it's just that…" she couldn't find the right words.

"What Abi?"

"Well, look, we're like a married couple now so I have to be the most important person in your life, you have to look after me…" she raised her voice and laughed. "and you have to worship my pussy. Am I making sense?"

He thought it through for a second. "Yes, I understand completely and agree. What you're saying is that if I had to choose between you and Mummy I should choose you."

She looked him in the eye. "And?"

"I said I agree, I would choose you, after all we are going to get married."

Abi could have cried. "Are you asking me to marry you?"

"Yes, I guess I am. So, what do you say?"

She leaped up and jumped onto his lap and started smothering him with kisses.

"Oh God, I am going to do things to you later you have only dreamt about, pain and pleasure! Oh God, let's start now please!"

Someone coughed further up the carriage and Abi made a face at Callum.

"We had better wait then, how much longer till we're there?"

Callum looked at his watch. "Good news, about five minutes."

She smiled and nodded. Marriage! she was getting married! She felt like crying.

He was correct, five minutes later the train pulled into Virginia Water and they exited onto the platform.

She grabbed his arm.

"Where shall we go on our honeymoon then?"

He answered her without a smile, "Forget all that for the time being; we have other things to do, let's go."

She was about to argue but left it. He was right, and she followed him towards the exit. Callum made straight for the taxi rank and they got in a queue behind one other couple.

"I want to go to America."

He looked at her, not understanding.

"On honeymoon."

"Don't mention it again until we have finished the job."

The couple in front got in the cab and they were next. A minute later, a cab pulled up and they got in the back and he told the driver where they were going. He pulled away from the rank and headed through the town centre. They were in the main high street when Callum suddenly shouted.

"Stop the car!" The driver wondered what was happening but pulled over and stopped.

Callum threw a ten-pound note in his direction, grabbed Abi and jumped out of the car.

"Callum! What the hell is going on?"

He took a deep breath and started strolling slowly along the pavement.

"She's over there across the road, outside the Costa coffee shop."

She looked across and saw a slim, very attractive woman in her fifties, smartly dressed, nice jewellery, she obviously had money. She was talking to a huge gorilla of a man who was by her side, must be a bodyguard, she thought.

"So that's Lexi then?"

"Yes."

Abi hated her.

"She disgusts me. Have you fucked her?"

Callum swallowed; he knew she would know if he lied.

"Yes, ten years ago before I went into...."

Abi was furious. "She's a bag of bones! How could you have fucked that? I hate her! She's a disgusting person! Let's do her now."

They were walking slowly, casually looking around and at Lexi.

"There's the bodyguard to consider and we are in the middle of the high street. It might not be the right time or place."

"I hate her Callum; you deal with the bodyguard and I'll cut her up."

"I don't think it's..."

"That bitch! She's flaunting her wealth, her tits..." Then she laughed scornfully, "What she's got there are so small, I want to take my time cutting her. Do you want to fuck her again?" She asked, looking at Callum suspiciously.

"No, I do not. Then, it was just to get back at him."

"Acid in the face would be good, it's becoming so popular." She spat in the gutter. "She's filth."

People were looking, Abi was being loud and almost out of control. Then he glanced around and was horrified because Lexi and the guard were looking straight across the road at them. He grabbed Abi's hand and pulled her with him as he walked in the opposite direction Lexi had been travelling.

"Don't pull me Callum! That bitch is laughing at me, I can see her, I need to cut her!"

Callum stopped and spoke in her ear, "Calm down, people are looking at us and so is Lexi and the bodyguard. Their time will come, keep calm or there could be trouble we don't need right now."

Abi took a deep breath. "I'm fine. Shall we just stroll then."

"Good." They began to amble along the shop fronts, chatting amicably.

Callum was slightly worried, Abi seemed more out of control than him.

CHAPTER 40

Karen Foster woke up and regretted it instantly; she turned her head to the side and it felt like a train had run her over.

"Fucking hell! I feel like shit!"

She closed her eyes and prayed for more sleep. Five minutes later she knew sleep was not returning and she would have to get up and take some aspirins. She heard a noise as the door opened. She closed her eyes and remained motionless, the door squeaked as Nina went to shut it.

"I'm awake."

There was silence for what seemed an eternity.

"And how are we feeling this morning?"

"Just bring me a pint of water and three aspirins please."

"Why do you do it Karen, you never learn, do you?"

"Forget the fucking lecture. If you won't get me some water and aspirins, I'll get it myself."

"I'd like to see you try."

Karen made to get out of bed.

"Alright, I'm going stay in bed."

Karen had had no intention of getting up.

"Thank you, darling I really do appreciate it."

Nina left, muttering, "Like fuck you do"

It was ten thirty and Nina was getting fed up with the drinking. Karen was reliant on alcohol which she thought meant she was an alcoholic. It was always the same, she got drunk, couldn't remember what the hell she'd done or said, and then the remorse and endless apologies. She took the aspirins and water back to her.

"Did I do anything…" she paused. "Anything really terrible?"

"You asked that nice Romanian copper if he wanted to have a threesome with us."

"Oh, God help me, did I?"

"Yes, you did, the good news is he was so drunk he may well not remember, so if he says anything just deny it."

"I'm so sorry Nina, it won't ever happen again, I promise."

"Don't be ridiculous, I've heard that a hundred times."

"No, but this time, I mean it."

"I've heard that a hundred times as well."

Karen pulled the pillow over her head. "Come back to bed, I need a cuddle."

"No chance." Nina was angry as she stormed out of the room, slamming the door.

Karen finally made it to the bathroom at midday. She was in there for an hour, lying in the bath. Then she came out of the water and made herself presentable. She got dressed in a loose fitting white kaftan and joined Nina in the kitchen. They didn't speak as Karen poured herself a black coffee from the already made filter machine.

"I'm moving out."

Karen wasn't prepared for that and instantly felt sick and wobbly.

"Please say you're not serious."

"I'm very serious, I'm sorry Karen, I can't take any more."

"But what…" Karen was about to cry but managed to stop herself.

"I've had enough, you need to get help. I'm going to Paris."

"Paris?" Karen was shocked.

"Yes, it's all organised. I'm staying with friends."

"I could come with you."

Nina looked at her and shook her head.

"I'm want to get away from you, you need to get a grip on reality."

Karen was hurting so much but her instinct was to fight back.

"Go then! See if I care! You're incapable of looking after yourself anyway, you'll be back."

"Karen, I'm not coming back; I'm starting a new life. It's been fun but it's over."

Karen nearly fell as she stumbled back to the bedroom, crawled back into bed, and pulled the multi-coloured duvet over her head.

Nina packed a large leather holdall and was gone twenty minutes later. Karen wasn't sleeping, she heard the door shut and she burst into tears. The terror of being alone was back and she cried and cried.

CHAPTER 41

"Dalca and Albescu have disappeared."

"Jesus, I don't believe it; there must be a property somewhere you don't know about."

"I will consider it and come back to you as soon as I can. I hope I can deliver them to you again but next time, no mistakes."

"It was my fault, I didn't understand the system; it might be better if I take care of them myself like the other two bastards."

Boian was very pissed off, the two Romanian traffickers had disappeared from there flat. His contact assured him that if they had gone back to Romania he would have heard; they were definitely still in London.

"I'm not going to comment on that; twenty years in prison might well be more painful to them than a quick death," the contact said.

"Oh, it wouldn't be quick, but I know what you mean. Anything else?"

"The girl that stayed she is alright."

"As far as I know yes, she is staying in a hostel and has found a job, Tatiana Negrescu is a very resourceful and mature girl she will do well in the UK. I'll call her this week sometime."

"Okay so I'll come back to you as soon as possible."

"Good, look once again thank you for your help."

"It is the least I could do, we speak soon." And the line went dead.

Boian was in the safe house and sitting at a battered old antique desk in the lounge. It had taken two days to get over the night out with Karen and Jeff. He now had a good idea why Jeff had left early, and he had sworn to himself he would never repeat that evening. He liked Karen Foster, in fact he fancied her but the drinking, he wasn't sure it would be sensible to get involved.

He was frustrated because the minute they took the surveillance off the two traffickers they had disappeared. The full surveillance had been changed to periodic, and on the first visit, the car had gone, and they were found to have vacated the flat.

He sipped his coffee and grimaced; it had gone cold.

He hoped the contact would come back with the information he needed.

***

It was still hot; the weather had held and according to the forecasters, July promised to be a glorious summer month. Boian pushed open the back entrance door and strode into Sutton Police Station. He was slightly apprehensive in seeing Karen and Jeff but knew that Karen would be more embarrassed about the drunken night than him. He made his way up to the fifth floor, it was nine thirty and the main office was a beehive of activity. He stopped and glanced over at Karen's office, he could see her sitting at her desk working on a pile of paperwork. He decided to take the bull by the horns by going over and knocking on her door and entered.

"Good morning Detective Inspector Foster."

Karen looked up and nearly smiled at Boian formality.

"Good morning Officer Lupei, and how are you be on this charming Wednesday morning?"

He stared at her, she looked tough and vulnerable at the same time, the feeling of wanting to hold her, to comfort her swept over him; he was shocked the feeling was so powerful.

He hesitated, speaking slowly, "Karen I…"

She interrupted him. "No lecture please Boian. I know that my behaviour was…"

"No lecture Karen. Look, let's meet after work, I hesitate to say, for a drink," he smiled.

"I'll, eh… have to consult my diary. Hey, yes ok then, I'd like that."

"Good. So meet you where?"

"I'll pick you up at the safe house seven thirty."

He nodded and turned to leave, he turned around as he heard Karen speak.

"She left me," she paused. "Gone for good."

He was truly sorry, but in a way, pleased. "I'm sorry."

"Don't be, I deserved it. Maybe it was meant to happen."

Boian smiled at her, "See you tonight."

"I'm looking forward to it."

CHAPTER 42

Oliver was sitting in the last booth as always; he liked to see who was entering Manze.

Ben put his knife and fork down and took a deep breath.

"Never changes, always the same delicious grub."

Oliver laughed, "If you could, you'd eat in here every day"

"If only!" said Ben.

Oliver finished his food and drained the last of his tea.

"So, now we can talk."

Ben wiped his mouth with the back of his hand.

"I wondered what was on the agenda."

Oliver looked thoughtful.

"I've told you about the nutter Callum."

He was looking straight at Ben.

"Yes, go on."

"Well, the forecast is that he will come after dad, Lexi, me and maybe Becca and the kids. The only thing we don't know is when."

"Makes sense."

"So, I'm not for sitting around waiting for that lunatic to attack the family. We need to make some enquiries and find out where the bastard is and take care of him once, and for all. What do you think?"

"Attack is often the best form of defence."

Oliver wagged his finger at Ben. "Now you're talking. I want three of the new team working on this full time. Tell you the truth Ben, I'm scared, not so much for myself but for the rest of the family; I mean, if you know there's someone out there who wants to kill you it can be terrifying just to go to the local shop. They all have plenty of protection but if we could find out where he's holed up, we could take care of the problem."

Ben nodded. "I'm one hundred per cent in agreement, but where to start?"

"Come on Ben, use your gut instincts. They said there was no inside help, I don't believe that; someone must have helped him to escape. Also, check on his mother Doctor Sharon Travis, apparently lives in Canada. Three guys should be able to get things moving very quickly."

"I'll get the guys together tonight, we'll start straight away."

"I want you to be involved. If you find him, there's a reward kitty of two hundred and fifty thousand for the team."

"Very generous."

"It's important to me; this all needs to be finished once, and for all. I can't have my family living in fear."

"Okay, don't worry, we'll get the nutter and then you'll be able to sleep soundly."

***

Three days later Ben met with Oliver again at Manze.

They shook hands and then ordered double pie and mash each and sat in the last booth.

"So, I can't wait. What have you found out?" Oliver asked expectantly.

"Sharon Travis left Canada a month ago to visit the UK. She comes over twice a year to visit the son in Broadmoor. The hospital she works at in Canada says she has not returned to work, so she's still here and I bet if we can find her we'll find him."

"So, she must have helped him escape." Ben looked thoughtful. "That seems to ring a bell."

"I think so, we've also made enquiries at the hospital - someone knows someone who works there. Anyway, apparently one of the guards has mysteriously disappeared. Just didn't turn up for work one day and not seen since then. It gets even better." Ben paused and continued, "The man, Tony Bridge, lives close to the hospital so I sent Andrew round to have a nose around. No one was home so he got in and had a sniff around. Bridge is apparently a single bloke with no attachments. Well, Andrew found evidence that a woman has been living at the house and recently. The police don't know any of this; they're fucking useless."

Oliver looked thoughtful again. "So, in summary?"

"I believe his mum visits the hospital to see Callum, meets Bridge and they get together, she then somehow persuades him to help Callum escape and they are all together somewhere playing happy fucking families."

"Bloody hell! it sounds feasible."

"I agree but knowing all that does not help us find them. I can't find reference to any property which they might have in the UK; so, it's a bit of a brick wall at the moment, and it's cost me ten grand."

"Spend whatever it takes and put it in as expenses. So, what are you going to do next?"

Oliver didn't speak immediately.

"Have to be truthful Boss, I'm not sure. What do you think?"

"I think you've done a fantastic job in a very short time but as you say, it doesn't help us find them. I need to think, get some more teas."

Ben nodded and got up.

Oliver rubbed his eyes, he needed to come up with a plan.

Ben came back with two new brews.

Oliver smiled at him as he sat down.

"We may not be able to find him so maybe we create a situation where he cannot resist coming to us."

"Dangerous."

"Yes, but if it works, it's finished."

"You going to tell the old man?"

Oliver thought for a second.

"I'll have to, he's been through all this shit before so might help; he might even say forget it, we'll see."

"Well, when you need me to do anything, shout, otherwise I may just follow up a bit more on where the family of nutters could be."

"Okay, speak soon." Oliver left as Ben got on his phone.

CHAPTER 43

It was nine pm, Abi and Callum were sitting upstairs in the small lounge, both with large glasses of red wine. A part-time barmaid was downstairs serving the few customers that had come for a drink. Seeing Lexi in the high street had thrown a spanner into the works and Callum had decided that he had had to get Abi home before she did something completely crazy. Callum drained his glass and reached out for the bottle and filled it to the brim, he slurped the top and put it on the coffee table.

"God, I needed that." He paused, thinking of what to say, "Abi, what were you thinking? You almost lost total control."

Abi said nothing. She sat sipping her wine and looking very miserable.

"I know, it's just that the thought of you touching that stick insect bitch gets me so riled I just lost it…"

"Relax it's not the end of the world. I over reacted she wouldn't have recognised me from a foot away let alone across the street."

"Anyone who disrespects you has me to answer to, that's how it is and that's how it's going to stay. We are together like we did the fuck jobsworth at the station. I wanted to cut her up, Callum, do you understand?"

"No one wants to deal with the bitch more than me, I was actually thinking of acid in the face. Tony Bolton will be dead, and she'll be in a living hell."

"Yes, that sounds good but where the hell would we get acid from?"

"We can buy pure acid on the net, but extra strong bleach would do just as well."

"I've got some very strong stuff for the drains that would probably be okay."

Callum drank quickly and now looked visibly relaxed.

"When are we doing it then?" asked Abi excitedly.

"There's no rush."

Abi leaned forward, exclaiming, "It's hanging over us! We need to get it done as soon as possible! It needs to be sorted and then we can get on with our lives. How many are there to deal with?"

"Uncle Paul Bolton," he said with a sneer. "Lexi and Oliver, if anybody else, including kids get in the way, we deal with them as well."

"In that case, we need to get them altogether and that could be tricky."

"Yes, I hadn't given that some serious thought. We could always split up."

"No, no, no! I need to be with you! You are my rock, I'm definitely not going to be on my own."

"Hey, no problem! We stay together then. Anyway, I like you having my back."

Abi visibly relaxed.

Callum smiled, "So, let's have a good drink, you can get into the black leather while I pick out some of your sexy underwear and put some lipstick on."

Abi lifted her glass in a toast and laughed out loudly. "Now you're talking!"

***

Sharon was back at the rented house. She'd got over the trauma of the murder of Tony, but still got the wobbles when she stood on the kitchen floor where he had died. She didn't see that much of Callum, he was always working at the pub and had effectively shacked up with Abi for good. The wedding news was astonishing, never did she think her little angel would be married and possibly even be starting a family. She felt surplus to requirements and gave serious thought to going back to Canada. The house was deathly quiet, she sat around moving from chair to chair and from room to room. She now cooked for one and was bored to tears. She had also got very used to the sex with Tony who had been an animal in the bedroom, and for that matter, also in every other room in the house, and she had loved every second of it. Now she relied on her good old faithful dildo and a rampant rabbit vibrator Tony had bought her. She was beginning to think maybe Tony was right, she should leave Callum and Abi to get on with their lives and leave.

CHAPTER 44

She pressed the doorbell, she was excited and nervous, the door opened.

"Hello Karen, come in while I get my coat on." He stood to the side and she walked past him, brushing against him as she did so. He smelt her perfume and sucked it deep into his lungs.

She had spent two hours getting ready. She was wearing a simple pair of black trousers with a black shirt and black wool cardigan, her gold necklace was the final touch to really finish the look off.

"You look fantastic!"

"Thank you," replied Karen with a smile. "Just something I threw on quickly." And she smiled again. "You look smart yourself."

He laughed as well; the ice was broken, and they were on the same wavelength.

He grabbed his short coat.

"Are you going to be warm enough?"

She liked that, he was a considerate man.

"Jacket's in the car, shall we go?"

He looked at her, wanting to push her against the wall and kiss her and then drag her to the bedroom.

She looked at him wishing he would push her against the wall and kiss her and then drag her to the bedroom.

"I'm ready."

He pushed the front door open and she followed him out.

"So where are we going?"

"I'm taking you to a very quiet intimate restaurant not very far from here; it's called La Cage Imaginaire."

"So, a French restaurant, I love French food."

He walked ahead of her and opened the driver's door. She wasn't used to this from women or men and wasn't sure she liked it.

"Thank you, you're such a gentleman."

"Not all the time Karen," he laughed.

She started the engine and pulled away from the kerb. Ten minutes later she parked at a metre in Flask Walk.

"I don't see the restaurant."

"Follow me."

"Karen."

Bermondsey Pie & Mash

She stopped and smiled at him as he said, "You look cold hold my arm."

She wrapped both hands around his arm and they walked on. They came to a quaint cobbled street and Karen led him down it towards what was obviously the restaurant.

"This is a wonderful setting."

"It's beautiful isn't it," and she hung on to him for dear life as she stumbled on the cobbles in her high heels. She didn't bother telling him she had brought numerous men and women to the restaurant with the sole intention of seducing them after the meal.

It was a lovely evening and the restaurant French doors were open at the front. The restaurant was busy, there was a lively sound of laughter and chatting on the cool breeze.

They entered and were shown to a table for two in a small alcove on one side. It was perfect, thought Karen.

"Have you been here before?" He asked innocently.

"Once or twice," she replied casually.

"So, what do you recommend?"

"First, some champagne." She signalled to the waiter and ordered a half bottle of Moet et Chandon. Boian didn't say a word but he was pleased it was a half and hoped and prayed she didn't get drunk.

"And the food?"

"I'm a bit traditional but they do frogs legs and rabbit and beef Bour..." she couldn't finish the word.

"Boeuf Bourguignon."

"Yes, that one," and she laughed.

Karen ordered Scallops while Boian went for the frog's legs, main courses were fillet steak for Karen and Boian had the seabass.

Karen ordered a bottle of house red and a white, she figured they would be there for two or three hours and they wouldn't need any more than that.

They chatted about everything and anything, Boian told her all about beautiful Romania and she told him about her career with the Met. There was a natural chemistry between them, and for Karen it was one of the most enjoyable evenings she had had for a very long time. They enjoyed cheese and biscuits and before they knew it, the time was ten thirty.

"Karen, you picked the perfect restaurant, the food and wine have been wonderful but the best thing of all has been your company."

She felt moved, no one had been so nice to her for ages.

"Don't! I'm getting all embarrassed."

He laughed. "No need to, it's been a very special night; and now I will get the bill."

"Boian, no, I told you it was my treat, well sort of, the Met will be paying."

"Are you sure?"

"Of course, it's Detective Inspector expenses."

Karen paid and knew the twelve and a half per cent gratuity added to the bill, did go to the staff so she did not leave a tip. They strolled to the car arm in arm, like a couple of young lovers.

Karen pulled up in front of the safe house, there was a short silence.

"You must come in for coffee and a night cap."

"Are you sure?"

He learned across and kissed her gently on the lips. "I'm very sure."

"Well, in that case I must obey." And she pushed the car door open and stepped out.

Karen was sitting on the sofa while Boian busied himself in the kitchen, making coffees and pouring brandy. She was nervous, she hadn't been with a man for over a year; she hoped she still knew what to do.

He came back in and moved a glass coffee table to their front. He sat down next to her and kissed her again gently on the lips.

"Why don't you kiss me properly?" and she moved closer and leaned towards his lips.

He increased the pressure and then she felt his tongue probing into her mouth, she reciprocated, and the embrace lasted several seconds.

"That was better, now for the coffee and brandy and then…" she reached for her coffee.

They had finished their drinks and she looked at him expectantly as she touched his arm.

"Karen, slowly, there is no rush."

"I know, sorry." She had almost assaulted him, thinking it was passion; she was used to making love when drunk. It was a dramatic change to be just a little tiddly.

"I need to relax, it's been some time since…"

He slowly undressed her, kissing her neck and shoulders, working his way down, caressing and kissing her intimately. He was strong, he manoeuvred her exactly where he wanted her, and she loved it; she let him take control. His hands and his lips were everywhere, even his toes. She loved the caresses of a woman but when a muscular man knew what he was doing it was pure pleasure to be taken. It went on for an hour until she could take no more.

"Boian! I need to climax! Please, I am so close!"

He changed position so he was on top of her missionary style, her face was almost level with his belly button, and he stroked.

"That's it Boian! Perfect! Oh God help me! Gosh! it's so good! Yes! Yes!" And she erupted in climax and then he exploded as well. It was perfect.

She caressed his shoulder.

"Was it, you know..."

"You mean was it good for me?"

"Well yes, urm, was it?"

"Karen, it was incredible, and in another ten minutes you won't be able to keep me away."

"Oh, good I'm ready whenever you are." She moved her hand and started stroking his cock; she could feel it growing in her hand and she closed her eyes.

CHAPTER 45

"That bitch is such a good fuck."

Ciprian Albescu collapsed onto the kitchen chair, he was catching his breath and wheezing. He had needed a fuck and Tatiana Negrescu was available twenty-four seven for his and Dalca's pleasure.

Dalca laughed. "You look worn out, you need to do some exercise, get fit. When you fuck the bitches, they need to be fucked good, she's probably laughing at you." And he laughed even more.

"I can get fit."

Dalca laughed again. "You are a pussy, you don't know the meaning of the word fit. Look at me, when I fuck a bitch they are fucked good and cannot move for hours."

"Bollocks! I am going to get fit, just you wait and see."

Dalca laughed again. "I will believe it when I see it," and he kept laughing which really began to piss Albescu off.

Albescu made a coffee and went back to see Tati.

He entered her room and stood looking at her.

"You want seconds," she said opening her legs.

"No, I am tired, but you are good, very good."

"Thank you," she said as she closed her legs.

"Am I a man? You know..."

Tati knew she needed to be careful.

"More than enough man for me."

He didn't speak and then slowly shut the door.

"What about Dalca he is..."

Now she knew she had to be very careful.

"He is very hard and likes the back passage too much, I prefer you fucking me."

"Really?"

"Yes, but don't tell him I said that he would kill me."

Albescu smiled. "Don't worry, you are our only meal ticket, he will not harm you."

She slowly opened her legs again, revealing a smooth shaved pussy.

"Are you sure you didn't want seconds?"

He felt the bulge in his jeans growing.

"Get on all fours I want you from behind."

Bermondsey Pie & Mash

"Yes master."

***

Albescu was tiring but pushed and pushed his legs. The hill was steep but he was determined to get to the top without stopping. He had stolen the bike three days before and went out every day for two hours. He would show that pig Dalca who was fit. His legs were burning, his thighs on fire, but still he pushed; he was nearly there and then suddenly, he was storming over the brow and hurtling down the other side. It was a quiet early Sunday morning, no one was about and there were hardly any cars. Albescu took his feet off the pedals and let the bike freewheel down the hill.

***

The black people carrier was parked across the road down a side street facing the entrance to the flats. Boian Lupei was in the front passenger seat, next to him was one huge, hard man while similar looking man another was in the rear. Suddenly, Boian shouted.

"He's moving let's go!"

The three men all came alive. The driver started the engine and pulled out to follow the cyclist. It wasn't difficult as there was no traffic and the roads gradually got steeper, so the cyclist couldn't go that quickly. Boian was very excited. His contact had come through with the address of a new flat and they had soon identified Albescu and Dalca. The cyclist, who they knew to be Albescu, was huffing and puffing as he strained to make it up the hill; now he was at the brow.

"Now speed up!" Boian ordered excitedly.

The man at the back opened the side door and took hold of a baseball bat. The car was speeding down the hill and was just behind the cyclist.

"Do it now!" The driver sped up and they pulled alongside him and then swerved in front of him. The cyclist shouted but to no avail. The car hit him, and he went flying onto the pavement and into the wall of a house. He crashed into it at speed and was dazed as he stumbled to his feet; and before he knew what was happening was grabbed by two men and dragged into the back of the people carrier where he was thrown to the floor and the baseball bat shoved in his face.

"Keep quiet and do not move or I will smash your skull open."

Albescu was wide eyed as he recognised Lupei as one of the two men. The car pulled off with a jerk and did a swift U-turn and went back up the hill.

"What do you want from me? Let me go!"

"Shut it!" and the large man applied pressure to his neck with the baseball bat.

The car drove into an old industrial estate and pulled around to the back of a derelict looking factory. They drove into the factory through an enormous goods entrance and stopped. Albescu was more than terrified; he kept thinking of being buried alive and couldn't control the fear. He peed himself in the car.

The guard smelt it and shouted, "Jesus the bastard is pissing himself!"

Boian answered, "He has reason to. Get him out."

The guard at the back pulled open the side door and literally kicked Albescu out onto the hard-cold concrete floor.

"It wasn't me, you know that," Albescu said quickly, his eyes round with terror. "Dalca is the boss! He's the one who should be here not me, ask the girl, she'll tell you!"

Boian stopped dead in his tracks. "What girl is this?" He was staring intently at Albescu.

"Negrescu, Tatiana Negrescu."

Boian was confused and then it hit him like a sledgehammer. "Where is she?"

"In the flat with him, she much prefers me, I treat her good, Dalca is a pig he beats her and fucks her up the arse all the time."

Boian felt sick, he could hardly speak. "When and how?" he screamed at Albescu.

"We were just driving around, then we saw her. I said to leave her alone; it was him, he did it all, ask her, she much prefers me."

"How many days has she been in the flat?"

"A week, not long; it was Dalca, he had an..."

"Shut the fuck up you moron!" And Boian landed a hefty kick into his stomach.

He coiled up in agony, moaning with pain.

"You two animals took her back again into hell?" he was shouting. "Do you have no conscience? She has a mother and father, she is a young girl, a daughter, and she's Romanian; she is of your own people!" He put his hands to his head and the tears flowed, he could not control them.

Albescu didn't understand; he spoke quietly, "She's just a bitch, that's what they're for."

Boian heard. He wiped his face and stared at Albescu then he turned to the nearest man.

"Bring me the bag." The man opened the boot of the car and pulled out a holdall from the boot of the car. He put it on the pavement beside Albescu and and pulled the zip open. He pulled out a meat cleaver and handed it to Boian.

Albescu started quivering with terror. "No please! I told you it wasn't me! Ask the bitch, she likes me! She really does! She was only telling me a couple of days ago she much prefers me to Dalca! I was going to let her go, honestly, I was, it was all him it always has been him! I just do as I'm told." He saw Boian lift the cleaver above his head and bring it down towards his ankle. He screamed and lifted his legs and his hands to protect himself but he was too late.

"This is for Simona Dumitrescu, Ana Funar, Tatiana Negrescu and all the other girls."

He accompanied each name with a vicious hack to his feet and legs. His aim was good, and he applied all his strength. The brand-new razor-sharp meat cleaver cut through his foot at each aim. The blade cut into flesh and tissue, cutting, and slicing flesh and bone. At the first blow,

Albescu gave a blood curdling scream and tried again to move out of the way. The cleaver went up and down again, and again. Then Boian aimed for the knee and it was a perfect hit; again flesh, tissue and bone splattered everywhere. The screaming didn't stop as the cleaver went up and came down inflicting massive wounds all over his body. Boian was being careful, he didn't want the animal to die quickly; he wanted to make it last, he wanted the bastard to pay for his crimes, to pay for the living hell he had put the girls through. A second later he stopped to gather himself and rest. He looked down at the bloody, crumpled mess lying at his feet. Albescu was bleeding to death but it would still take some time; there was gurgling, rasping noise coming from his throat.

Boian bent down and shouted, "You're an animal and you'll die like one! It won't be too long. Can you feel life draining out of you? I'll make sure all the girls hear about this; they will sing from the rooftops, they will be so happy. Oh, and don't worry, Dalca is next; he will regret the day he was born!"

The bloody mess stirred and whispered, "You coppers are all wankers, fuck you."

Boian smiled and then noticed the gold ring on his right hand. He bent down and stretched out the arm, and the cleaver came down at the wrist and he pulled the hand away. He laughed loudly as he lifted the hand to show the other two men; blood was dripping all over him as he swung the hand left and right laughing hysterically.

And then the blood lust left him. He had done enough, and he was very pleased Albescu was dying before his eyes; the puddle of blood was growing by the second, and it wouldn't be long before he expires. He threw the hand onto the concrete.

"Find something to put the hand in, I have a use for it," he ordered the men.

The two men looked at each other, hoping the other would move first.

***

Dalca was getting more, and more worried; all sorts of reasons ran through his head and none of them were good. Albescu had not returned from his bike ride. He looked at his watch yet again, he was an hour overdue. He strode into the kitchen to make another coffee, Tatiana was eating toast and sipping at a coffee.

"So, bitch, do you know anything?"

"Know anything about what exactly?"

"Why Albescu is late back?"

She laughed. "How the hell should I know?"

"You been cooking something up with him?"

She shook her head, he looked at her and felt a stirring in his jeans, he thought a quick fuck might take his mind off Albescu.

"Lift your nightie."

She immediately grabbed the two sides of the flimsy see through nightie and lifted it, showing her naked pussy and arse.

He lost interest as quickly as it had stirred.

"Maybe it's time we got another girl, you're boring me."

"Please yourself," and she strode out of the kitchen.

He put the kettle on and spooned some Maxwell house into a cup. He heard a noise outside the front door and smiled, Albescu was back. He quickly pulled open the door but there was no one. He looked down and saw a small brown cardboard box was sitting on the door mat. He looked around and listened, it was quiet. He picked the box up and shut the door and went back to the kitchen. He took a sip of coffee as he looked at the box, and then flipped opened the top. Inside was a strange smell and something covered in an old cloth. He lifted it up and then threw it onto the table; thick dark blood dripped from the cloth, he took hold of the edge of the cloth and pulled it back.

He gasped and jumped back as he saw the hand; and then he saw the ring and knew it was Albescu's hand! He was very shocked and couldn't think. At the same time the door crashed open and men were grabbing him and throwing him to the floor. It happened so quickly, and it was as though he was dreaming, and he couldn't understand what was happening. Boian ran down the corridor, pushing the doors open until at last he found her. She was sitting on the bed. She saw him and just burst into tears; he pulled her up and hugged her close.

"It's over and this time for good. You're going back to Romania and not leaving my side until you go."

She pulled herself away from him.

"I'm alright."

"Are you sure?"

"Yes, I'm okay. What happened to Albescu?"

Boian decided to make it simple. "He's dead and won't be troubling any more girls. But listen, that is our secret, you understand?"

"Yes, I understand," she paused and asked, "and the animal Dalca?"

"I will deal with him shortly."

She moved so quickly he was caught by surprise, she was out of the door and into the kitchen; two seconds later, she saw Dalca on the floor. She opened the cutlery drawer and pulled out the short vegetable cutting knife. She bent down and put the knife across his face and said, "This is from me and all the girls," and she plunged the knife into his neck and pulled it across his throat. The throat opened and a fountain of blood shot into the air. Just then, arms grabbed her and pulled her back. She didn't care, at least she's had her own personal revenge. She heard the gurgling as he tried to breath, blood was pumping onto the kitchen floor; he tried to sit up, but he fell back and stared with glazing eyes at the ceiling it was suddenly so close.

She stood over him.

"Enjoy burning in hell Dalca, because that is where you are going."

He shuddered, and his legs kicked once or twice and then he was still. she smelt urine and saw he had peed himself.

She turned away from him and made for her bedroom.

Boian stood in the kitchen and looked down at Dalca.

****

"Now it's all over." He was in the car being driven back to the safe house in Hampstead.

"You haven't called the police, is this…"

Boian interrupted Tatiana, "Yes, it is private, the local police know nothing of this. Money has been provided for your ticket back home; you are going today."

She burst into more tears. "Thank God for you Boian, thank you."

"Now, I must make a very important call."

"It's Boian. It all went well, what we didn't know was that they had found one of the girls again and put her back to work. She is going home tonight."

"They will never trouble another young girl."

"I couldn't have done it without you, thank you so very, very, much."

"Yes, I hope so. Goodbye."

Tatiana was curious. "Was that someone who helped you?"

Boian didn't answer straight away, then said, "Yes, we would not have been able to find them and you without the man's help."

"Am I allowed to know his name?"

"I think so, it is Florin."

Tatiana looked thoughtful.

"I think I have heard that name before."

"He is the doctor who came to see Ana Funar, he is a true Romanian who has helped us so much. I owe him a great debt."

"Why did he help you?"

"Because he knew they were going to kill Ana and did nothing about it. He was trying to make amends."

"Well, thank God for him as well then."

CHAPTER 46

Paul had originally wanted to hold the party at the house with a marquee, caterers, and a live band. But whenever he talked about it, Lexi felt uncomfortable. They had never had a marquee in the garden since Katie's eighteenth birthday, and she couldn't bear it because of the happy memories of that event, then followed by her terrible murder at the hands of the lunatic Callum. So, in the end Lexi won and at Oliver's recommendation the party was booked in the Hilton Hotel, Park Lane, London. Paul was quite relaxed about it and in the end, thought the venue would be perfect. Lexi took on the task of planning what was a celebration of the new clubs and a new beginning for the family. She started writing the guest list, liaising with the Hotel party planner Carla Westburgh, and the menu planning, wine list and guests' presents. The party was to be in August, only three weeks away; there was a lot to do.

***

"I've drafted in people from all over the place, I want you to vet them and get rid of anyone you don't think can hack it. "

"How many in total?"

"About twenty."

Ben thought for a second. "So, plus our guys, we have thirty odd; should be enough I reckon.

"The Hilton is huge and there will be about two hundred guests, it's not an easy operation."

"No, it's not. You sure this is a good idea?"

"The old man wants it sorted and has agreed, but the one proviso is that Lexi, Becca, the kids and myself have water tight security."

"We'll need more than thirty then, I have to swamp the hotel with plain clothes people. Do you think he'll come?"

"We've arranged for the party to be widely publicised in all the papers, he'll hear, and he won't be able to resist. Imagine us all in one place; he'll be jerking off at the thought of it."

"I'll need weapons, a lot of weapons."

"I've already sorted it, it's costing a small fortune, but weapons are on the way from Serbia as we speak."

Ben was suddenly very interested.

"What have we got?"

"Glock pistols and semi-automatic rifles. Mostly pistols, but where the fuck would you hide rifles?"

Ben laughed. "Rifles are no good, and make sure you get plenty of ammo."

Ben looked thoughtful again. "He's not likely to have a bazooka or grenades, is he?"

After a long pause, Oliver said with a frown, "Bloody hell I don't know. Could he actually get that sort of gear?"

"Money can buy anything, but he would find it hard to buy that type of weaponry without it being publicised," Ben said confidently.

"You sure?" asked Oliver anxiously.

"Pretty sure; I mean, where the fuck would you buy a bazooka?"

"I'll make some enquiries from my contacts."

Ben was feeling slightly apprehensive, he still wasn't sure the party was a sensible idea.

Oliver could sense Ben's concern. "Don't worry Ben, we'll have the hotel tighter than a duck's arse."

"And for that reason, he could well leave it."

Oliver shrugged. "C'est La vie."

"We'll see," Ben said doubtfully.

"Snap out of it Ben or do you want me to get someone else to sort it?"

Ben couldn't believe what Oliver said, he replied vehemently, "No leave it to me, it'll be fine."

Oliver rubbed his hands. "Great! Now, how about some pie and mash?"

"Now that is a bloody good idea, let's go," Ben laughed.

***

Boian Lupei hugged the girl tightly.

"When I get back home, I'm going to give you a call."

The girl started to cry, sniffing loudly. "Thank you, thank you for everything; if it hadn't been for you…" and she cried even more. She rested her head on his shoulder.

"It's okay," Boian said soothingly. You're going to have a full and wonderful life from now on."

She smiled, "I'm never leaving home again, never!"

"You better go and catch your flight."

She nodded and slowly pulled away from him. She took a step backwards, took a deep breath, then turned around and walked to passport control. She handed her ticket and passport over to the man in uniform and then turned. He was still there; she smiled at him and waved, he waved back.

"Carry on miss," the uniformed man said as he handed back her passport, and boarding pass to her.

She turned and took her documents back and moved away from the check-in desk and started walking towards departure area. She couldn't help glancing back once more. He was still there, and he held his right thumb up and she did the same as she went through the open doors into the departure area.

An hour and a half later, the British Airways Jumbo jet roared into the sky heading South East to Romania.

She was sitting at a window seat next to an elderly lady. She couldn't help it, she was crying again as she thought of Simona, Ana and all the other girls.

"Are you alright my dear? Shall I call the stewardess?"

Tatiana Negrescu looked up at the kind lady.

"No, I'm fine; it's just that..." she paused. "I'm going home." And she cried some more.

***

Abi was flicking through the morning paper and got to the "About Town" section; she loved the tittle tattle of celebrity. She scanned down looking for something interesting and then nearly jumped out of her seat.

She shouted, "Callum! Come here quickly!"

She heard him bounding up the stairs and pushed the door open.

"What's happened?"

"Nothing to worry about, calm down."

"Hell, I thought something terrible had happened!"

"Quite the opposite, good news!"

They looked at each other. "Yes, well, tell me then."

Listen to this and she lifted the paper so she could read it easily.

"The well-known nightclub owner Paul Bolton is holding a party at the Park Lane Hilton to launch his new clubs. Paul was recently deported from the United States for tax evasion. The champagne will flow, and guests will be treated to a magnificent meal and star entertainment."

Callum was beaming. "Manna from fucking heaven!" he shook his head laughing. "The gods have answered our prayers! Brilliant news!".

Abi said thoughtfully, "Prayers?"

"Well, you know, I mean, I haven't actually been praying. Anyway, it's great news, isn't it?"

"They'll all be there, Bolton his wife..." She couldn't say her name because whenever she did she went into a frenzy of cursing. "The son, kids, all of them together; but to kill them all we need a bomb or a tank."

"Bloody hell! I hadn't thought of that...," he scratched his head. "I need to think"

"We haven't got long to get a plan together," Abi said.

"How long?"

"Three weeks."

"That's long enough."

***

Karen was sitting in cream coloured silk pyjamas with her feet tucked under her bottom. She was sitting on the green sofa in the lounge, sipping at a glass of white Pinot Grigio. She smiled to herself, she thought she could have found the one. Boian was a copper, albeit a foreign one but he knew the stress, and strains of the job. He was tall, handsome and had a big cock. She was surprised how much she had enjoyed having one inside her; it had been a long time. She took another sip of the wine; she had taken a vow to keep off red wine for the immediate future. she looked at the wall clock and suddenly felt awful. It was eleven O'clock, much too early to be chugging down wine, white or red. She wondered when Boian would be going back to Romania; she wondered if she could get him to stay, she wondered if he liked her as much as she liked him. She finished the glass of wine, got up and walked to the kitchen. She opened the fridge and took out the half-full bottle of wine. She turned the screw cap and went to pour then she hesitated and stopped; she screwed the cap tight and put it back in the fridge. She took a deep breath and made for the bathroom to have a good soak in a hot bath.

***

"There's something you're not telling me."

Paul sighed; he had meant to tell her but just hadn't gotten round to it.

"I'm just thinking of the party."

"What about it? Everything's under control; what exactly is it that's worrying you?"

"Well, it's a target."

"What?"

"Lexi, we know Callum's out there somewhere. We'll all be in the same place, he could come."

Lexi stared at her husband and thought about what he had said.

"What you're really saying is that we are the tethered goat and he's the lion, is that it, Paul?"

He made a face and started slowly, "Well…"

She was angry and interrupted him, "Just say it for God's sake!"

"He gathered his thoughts together and said in a firm voice, "Yes I want it finished with; the whole plan is a ruse to get him to come out; he has to die then we can all live in peace."

Lexi was shocked. "I can't believe after all the years, and after all the things we've been through, you wouldn't tell me what had been on your mind! But why is that, Paul? What's changed?"

"I honestly don't know, maybe it's just me getting old; I didn't want to worry you. Look, I can't explain it."

They stood there looking at each other, not understanding.

Lexi was the first to speak.

"Oliver, Becca the children will all be there, I have to warn you, if something goes wrong and anything happens to them…"

She left it there, knowing he understood there would be repercussions.

"It will be fine don't worry." But even he wasn't sure anymore.

Lexi turned and walked away, trying to work out what the hell was going on with Paul.

Bermondsey Pie & Mash

CHAPTER 47

The Park Lane Hilton was a mass of glass and chrome. It was luxurious but in a different way to the classic hotels like the Dorchester or Claridge's. Callum and Abi had arrived at one thirty and spent five minutes in the reception hall looking at exits and studying the general layout of the hotel. They had arranged a meeting with the hotel party planner, a Ms Carla Westburgh. They had both dressed up, with Abi wearing her party best outfit of cream dress with a short black jacket; Callum was dressed in a blue suit and his usual disguise. They finished looking around and made for the imposing reception desk which was manned by several uniformed staff.

"Good afternoon, we have an appointment with a Ms Westburgh."

An attractive uniformed young lady smiled, "Good afternoon, your names please."

Callum answered, "Mr and Mrs Jay."

"I'll inform her you are here. Please take a seat." And she pointed with her open hand to a set off comfortable lounge chairs at the side of the reception area.

Carla Westburgh strode across the reception area; the desk had told her where they were sitting and what they were wearing. She Saw them and smiled as she held out her hand to Abi.

"Mr and Mrs Jay! Welcome to the London Park Lane Hilton."

"Thank you."

She shook hands with Abi and then by Callum. He immediately noticed her long legs and ample bosom and imagined her naked and felt a hard on developing.

Carla took them to the morning lounge and coffee was served. She told them there were four hundred and fifty-three rooms and fifty-six suites. Some of their guests would be coming from long distances and rooms were available should they so desire. There were three restaurants and on the twenty eighth floor, there was a Michelin starred eatery called 'Galvin at Windows' which had incredible views across London. There was a total of five bars and a full room service. She also suggested Abi might like to take advantage of the spa.

They left the reception area and moved to the lifts. A minute later, double doors were opened into a massive ballroom with what seemed to be hundreds of round wooden tables.

"Obviously it looks like the pictures in the catalogue when the tables are all set up, and decorations have been done."

Abi looked around in awe. "It's so big!"

Before Abi could say anything else, Carla interrupted, "We'll section off a room to accommodate your number. It will have its own entrance and bathrooms, so it will be very cosy."

"I saw in the paper Paul Bolton is having a party here which I think is a similar size to ours. Is that in this room?"
"We don't discuss individual clients but…" She lowered her voice, "Yes the Bolton function will be in this room."

 "What about a band? Can you recommend anyone?" Abi asked,

"Most people do have their own; the Boltons for instance have a band called the 'Wanderers'. Have you heard of them?"

"Vaguely. I seem to remember they had a hit some years ago."

Carla smiled, "I used to follow them when I was a teenager. I can't wait to see them. Yes, I could give you a list of bands."

"Don't worry, we'll find one thanks," Abi said quickly.

"Okay. So, let's go and have some more coffee and discuss some more of the details."

Thirty minutes later, Abi and Callum shook hands with Carla. Then, Callum asked Abi to sit and wait for him at reception. Forty minutes later he returned.

"Bloody hell, Callum! I was getting worried! What the hell have you been doing?"

"I got some maintenance clothes and have been wandering all over the areas the guests don't see; the back stairs, the roof, you name it, I've been there."

Abi smiled. "You are just so clever." She couldn't stop smiling. "If only we could get a room."

"Come with me." He grabbed her hand and walked her down a long corridor; she saw the toilet sign and knew what he was up to.

He entered the ladies and checked the cubicles, they were all empty, he opened the door.

"It's empty," he said with a big smile on his face.

They were soon locked in a cubicle grunting and panting, not caring if anybody came in or not. Fifteen minutes later they left the hotel for the journey home.

"It's been a good day."

"Yes, Mrs Bolton, it has."
It was the first time he had called her that and she loved it.

CHAPTER 48

Karen pushed back the cover and carefully got out of the bed; unusually, she felt fit and healthy. Most Sunday mornings she woke up with a ghastly hangover and most of the day would be spent trying to recover so she could go to work on the Monday. She licked her lips, they were moist, and her mouth felt fresh; again, unusual as her mouth usually felt like the bottom of a bird cage. She rubbed her eyes and then slowly pulled back the curtains. The room was flooded with light and she noticed it was a glorious day through the dirty windows. She tiptoed to the kitchen, took a paper filter and coffee out of the cupboard, filled the machine with water and turned it on. She heard the comforting gurgle as the water started to filter through the coffee; she inhaled the lovely aroma as she went to the fridge.

She had stocked up with bacon, one hundred per cent pork sausages, black pudding and button mushrooms. She grabbed them all together and placed them next to the stove. She took a tray of eggs out of the bottom cupboard and a tin of Cross and Blackwell baked beans from another. She stood and looked at the array of food and smiled to herself. Ten out of ten for effort, she thought; all she had to do now was cook them, so they could be eaten. The coffee aroma was so delicious she had to have some and quickly poured herself a half mug full. She then sliced the black pudding and put them into a baking tray along with the bacon, sausages, and mushrooms. She opened and poured the can of baked bean into a plastic bowl and placed it in the microwave; everything was going according to plan.

"Good morning!"

She turned and smiled at the same time.

"Yes, it is a very good morning. Did you sleep well?"

Boian laughed, "Oh, I slept like a baby! That is the correct saying, is it not?"

"Yes, Boian it is." She went towards him and threw her arms around his neck and cuddled him. He was in his white pants and in a second, he had a huge erection.

She stepped back and laughed loudly, "Well! That didn't take long!"

He looked down at the bulge in his pants and laughed.

"That's what happens when you just look at me let alone touch me, and I can see your nipples through the nightie. I think we should go back to bed; what say you?"

She paused then said, "I say yes, but let's have breakfast first. I'm treating you to a full English."

"A full English followed by a naked sexy Karen; what more could a man want in life?"

She smiled. "I hope…" she paused, then carried on quickly, "everything is ok between us."

He frowned. "Everything is great. Why do you say that?"

"I guess I worry, that's all. Have some coffee while I try not to burn breakfast."

She turned to commence unpacking the food. He came behind her and ran his hands around her back and took hold of her breasts and gently squeezed lightly, playing with her nipples.

She squeezed his powerful strong hands to her breasts and then turned crushing her lips to his.

"We'll have breakfast later then," she conceded.

It had all happened so quickly they were both in shock. He had spent one night and then they decided he should stay; it was as simple as that. He hadn't wanted to return to Romania, and meeting and falling in love with Karen had pushed him to make the decision to stay. He had no job, but they could manage well enough until he found something.

***

"Come on! We don't want to be late!"

Paul was trying to be very upbeat but beneath the confidence and bravado he was a worried man. He had even considered cancelling the party. He couldn't shake off the belief that he was putting his family at unnecessary risk. He was sure that the lunatic Callum would make his move, but would they be able to stop him and bring an end to them all living in fear?

He shouted upstairs again, "Are you ready?" He muttered under his breath "Bloody women! Take hours doing nothing."

"I heard that! And I've been as quick as I can!"

He looked up as Lexi came down the stairs. "Wow it was worth the time and the wait; you look stunning!"

Lexi was in a flowing chiffon peach evening dress, diamonds flashed from her fingers ears and neck.

"Did I buy you all that bling? They look incredible!"

Lexi laughed, "It's all fake, but very good quality fake."

He shook his head thinking, what was the point in buying the real thing when the fake stuff looked so good.

"I presume we are meeting Oliver and Becca at the hotel."

"Correct darling, so the cars waiting."

Lexi wandered off, "I'll be two minutes"
She went to the kitchen and picked up her Samsung mobile phone from the worktop and then strolled back to the entrance hall. She didn't want to go, she was scared for the grandchildren and thought it insane to invite trouble.

"I'm ready."

Paul opened the front door and they stepped out.

***

"Is everybody in place?"

Oliver was standing next to Ben on the band stage in the Hilton hotel ballroom.

"Everything's pukka, boss."

Oliver looked out over the thirty-five beautifully decorated tables; the colour scheme was peach. The tables looked amazing with brilliant decorations and a multitude of balloons and streamers hanging in bunches and floating into the air on every table.

They both scanned the room, there were guards at every entrance and scattered throughout the room.

"What about the back of house?" Oliver asked.

"Stairs are all covered, men in the kitchens, we're good to go."

Still, Oliver couldn't relax. "Waiters, he could easily disguise himself."

"I've got men on the doors, and all the waiters and waitresses have been vetted; they'll all be checked again night."

"Do you think he'll come?"

Ben shook his head slowly, "Who the hell knows? Even if he does, when he sees the security, he might just take off again."

"Maybe it was just a stupid idea."

"Ben said seriously, "I don't think so, but if we really want to flush him out, we would have to hide the security."

"No way am I doing that! The old man would go into one! Forget the idea.!" Oliver looked around, people were beginning to drift in from the bars.

"We go as we are," he said decisively.

"Okay boss," and Ben moved off to check the kitchen area for the umpteenth time.

The ballroom soon filled, and it was five to eight which was sit down time. Oliver had taken his place at the top table with Becca; Matthew and Robert had been placed on a table in the middle of the ballroom, with an armed guard sitting next to them.

Paul and Lexi were waiting in a small ante-room, enjoying a glass of perfectly chilled Dom Perignon champagne. The door opened and a portly man with a large silver moustache and dressed in a bright red jacket entered. "Good evening, I'm Phil Taylor, master of ceremonies. Time to get some applause," and he held the door open for them. They stood up and went through, but Phil stopped them as they entered the ballroom.

"I'll announce you and then you make your way to the top table. Walk slowly and enjoy it."

Phil then walked to the top table and stood behind Oliver. Phil rang a hand bell and immediately, there was silence. Then and shouted, "Hear ye! Hear ye! Please welcome the guests of honour, Mr and Mrs Paul Bolton!"

The crowd rose to their feet, clapping. Paul and Lexi started the walk through the crowd shaking a few hands on the way. The atmosphere was presidential and electric and certainly aided by the gallons of free champagne the bars had been pouring for the guests. The band crashed into life, adding to the overall effect. At last they arrived at the table and Lexi sat down. The guests copied her and sat down. Paul remained standing as the band slowed to a very quiet background hum and then stopped altogether.

"My Lords...!" Paul stopped and looked from side to side. "Forget that! I don't know any!" A ripple of laughter from all around the ballroom. "Friends! Welcome to our little shindig. We are back in the UK for good...!" The beautifully dressed guests cheered. "Tonight, is a celebration of us returning to our roots; we are back in the club business!" he looked at Oliver. "Well done to my son Oliver who had masterminded our return." He smiled. "And my speech will certainly be incomplete without mentioning my dear wife Lexi out of any speech. I love you Lexi, that's it. So now let's rock the night and party...!" Que more cheering and whooping.

Ben wasn't cheering or whooping because his heart was beating fast and his mouth was dry. He was patrolling the corridor outside the main entrance to the ballroom. He spoke into his mouthpiece continuously, checking on key locations; everything was as it should be, so far so good he thought. He cursed as he ran his fingers around the neck of the formal dinner shirt he was wearing, trying to loosen it. He pushed the double doors and strolled back into the ballroom. He made for the top table, saw Oliver, and nodded at him, giving him a-thumbs up and just at that moment, he jumped as a bang went off at the table he was next to. He went for his gun and then realised it was a firecracker. He took a deep breath; it was going to be a long night and he needed a drink which unfortunately he couldn't have till it was all over.

Oliver wasn't enjoying the evening either. He was waiting for a gunshot, an attack of some sort; he couldn't relax. He kept touching Becca's arm, not sure whether it was to reassure

Becca or himself. He glanced at where the children were. Something was not right, Matthew was missing. He leaped to his feet and ran towards the table; Becca wondered what was happening. Paul jumped up and moved, Ben saw the movement out the corner of his eye, drew his pistol and looked for the threat. Oliver got to the table, he could hardly breath as he shouted at Robert.

"Where's your brother?"

Ben arrived brandishing his pistol, guests were getting up, a woman saw the gun and started screaming, guards rushed in from outside, guests started grabbing their bags and rushing for the doors.

"Gone toilet, daddy!"

"Shit!" he muttered. He rushed back to the top table and grabbed the microphone.

"Stop where you are please! False alarm! Sit back down! It's nothing, please sit back down and have a drink, everything's fine!" Guests were frowning and shaking their heads wondering what the hell was going on. Paul was soon by Oliver's side.

"What the fuck is going on?"

"I over reacted; Matthew's gone for a pee. It was stupid of me."

"Don't worry we're all on edge. Sit down and have a drink."

Ben's heart was in his mouth. He slipped the gun back into his shoulder holster, beads of sweat were forming on his forehead. He tried to remain calm as he spoke into his mouthpiece.

"Stand down everybody! Get back to your stations." He moved to stand behind the top table and started a call round key senior security guards. Steve Toppin was controlling the back stairs and didn't answer.

"Steve, are you there?" Ben's heartbeat was going through the roof again. "Shit!" He paused then called again, "Steve! Are you there?" No answer.

He started walking very quickly, afraid to run in case it caused panic. Oliver saw him and pushed his chair back and rushed after him.

"Ben! What's happening?"

"Back stairs! He's not answering!"

They rushed to the side of the ballroom and pushed open one of the many doors. They took the stairs two at a time and stopped on a landing.

"He should be here, let's keep going," Ben said, now very worried.

They descended into a very wide, and endless corridor whose ceiling was covered with hundreds of pipes of all shapes and sizes. Ben was worried there was no security anywhere at all.

"Fuck! what is going on?" And then he heard laughter. They followed the sound, and turning a corner, there they were, four of the team laughing and smoking cigarettes.

"What the fuck is going on here?" shouted Ben angrily.

Steve piped up in reply, "Just a quick fag break, boss."

Ben and Oliver were in shock, but it didn't last long.

Oliver growled. "You have put my family at risk! All of you get out of the hotel now! I don't want to see your ugly faces ever again."

Steve was also shocked. "We were only…"

Ben stopped him. "Stop talking and get the fuck out of the hotel."

The four men trooped off down the corridor.

Ben was straight onto his team.

"Max bring three men to the back-staircase door six as quickly as possible, and I mean like now."

Oliver was beside himself. "Fucking bastards!"

Ben looked glum. "Sorry my fault."

"It wasn't. Let's get back upstairs. Don't ever employ those bastards again."

Ben just nodded, and then they heard a shout.

"What's going on?"

Oliver couldn't believe it as Paul appeared, marching down the corridor.

"Nothing's happening dad, don't worry."

"Of course, I fucking worry! Jeez! This was a bad idea! I'm on edge and can't even enjoy the champagne." Then he laughed; it was infectious, and Oliver and Ben chuckled as well.

"Ben, get back to work, I'll follow with dad."
Ben recognised Paul, nodded, and moved off quickly.

Four hours later the party was over, and guests were leaving to go home. It had been a great success; even Paul, Lexi and Oliver had enjoyed it in the end. As soon as the music stopped, Ben had sneaked a large whisky; he had been as taut as a bow string all night and was just happy that it had all gone smoothly with no real hitches. He did one more tour of the ballroom and doors and then called the team in. Ear-pieces and walkie-talkies were handed in, brown envelopes were handed out and everybody went home happy bunnies. Ben stood in the middle of the ballroom, looking at the mess.

He took a deep breath and decided to go home for an early night. He made his way to the main Hotel entrance and stepped out into the night. Park Lane traffic was busy as always, day or night. It was a glorious, warm night; the sky was clear, and stars shimmered in their thousands. He undid his bow tie and loosened the top button of his white dinner shirt; he then decided to he'd take a short walk.

Just as he took the first step, he heard a familiar voice from behind him.

"Ben, I wondered where you were! You're not answering your phone!"

"Ran out of battery. What's up?"

"I've sent Becca and the kids home with two bodyguards. The night is young, I thought you might like a drink or two?"

Ben smiled and laughed. "Talk about a stressful evening, so yes love to. Where shall we go?"

"Easiest is the bar in the hotel," Oliver said cheerfully.
They both turned and headed back into the reception entrance. Five minutes later, they were sitting by the window in the cocktail bar on the fifth floor, sipping martinis.

Ben grimaced. "Never get used to these drinks; might have been alright for Bond but give me a pint any day."

"Next one's a pint then"

"We're not making a night of it are we? I'm exhausted."

"Don't worry, after a few drinks you'll get your second wind and then we'll hammer it."

Ben lifted his martini. "Shaken not stirred," and he drained the glass. "Now, where's that beer?"

They drank slowly, and it was soon one thirty.

"So, he didn't turn up."

Oliver looked thoughtful. "He knew there would be masses of security. It's a shame but I'm not that unhappy."

Ben agreed. "Could have been messy with so many people."

Oliver took a deep breath. "He won't go away, you do realise that? The man is a lunatic. He killed my sister Katie, they were in a hotel, he'd had sex with her and then he strangled her. Nutter, a complete nutter." He took a long slug of the whisky he had ordered.

"I'm sorry boss, sounds to me like he needs to be taken care of, and I mean permanently."

"He's been in that nuthouse for ten years, God knows what he's like now."

Ben shook his head. "Ten years in Broadmoor, what could be worse than that?"

"Why do you think he didn't take the bait?"

"Put yourself in his position, huge security, can't take a shot from a distance, plus you say he probably wants to kill all of you. How would he do it? Run in here with a pistol or knife? He wouldn't survive." He went quiet and Oliver noticed a change in his demeanour.

"What is it?"

"I'm in his position again and had a terrible thought."

"Well, what the fuck is it?"

"Don't worry forget it."

***

Paul and Lexi were sitting in the back of the luxurious Mercedes.

"Turned out to be a lovely evening."

Lexi smiled. "Thank goodness, yes, it was fun to see some of the old crowd."

Paul smiled. "I told you there was nothing to worry about; so, when we get home then…"

"I'm very tired Paul and I can feel a headache coming on."

He didn't take his eyes off her and then she couldn't hold it any longer and burst out laughing.

"All that champagne has put me in a right mood."

Paul didn't smile as he asked, pretending he didn't know what she was talking about. "Mood for what?"

Bermondsey Pie & Mash

"You know I like to surprise you sometimes, well I apologise in advance for my bad language so, in the mood for a damn good hard fuck. Are you up for it, Mr Bolton?"

He looked down at his groin. "I'm already getting up for it." And he grabbed her and kissed her long and hard on the lips.

It took forty-five minutes for them to reach home. Some of the lights were on and Paul looked for the security guard but couldn't see him. They exited the limo and made straight for the front door. Paul had already decided he was going to take her into the lounge and rip her clothes off and have her on the sofa. They entered the vast entrance hall and took their coats off. He grabbed Lexi's hand and almost dragged her into the lounge, pushed her onto the sofa and knelt in front of her. He pushed her knees apart, ran his hands up the inside of her flimsy peach dress and felt for the sides of her knickers; he took hold and started to pull them down when he heard laughter. He turned to see what the hell was going on.

"Hello Uncle Paul," Callum peered around him. "And there's the lovely Lexi; what a sweet couple you make. What were you about to do Paul? Were you going to be coupling, you know, fucking?"

He was holding a long knife in his right hand and a pistol in his left.

Another voice, a woman dressed all in black, walked into the room.

"Bodyguards taken care of; so sorry Lexi, there's buckets of blood on the cream carpet."

Lexi was shaking, and her eyes were round with fear as she saw the bright red blood dripping off Abi's hand. She remembered the last time Callum had attacked her; now she was in shock and couldn't think straight.

Paul was also shocked but quickly gathered himself together and took the offensive.

"You bastard! I can't believe you would dare to come into my house!" he glanced at the young woman. "and who might this be?"

 "The future Mrs Callum Bolton," Callum smiled.

Paul looked at the woman, his eyes flaring with anger and disbelief, that these two monsters dared to intrude in his home. "Did he tell you he strangled my eighteen-year-old daughter, he was having sex with her and then murdered her, he tried to throw acid in my wife's face, he's killed so many people the authorities have lost count; and you're going to marry him?"

Abi smiled at Callum indulgently, "You've been a very naughty boy Callum and you know what happens to naughty boys?"

Lexi and Paul were both looking at the woman, thinking she must be as mad as him, even worse!

"I can't wait," Callum smiled at Abi. "Abi, would you be so kind as to fix us a drink?"

"Seeing as you ask so nicely, of course hon."

Abi had already clocked the expensive walnut booze cabinet and passed Lexi as she strode towards it.

She hissed out the side of her mouth, "Fucking bitch! You'll get yours in a minute."

Lexi was terrified but took her lead from Paul.

"You must be a real slut to be sleeping with that piece of shit!"

Abi started rocking with anger and pointing at Lexi. "Bitch! I'm going to so enjoy cutting you up!" and from the inside of her jacket she produced a huge twelve-inch blood-soaked razor-sharp hunting knife.

"On second thoughts, before you do that, tie her hands behind her back." Callum said as he aimed the pistol at Lexi.

Abi didn't need a second prompting. She leaped at Lexi ferociously, knocking her off the sofa and onto the floor. She grabbed Lexi's arms and yanked them behind her back; Lexi grimaced and groaned in pain as Abi secured her wrists tightly with plastic ties.

Paul moved towards Lexi.

"Stay where you are Paul! Sit on the sofa!" Callum screamed, then strolled towards him. "I'll never forget what you did to my daddy. You've had a privileged life while my daddy has spent years in the wet cold ground. You and your bitch love the good life, eh? Look at this beautiful house." Callum went into a trancelike state and then called Abi to him. He whispered into her ear and she disappeared quickly out of the door.

Callum walked to the drinks cabinet and poured himself a large whisky from a cut-glass decanter. He knocked it back and turned to Lexi and Paul. He smiled and opened his mouth to speak, then stopped as the sound of shattering glass and a loud whoosh of air burst into the silence. Paul knew what it was and was desperately trying to think of what to do next. Abi came rushing back in, almost bouncing with excitement, laughing manically; and then Paul knew for certain she was as mad, or even madder than Callum. More loud noises could be heard, and the shattering and exploding of glass followed by the unmistakable sound of the crackling and hissing of fire and the smell of burning.

"You are both sick! Very sick!" Paul was interrupted by a massive explosion somewhere to the exterior of the property. He thought it was probably the garage as he had petrol in there. Everybody ducked as more explosions erupted closer and closer to the lounge. There was a further whoosh, and a blast of hot air exploded into the room.

Callum looked at Abi then took handcuffs out of his pocket and shouted to Abi.

"Drag the bitch here!"

It was getting hotter and then the smoke appeared; thick, black, choking smoke was entering the room. Carpets near the door entrance began to burn; it was mayhem.

Abi dragged Lexi close to the sofa and Callum snapped the handcuffs onto the pair of them and smiled down at them. He took a flick knife out of his pocket and clicked it open. Paul began to pray silently. Callum turned Lexi over and suddenly slashed and cut at the tendons on her calf, she screamed in agony as the tough band of fibrous tissue snapped. Paul tried to attack Callum but could not reach him. Callum brought the pistol butt down towards Paul's head and there was blackness. The smoke was becoming thicker and thicker, Lexi was struggling to breath and Paul was unconscious.

Lexi tried to stand but the pain was unbearable, and she collapsed. She shook Paul, but it was no good, they were going to die from smoke inhalation. She thought it was preferable to burning to death. The fire had entered the room and the curtains quickly went up in flames. The thick black smoke was now enveloping the whole room as Lexi tried to hold her breath. She grabbed hold of Paul by the arms and tried to pull him towards the door; he was so heavy, she gave up and fell on top of him and resigned herself to dying.

***

"I won't forget it, tell me and I'll decide whether it's worth worrying about or not."

Ben blurted it out. "Well, he would have known there would be huge security, but when it's finished, when everybody relaxes thinking nothing's going to happen, if it was me, that's when I would strike."

"Yea, so get to the point"

"The point is I would be waiting at the house for them to return."

"Oh fucking cow!" Oliver grabbed his phone and pressed speed dial one; it rang and rang and rang.

"Pick up, pick up for God's sake!"

Ben grabbed his mobile. "Who are you calling?"

"The old man!"

Ben pressed contacts and then Lexi. "I'm onto Lexi, it's ringing." He listened and listened. "No answer!"

Oliver clicked off and frantically re-rang Paul's number, it went straight to voicemail "Fuck!" he shouted.

"Ben, get the car running! I'll be right behind you! QUICK!"

Ben ran for the door, shouting at the concierge to get the range rover.

Oliver started walking towards the door, with the phone glued to his ear. "Can you help? I think Callum might be at the Virginia Water house...!" he listened as he broke into a run. "Thanks! Pray we're in time!"

One minute later, the range rover hurtled onto Park Lane and Ben slammed his foot down on the floor.
"M4!" Oliver shouted.

"Put the sat nav on!" Ben replied.

"Don't worry! I know the way! M4 M25 then come off at Egham! It's 24 miles!"

Ben was driving at breakneck speed through Kensington, careering around corners with smoke pouring off his tyres.

"We could get stopped by the law!"

"Don't stop for anybody! Just fucking drive!" Oliver shouted.

***

Callum and Abi were heading down a winding tight country lane towards the pub.

"Roasted Lexi, it has a nice ring to it."

"I do admire you Abi, we both are like peas in a pod."

"All that smoke, the flames licking at her! I expect she was screaming! Oh, the joy of it!"

Then Abi frowned, and Callum quickly asked, "What's wrong?"

"I just wish I could have watched her burning, that thin breast-less bitch! How you could have gone near her, I just don't know."

Callum wanted to change the subject because whenever Abi started talking about Lexi, she couldn't stop.

"So now we need to focus on Oliver, Becca and the kids."

"The kids?" Abi was surprised.

"The Bolton seed has to be completely destroyed, if not they will have won, you do see that?"

Abi thought for a few seconds.

"I do see, the seed must be destroyed, of course it makes sense. So, when?"

"Let's get home and have a drink to celebrate, and I'm feeling very horny; after a good fuck we'll talk it through."

"Sounds wonderful, especially the good fuck part."

***

Ben had never driven like this in his life. He was sweating and on edge as he continued from Egham to Virginia Water at a hundred and ten miles per hour. There had been no traffic due to the late time and with clear roads they had made incredible time.

Oliver shouted, "Straight road for a mile and we are there!" He looked up and saw a glow in the distance "What the...!"

Ben saw it too. "Fire! Oh shit! You don't think...!"

"I do! Faster or we could be too late!"

Ben couldn't go any faster as he gobbled up the distance.

They got closer and could see the thick, black smoke swirling into the air and then they saw the house fully ablaze, glass windows still exploding; the noise was ear shattering.

Ben screeched to a halt outside the gate and Oliver jumped out even before as the car came to a shuddering stop, closely followed by Ben

The heat was intense, but it didn't stop them. Oliver was in the front and he kicked the front door as hard as he could and thank God it burst opened, black smoke pouring out. He felt Ben grab his arm. "We're too late it's hopeless."

"No!" screamed Oliver. "Dad! Lexi!" He was shouting as loud as he could. He took off his jacket and put it over his head and entered the hall. Fire was everywhere, choking, black smoke was getting worse by the second.

"Dad! Lexi! Where are you?" He knew it was hopeless and then he thought he heard something.

"Lexi! Is that you?" he screamed into the fire and smoke.

He took a few more steps, the heat was staggering.

"Lexi, is that you?" he shouted again.

He heard her shout, "In the lounge!"

"Ben! They're alive! Will you help me?"

Ben ripped off his jacket and shouted, "Let's go!"

Oliver was in front and he rushed for the burning lounge door, Ben was holding onto the back of his belt. Oliver couldn't see much because of the smoke but he knew exactly where the lounge door was and soon he kicked it open amidst the flames and smoke.

He squinted his eyes; it was difficult to see anything.

"We're over here!"

He heard Lexi's hoarse voice and made for the voice. It was difficult to breath; the thick black smoke was choking the life out of all of them. Ben's hands began to tremble and loosen their hold at Oliver's belt as he began to lose control.

At last Oliver placed a hand on Lexi's shoulder.

"It was Callum and a woman," Lexi managed to say in a raspy voice as she struggled to breath. "We've been handcuffed, pull both of us." She was coughing and her hair had been burnt off. Paul's clothes were on fire and Ben lunged towards him to try to try and smother the flames. The smell of burning flesh got in his nostrils and he gagged.

Oliver took Lexi's hand. "Grab Dad Ben, we haven't got long!"

Oliver pulled Lexi across the floor and Ben dragged Paul on his side. Suddenly sparks flew, and Lexi burst into flames. Oliver stopped and smothered the flames with his jacket, he could feel his hair burning, he wouldn't give in.

"Pull for all our lives Ben!" And they started again towards the door, they were almost there, it wasn't far to go. He had to breath, his head felt as if it wasn't there, his legs turned to jelly, he couldn't think; he could feel himself sinking to the floor. "Ben!" he shouted but Ben was already lying on the floor, unconscious.

He opened his eyes one last time, knowing they had failed, and then it happened. Powerful hands grabbed him and lifted him into the air. Blissfully, he closed his eyes, unconscious.

***

The car pulled up outside the burning house.

Karen and Boian jumped out. There were three fire engines, two ambulances and numerous police cars.

She heard shouting and rushed to the gate, she flashed her badge, but an officer held her back.

The property was an inferno, no one could have survived; tears filled her eyes as she closed in on the shouting. It happened quickly, three fire-men appeared at the front door of the burning property, carrying bodies. The last man was also dragging a man who she couldn't identify. More fire-men rushed forward to help. As they got closer Karen could see all the bodies were badly burnt; then she recognised Lexi and her hands went to her face in shock. Lexi's clothes had been burnt off her body. Karen turned away, unable to look. She heard the swish of water as buckets of water were thrown onto the bodies, one of them cried out in pain, someone was alive! She turned back round to look. The bodies were laid down on a grass verge next to the ambulances. Paramedics were on them in seconds, setting up drips and giving oxygen. Karen was soon at Lexi's side.

"Lexi, it's Karen. You're going to be all right, you all are." Karen couldn't hold back the tears. Lexi was severely burnt, she looked like a charred corpse, as did the other three.

"Karen grabbed the shoulder of one of the paramedics. "Will they make it?"

"They have a chance, keep talking to them, it's the shock that kills; keep talking to them."

Karen swallowed hard and moved over to Paul and knelt beside him and gently took hold of one of his charred hand. "Paul, listen to me, Lexi is alive you all are, and you will all survive. Can you hear me, Paul?"

Boian had joined her and was trying to comfort Oliver who had begun to speak.

"What happened?" Karen rushed over to him. "Lexi and Dad are alive, you'll be fine."

"Ben?"

Karen assumed that was the other young man lying next to him.

"I don't know." She turned to Boian, "Check on him, please darling."

"Callum, it was Callum and a woman," Oliver said in a gritty voice.

Karen wasn't surprised but was surprised that he had got through the security.

"Stop worrying, you'll all be in hospital very soon."

"Tell Becca, and guards for Dad and Lexi"

"I'll take care of it, relax."

A minute later Paul, Lexi, Oliver, and Ben were loaded onto ambulances and were on their way to the specialist burns unit at St Peters Hospital in Chertsey.

Karen and Boian watched the ambulances drive off, blue lights flashing and sirens wailing.

Boian turned to Karen. "What do you think?"

"I have to believe they will all make it." She looked back at the house, a smouldering mess now that several hosepipes were showering it with thousands of gallons of water.

"Are you a good copper, Boian?"

He laughed. "I am a brilliant copper"

"Good, because you and I are going to find Callum Bolton and the mysterious woman. And when we do we are going to kill them."

***

The three ambulances pulled into St Peters Hospital Accident and Emergency department. They had been expecting them and knew they would be dealing with four patients who had a mixture of second and third-degree burns.

They were wheeled into A and E and four teams were standing by at the ready. Extra specialist burns staff had been called in to help cope with the emergency.

Paul, Lexi, Oliver, and Ben were all moaning in pain; in some respects, it was a good sign, they were alive, and they had been gotten to hospital in good time.

The first four things that happened were checking of the airways, then pain relief, oxygen, and I.V. solution drips. It was done quickly and professionally. Paul, Lexi, and Ben all had endotracheal tubes placed down their throats to aid breathing. Next, was to cut away the bits of clothing that were still on them. Lexi and Paul had suffered far more than Oliver and Ben due to the time they had been in the burning property. All four of them had blisters forming over different parts of their bodies, again Paul and Lexi had suffered more than the two young men. Paul and Lexi also had patches of charred black skin and bright red skin that appeared leathery and dry.

After a further assessment, Paul had an immediate escharotomy where he was given a deep cut around the shoulder to release liquid that had formed under the burnt skin. All four had signs of inhalation injuries that would take time to manifest in terms of seriousness. Blood samples were taken to measure for carbon dioxide poisoning. Antibiotics were given to lessen the chances of infection. The bodies were all cleaned as best as they could be, dead skin was cut and removed; small areas were washed, and burns were dressed and would be changed twice daily. Two hours after arriving at the hospital, all four patients were in a private ward together; they had been given as much pain relief as was prudent and they were all in controlled unconsciousness. Police guards had been placed at all entrances and exits to the hospital and to the burns unit.

***

Callum and Abi had been fucking for two hours, they were both exhausted and sat on the bed drinking a bottle of chilled white Sauvignon Blanc.

"I can see why people like starting fires; they call that something, don't they?"

"Callum smiled. "Pyromaniac; I know, it was just a spontaneous idea. I was a bit worried, I knew you had set your heart on acid or cutting."

"No, I liked it the thought of them burning..." she paused. "It sorts of suited them, if you know what I mean."

"Yes, I know exactly what you mean, especially Lexi, it was perfect for her."

"What about the others then?"

"Why don't you decide?"

"Okay, that's like a present. You're so good to me, I think I should show my appreciation."

"Well, if you insist," said Callum with a broad grin on his face.

"Do you want to slip into some of my knickers? It turns me on so much now I love it."

"Even better! Great idea!"

***

"So where do we start?"

Karen and Boian were standing at the window in her office in Sutton Police station.

Karen laughed. "You're the brilliant copper, you tell me."

"There's only one place ever to start and that's at the beginning."

"I agree, so let's list what we do know and go from there. One, we know Callum escaped from Broadmoor, add to that his mother, Dr Sharon Travis is in the country visiting him and a guard from the hospital has disappeared. So, let's surmise that Travis and the guard, I think his name was Tony Bridge, were instrumental in helping Callum to escape. So, the three of them are holed up somewhere, presumably in London or Surrey."

Boian grabbed the chance to speak. "It's a big area, we need to whittle it down to give us even a chance."

Karen nodded. "Of course, so the three of them must have rented a property, and I'm guessing Bridge would have had to do that because neither Callum nor his mother would have wanted their names on anything, not that Callum would have had the correct ID's and paperwork anyway. So, we find the property, we find them." She paused, "Trouble is, there are thousands of estate agents."

"Just go to the head offices of the chains, it's all computerised we could get lucky."

Karen clicked her intercom buzzer, she recognised Nicola's voice from the admin team.

"Can you and Jenny both come up, please."

"They may well have hired a car at some time," Boian said thoughtfully.

"This woman who seems to be Callum's partner may well have no record, so, if she's involved we won't be able to trace anything she's doing."

Boian persisted. "Still, check just the hire car Head offices of chains for Travis and Bridge."

Nicola and Jenny knocked and entered the office.

"Have sit down ladies and listen; if you have any ideas don't be shy."

Karen started speaking aloud. "Callum's been out on the streets for weeks; he's so unstable he could have killed or committed some serious crime. Ladies, check for missing persons, unsolved murders from the date he escaped, especially in Surrey and London. I don't know why, I just get the feeling he's in the Surrey area."

Jenny spoke up. "Why don't we check all the CCTV in the Virginia Water area, near Bolton's house. We can isolate the time, it's a bit of a long shot but..."

"No, good idea. They would both have been in the front of the car, we know what Callum looks like; unless he's in disguise, we could get lucky. It's a bit like looking for a needle in a haystack; but hey, we could get lucky."

For a few moments, they all sat there, no one spoke.

"Any other ideas?" Karen asked eventually.

The two admin ladies spoke at the same time.

"No."

Karen smiled. "Okay, go to it, and if you need help, shout; this is a priority."

CHAPTER 49

"So, what do you think then?"

Callum looked thoughtful and glanced at Abi, then he turned back to his Mother.

"Mummy, you must do what you think is best for you. I don't want you to go but I understand why you would want to." He turned back again to Abi. "What do you think?"

"It's mum's decision." She turned to Sharon. "If you're worried about Callum, don't be, I'm with him now and I'll make sure he's alright. But if you want to, you could stay and live with us in the pub."

It was three in the afternoon. They were sitting at the dining table, sipping at coffees. Sharon had made her mind up, she wanted to go back to Canada. She was more than worried though because she was sure the authorities were looking for her in connection with Callum breaking out of Broadmoor. The one thing they wouldn't have though was any evidence.

The doorbell rang.

Abi sprang up and skipped to the front door which she opened with a flourish.

She almost froze but somehow composed herself. "Hello."

She was staring at two police officers. She clocked the funny hats and then realised they were community police officers, in other words, not real coppers.

"Good afternoon. We're making enquiries about a reported missing person. The lady in question is a Ms Rita Philips." One of the officers held a small photo up in front of Abi's face.

Abi had a helpful looking smile on her face but was thinking what to do and say. She knew the name Rita Philips and recognised the woman in the photograph from somewhere, and then suddenly remembered her from her pub. She hadn't seen her for ages.

"The name doesn't ring a bell. Should I know her for any reason?"

The taller of the two officers holding the photo replied, "Not at all, Ms Philips is local though, she lives near the local pub; and you are?"

A slight panic was beginning in Abi's brain, she controlled it with a deep breath.

"Abigail Hansen, I actually own the local pub."

The lead officer smiled as the second one took out a note book and started writing.

"So, you must know everybody in the local area?"

"Truth is most of the time I have staff who run the pub. What was the missing ladies name again?"

"Rita Philips"

"Doesn't ring a bell at all. I could ask the staff if you like."

"Yes, that would be very helpful. Is this your property?"

Abi was getting annoyed, what the fuck was it to do with these two bastards? She imagined cutting them, the blood running down their uniforms; she was having difficulty keeping herself under control.

"It belongs to a friend of mine."

"And her name is?"

"Karen Banks."

She watched the officer with the notebook write the name down.

"I hope the ladies alright."

"I'm sure she is but we have to check, she's probably on a beach somewhere in Spain."

Abi laughed. "Wish I was on a beach somewhere with a nice glass of cold beer in my hand."

The two officers joined in the laughter.

"Well, thank you for your assistance. If you should hear anything, please get in touch with Surrey Police."

"Of course, good luck and have a great day."

The officers turned and walked away down the path.

Abi started shaking and she took deep breaths until they were under control.

As soon as she shut the door, Callum and Sharon appeared.

Sharon looked white faced. "God! I thought they had come to arrest us!"

"If they had, there would have been a lot more of them and they would have had guns." She turned to Callum. "You and I need to have a chat."

Callum couldn't speak; he had heard the policeman say the name Rita Philips and knew what was coming.

"Sharon, me and Callum are going outside for a minute, another coffee would be lovely."

Sharon was still in shock and could only nod as she scurried away to the kitchen.

"So, Callum do you want to tell me, or do I have to wheedle it out of you?"

"What's to tell?" he said sheepishly.

She looked at him. "I don't care what you've done, but I need to know so we can plan, and so I should know what to say to the police if they come to the front door again."

"Well I…"

Abi interrupted him. "I remember Rita Philips, reasonably attractive, and I seem to recollect she lived fairly near the pub. Come on out with it. What did you do?"

"Well, I urm, I did know her and she annoyed me and things got a little out of hand."

"A little out of hand, what exactly does that mean? She's missing, so you killed her?"

He couldn't speak for some time. Abi lifted her eyebrows. "Well?"

"Well yes, she's buried near her house. I didn't mean to kill her. She, well, you know, annoyed me and I got into a rage."

"Oh, dearie me, you're so sensitive, my love. I don't give a fuck about that trollop, but I need to know what is going on. So, what else have you been up to?"

"What else? Nothing, I promise."

Abi wasn't convinced.

"Look, if there was anything I would tell you."

"I want to hear the details."

"Details?"

"The trollop! What did you do to her?"

"Oh, I see. Well as I said, she annoyed me, so I hit her on the head with a piece of wood and she died."

Abi shook her head and thought seriously for a moment. "Where is the body?"

"Buried near her house."

"That could be tricky if they suspect foul play and start looking for it. I'm guessing your DNA is all over it."

"I guess."

"So at least you got a fuck from the trollop?"

"Shall we go in then?"

Abi smiled. "Yes we can, I'll be thinking about our situation and see if we need to make any changes."

"Okay," and Callum skipped towards the kitchen back door.

***

"We're not getting anywhere." Karen was frustrated at the lack of progress.

"The admin ladies are working hard, something will turn up, don't worry."

"You're always so positive, Boian, that's something I really like about you."

He laughed. "So, it's not just my good looks and huge cock then."

Karen laughed. "Well, the huge cock is certainly something not to be sneezed at."

Boian screwed his face up. "Sneezing at my cock! I'll never understand these funny English sayings."

Karen laughed aloud again and kissed him on the cheek.

"What was that for?"

"Just for being you."

The intercom rang, Karen pressed the button. "Yes!"

"It's Jenny. Can I come up?"

"Yes."

She turned to Boian and he gave her a "I told you so" look and she smiled warmly.

There was a knock on the door and Jenny entered.

"I'm very much hoping you have something for us," Karen said hopefully.

"Well, we have an interesting missing person and a death."

Karen rubbed her hands together. "Let's sit down and then you can tell us all about it."

Jenny read from an A4 piece of paper.

"A young female, name of Rita Philips has disappeared in a small village called Tadley in Surrey, then we have a forty-year-old man who was shot dead during a bungled burglary in Leatherhead, a male teenager was knifed to death in Reading but that's been attributed to a gang war. Then three recent deaths in London but all accounted for, oh, except the Railway worker at Paddington Station who was knifed to death in the toilet."

"In the toilet!" Karen shook her head. "What is the world coming to? Where is Tadley? I've never heard of it."

"Tiny village I guess, with a shop and a pub, probably, somewhere near Marlborough."

"Never heard of Marlborough either. Anyway, not a lot happening then. Any DNA testing that can help? And the woman in Tadley is slightly interesting; find out what the local police are doing and let me know."

"I'll check on the DNA tests and the Philips case."

Jenny left and Karen and Boian continued to brain storm how they might find Callum Bolton and the mysterious woman.

***

For some inexplicable reason Oliver recovered very quickly. His burns were more superficial and less severe than Ben's. The doctors believed it could have been because he was wearing a tee shirt under his dinner shirt. He was also young and fit and with a very positive attitude to life.

"I need to get back to work." Oliver was lying in bed, he was covered in dressings, but they were for minor burns as opposed to the seriousness of Paul's and Lexi's. Ben was in the bed next door and in a bad way, but his injuries were not life threatening.

A young nurse was sitting in a chair next to his bed.

"The doctor says you're not going anywhere for at least a few days. We need to do some tests to see if your lungs are ok and then we'll see."

"I need to get back to work," Ben insisted

The nurse shook her head and wondered what it was that drove men to feel they had to get back to work, as though for some reason it was more important than their health.

Oliver could speak but it was painful, he knew he had inhaled some of the choking black smoke and it must have damaged his airways. He looked across at his father and Lexi, they were still unconscious, but they did look a bit better. He heard a moan and turned towards Ben. He was opening his eyes and was obviously in pain. Something attracted his attention out of the corner of his eye, it was a policeman strolling past the entrance.

He turned back as he heard Ben trying to speak.

"What the fuck is going on?"

"Language Ben! There's a very nice young nurse here who doesn't like swearing."

Ben tried to laugh but coughed instead.

"Thank God you're alright. What about Paul and Lexi?"

"They're alive and fingers crossed, should make it."

"Never going near a fire again." Ben said hoarsely and started coughing.

"Thanks Ben."

"What for?"

"Couldn't have got them out without your help."

"You owe me a pint then." Cue more coughing.

"It's a deal but you could have coughed yourself to death by then," Oliver laughed and he too started coughing.

The nurse was at Ben's bedside.

"How are you feeling?"

"Alright but I need to get back to work."

The nurse's whole demeanour changed in a flash.

"You're not going anywhere until the doctor says you're fit to leave. If you are really stupid you could discharge yourself, but I wouldn't recommend it, and to be quite honest, I don't care what you do," and she stormed off.

"Who rattled her cage?"

Oliver laughed. "I said exactly the same thing to her, so it was me." He started coughing yet again.

They both laughed until Oliver once again became serious.

"We do need to get out of here, so we can deal with that bastard Callum and his bitch."

"Now, that, I am looking forward to." And Ben started coughing yet again.

CHAPTER 50

Abi moved back to the pub but didn't allow Callum to join her. She explained that it would be best if the pub customers thought he had left and moved on. The police were still sniffing around, and she didn't want any possible connection being made that could jeopardise either of them individually or together. Sharon was packing and had decided to take a leisurely route back to Canada via several European countries. She would leave in a week's time; summer was coming to an end with September around the corner.

***

Oliver and Ben were out of hospital and recuperating. Becca had asked Ben to stay with them while he recovered, and she was spoiling the pair of them. The blisters and minor burns were healing well. The issue was the damage done by breathing in the toxic, thick, black smoke, although there was no lasting damage to airways or lungs. The doctors had explained that it would take time to heal and the coughing could go on for months. They were both eating well and enjoying regular beers.

Paul and Lexi were woken from induced comas after a week. They were relieved and overjoyed when told Oliver and Ben were had recovered and in good health and had been discharged to recuperate at home. Paul and Lexi had suffered second and third degree burns and were in continual pain even though both were doped up with strong morphine to relieve their constant pain. Paul had severe burns to his legs, torso, and hands. He had tried to protect his face with his hands and it had worked to a degree. He had suffered minor burns to his face which would heal in time. Lexi had also suffered on her torso, legs, hands, and scalp. She too had been lucky; she had shielded her face from serious burns with her hands. They would both be in hospital for at least two months and then must continue with skin grafts and treatments for months. Paul didn't care, they were alive and had discussed buying a new home by the sea in either Spain or Portugal. They would retire and reside in the sun for the remainder of their lives. Oliver and Ben had been to visit them as had Karen and Boian. After the visit, the four of them sat in the hospital coffee shop and discussed Callum and his new-found woman.

***

Police dog teams poured into the woods and fields near the Foresters Pub. One of the locals told Abi van loads of police search teams had arrived and were traipsing over the whole area. She was annoyed but not that surprised, it had only been a matter of time before they started the search for Rita Philips' body. She immediately called Callum and told him to stay in the house. The local community hall had been taken over as the police Head Quarters and she knew it was only a matter of time. In fact, it had been only three hours after they had arrived, and gossip shot around the village that a body had been found buried near her house and that it was Rita Philips. Abi knew it was also only a matter of time before they cross checked the DNA and found out Callum was responsible. She also knew that once they had established he could be in the area, it would be flooded with armed police and if he stayed at the house he would almost certainly be arrested and then she could be next. She had sneaked out of the pub and got in a taxi which dropped her near to Callum's house; she walked the rest of the short journey.

The three of them were sitting in the lounge with glasses of red wine.

"So that's the situation, you live by the sword and die by it as well."

Sharon spoke next and looked directly at Callum. "You are a fool. I don't care what you get up to but how many times have I told you not to do it on your own doorstep. Decisions must be made and very quickly. Well, what have you got to say for yourself?"

"I'm sorry mummy and you Abi. I've let you both down very badly."

Abi shook her head. "I love it when you're all apologetic," and she gave him a huge smile.

Sharon was keen to move on. "Look you're the brains here Abi. What should we do?"

She spoke slowly. "Well, I have given it a great deal of thought and I suggest you two move back into the pub."

Neither Sharon or Callum could speak.

Finally, Callum spoke. "There'll be hundreds of police swarming all over the area! We're sure to be caught."

"You both move into the pub and we try to bluff our way through. As soon as they discover the DNA connection, they'll assume you have disappeared, but you'll be hiding right in the middle of them. They don't know who I am so we'll all be safe. I'll give the staff time off and when the police move on, we can decide what to do."

Sharon looked thoughtful. "It could work."

"We don't have a lot of choice," said Abi starkly.

Callum gushed. "Well, I like it because I'll be with the two women I love more than anything in the world."

Abi looked at Sharon. "He's so sweet, isn't he?"

Sharon spoke seriously. "So, it's agreed then. When shall we come back?"

"Tonight, after I've closed, I'll call you to say it's safe. I'm off and I'll see you later. She kissed Callum and Sharon and left.

CHAPTER 51

"So, we're making progress."

Boian answered with a smile. "I told you it will all come together."

Karen pressed a speed dial on her mobile.

"I've got some news for you."

She spoke for three minutes and clicked off.

"How are they recovering?"

"Slowly but they'll all make it."

A hundred police officers, many of them armed, were descending on the village of Tadley and surrounding areas. Cordons had already been setup on main roads to check vehicles entering and leaving the area. Karen had been informed that DNA found on Rita Philips had been matched to Callum Bolton. She had immediately put in motion a plan to swamp Tadley with as many officers as possible to find and arrest Callum Bolton and his associates. Were they in time? She asked herself, probably not but it was worth the effort. If he was with his mother and the mysterious woman or on his own, people on the run make mistakes. Karen and Boian arrived at the small ramshackle community hall and met the local officer who had overseen the missing person case. Shabbily dressed Detective Leigh Grant handed over the whole case to Karen and was thankful a very senior and experienced officer had arrived to take control. It was eight am and things were moving at a fast pace.

"So, Leigh cordons are in place?"

"Yes."

"You do understand Callum Bolton is a cold-blooded killer and won't hesitate to use violence against any of your local officers."

"I see, it's serious then."

Karen wanted to shout at him, "Of course, it's fucking serious! He's a psychopathic murdering lunatic!"

But she managed to control her voice. "Yes, please warn all your officers that he is not to be approached unless they are armed."

"I'll do that immediately."

"Good. So, do we have any intelligence from your missing persons enquiries?"

Detective Grant looked confused. "Such as?"

"Such as properties or persons that are of interest to us."

"I don't think so."

Karen looked at him and smiled, he obviously didn't have long to go to retirement and hadn't handled a major case for donkey's years.

"Thanks Leigh, you've been very helpful."

"Leigh was very happy and took his leave."

Karen turned to Boian and Jeff. "Right, let's get moving. Jeff, organise the search teams, we're going to visit all the local places of interest." She looked around and continued. "And that shouldn't take very long."

"First, stop in any village, the first place is always the local pub. Let's go."

Karen and Boian walked across the road and continued thirty yards down the road to the entrance of the Foresters arms. Police cars and vans were hurtling up and down the road, officers were on both sides of the road and had begun house to house enquiries.

The pub door was shut and locked. Karen located the bell and pressed, she wasn't sure whether it was working or not but waited for a few minutes to see. She lifted her hand and pressed it again and she heard a woman shout from inside.

"Stop ringing the bell for Christ's sake!"

The door opened, and a youngish lady was standing in the doorway in a pink dressing gown.

"Yes, what can I do for you?"

Karen took her ID out. "Detective Inspector Karen Foster, Surrey Police. This is detective Boian Lupei."

"Sorry I shouted, didn't get to bed till late last night. What can I do for you?"

"I realise it's early, but we would like to ask you some questions regarding the murder of Rita Philips."

"It's so early but of course come in I'll help in any way I can."

She opened the door and stood back. "Grab a seat in the bar and I'll be back in a minute."

She went up the stairs and into the bathroom. Sharon and Callum were standing by the door. She put her finger to her lips and mouthed "Police" Callum nodded, and Sharon went white.

The plan was whenever the bell rang they were to go into the bathroom. Abi washed her face and tied her hair back, she went to her room and stuck on a pair of track suit bottoms and a jumper. She took a deep breath and went back downstairs.

"It's so shocking, that poor girl," and Abi shook her head from side to side.

"Are you the land-lady?"

"I own the freehold actually, but yes I'm the land-lord as well," she smiled.

"I'm sorry, I don't know your name?"

"Abigail Hansen. I told your two officers everything I know which I'm afraid wasn't much."

Karen had a questioning look on her face.

"They came to see me when Miss Philips was a missing person, obviously it's got a lot more serious now."

"Yes, it has, she's been murdered, and we found her buried not that far from here."

"It's just shocking. I still can't believe it, and this is such a quiet respectful area."

"So, did you know Rita Philips?"

"I didn't but she may well have visited the pub at some time, I don't know."

"Do you have staff?"

She didn't answer for a second. "Sometimes, I lead a very quiet life but if I do go out then yes, I get cover."

"We'll want to speak to them. What are their names?"

"Susan Green and Michelle Barclay"

"They're local?"

"Yes, I'll give you their phone numbers before you go. I think Susan is away though."

"Any new strange men been around?"

Abi took a breath and concentrated. "You know, I honestly don't think so; we get some people in occasionally and you think they're a bit weird, but no one stands out."

"Do you know of any new arrivals in the village or surrounding area, think of maybe two women and two men."

Bermondsey Pie & Mash

"I'm really sorry I can't, I don't seem to be helping much."

"It will be all over the news soon enough. The man we're looking for is Callum Bolton, he escaped from Broadmoor and is very dangerous." Karen rummaged in her pocket and took out a photo of Callum. She passed it to Abi.

Abi studied the photo and almost smiled, it was a lovely photo and was presumably taken at Broadmoor hospital.

"Never seen him before and I would remember him."

"Oh, why's that?"

Abi wished she hadn't said it. "He's got a face you would remember that's all, he's never been in here."

Karen stared at her without saying anything and Abi stared back at her.

Abi was imagining sticking a knife into Karen's neck and seeing a fountain of blood spiralling into the air.

"So, we'll leave you to get on. I'll take the two phone numbers if I may, and if we need to speak to you again we know where you are."

Abi stood up. "I'm not going anywhere. I'll get those numbers for you."

Hundreds of vehicles were stopped and door to door enquiries revealed no leads. Karen and Boian were in the local shop interviewing the owner when the call came through.

"We're on our way now and get the forensic boys in as soon as possible."

Two Policemen had called on the property where Callum and Sharon had been holed up. No one was in, but they had found a to rent property board thrown into a corner of the front garden. They decided to be thorough and called the agent enquiring if anyone was renting the property. The answer came back that a Mr Tony Bridge had signed the rental agreement. Alarm bells rang, and they phoned the information into Head Quarters.

Karen and Boian arrived at the quiet country lane property. The two officers were smoking and on seeing the car immediately threw their smouldering cigarettes to the floor.

Karen jumped out the vehicle. "Don't worry, you deserve a smoke, carry on."

She and Boian marched up the path and looked in the windows, it looked deserted. They strolled around the side and did a complete tour and arrive back at the front door.

"Where the fuck are the forensics?" She looked around. "Bollocks! We will have to kick the

front door in, we'll say it was open."
"You sure?"

"Kick it in."

Boian prepared himself and gave the door a mighty smash, it flew open and Karen took the first step inside. She looked around, it was obvious they had definitely gone and Karen was straight on the phone.

"Jeff, they're on the run! Get everybody out of the village! We'll be back at Sutton later today, I want to have a quick look around the property."

Ten minutes later the forensics team arrived at the property and commenced searching and swabbing for DNA and finger prints.

"There's fuck all here for us, so we move on. They must have a vehicle, second, they will have to stay in hotels or more likely, small B & B's. So which way have they've gone is the big question. The good news, Boian, is that they will make mistakes. Let's get back to Sutton."

***

Sharon, Abi, and Callum were in the small upstairs lounge.

"It worked a treat Abi! You are without question a fucking genius!" Callum said, looking at Abi with admiration.

Abi preened and lifted her glass of champagne. "I know, I can't help it! A fucking genius!"

Abi and Callum were celebrating, but Sharon was looking glum and could hardly raise a smile.

"Cheer up mum! We're in the clear!"

Sharon looked at Abi. "What do you think Abi? Are we in the clear?"

"Short term, yes we are, so as Callum says, cheer up."

Sharon glanced from one to the other. "We got away with it this time, but truth is we're rats in a hole. We can't go anywhere, we have to keep quiet at all times, we cannot go near any windows; you call this winning, I don't."

The atmosphere changed from celebration to despair, but Abi was not having it.

"Callum, come with me, we need to celebrate properly."

Sharon closed her eyes, knowing what was coming.

Abi and Callum went next door to their bedroom and seconds later the grunting and noise

Bermondsey Pie & Mash

started. The night before it had been spanking that Sharon had to endure, she'd also caught Callum wearing a pink bra and knicker set which again disturbed her. She tried not to listen as Abi was shouting, "Harder! Harder, fuck me, you bastard!" She tried to ignore her emotions, but she was becoming aroused. She could hear the slapping and imagined Callum thrusting into Abi from behind. She stood and opened the door, she took the three steps to the bedroom door and opened it. She stood in the doorway, she could smell the sex as Abi and Callum rolled on the bed. Abi saw her and smiled, she gestured for Sharon to enter further. Sharon took the step and pushed the door shut behind her.

***

The two community police officers were strolling down the village high street. Everything had gone back to normal after the incredible excitement. The multitude of officers, dogs and even mounted police had disappeared as fast as they had arrived. The village had gone back to sleep and they were delighted and looking forward to investigating who had stolen a bicycle from outside the local shop.
It was three pm on a Tuesday, they were walking across the road from the pub and one of the officers called Tom Furness suddenly stopped.

"That's strange," said Tom.

"What is?" asked Ken Tutor, the other officer who also stopped.

"Pizza delivery at the pub."

They both looked over and saw a pizza delivery scooter man taking two huge pizzas out of the box on the back of the Scooter.

Ken was puzzled. "It's a pizza delivery, what's strange about that?"

"The pub closed at two, so who's the pizza for?"

"Who cares, perhaps Abigail's very hungry."

Tom took a step to cross the road. "Let's go."

Ken hesitated then started after Tom.

"What are you going to say? Perhaps you're going to ask her how many pieces of pizza she's going to eat?"

"She might be a hostage."

"What! Sherlock, I'm worried you've been watching too many late films."

Tom became more worried when he saw the curtain move in one of the upstairs rooms.

Tom was first at the door and rang the bell.

They waited and waited, and nobody came to the door.

"This is getting stranger and stranger," Tom said as he rang the bell again holding it down for a few seconds.

"Jeeze! Give your hand a rest!" Abi shouted as she opened the door.

"What do you two want?"

"No need to be like that Ms Hansen! We're just doing our job."

"Well, go and do it somewhere else, you bloody micky mouse coppers! What do you want?"

"We thought it strange you having so much pizza delivered."

She stood there looking at them in disbelief.

"Pizza? I bought some in as I've got friends coming over tonight, that is if it's okay with you?"

"You're on your own then?"

"Yes, I am! What of it?"

Suddenly there was a crashing noise from upstairs.

"What the hell was that?" Tom pushed past Abi and Ken followed.

Abi shut the door.

Tom looked around the bar.

"Ms Hansen, is everything alright?"

There were some more noises from upstairs.

"Everything's fine, it's a man friend, you know how it is."

Another crash from upstairs like a person falling down onto a bathroom tiled floor.

"I'm going up."

Tom made for the stairs and Ken followed.
Tom took out his baton and slowly ascended the tight steep staircase, his heart was pounding.

He got half-way and stopped in shock.

A man in bright red bra and knickers appeared at the top of the stairs holding a huge serrated hunting knife in each hand. The man started to slowly descend the stairs, one step at a time.

Tom shouted without turning around.

"Get out Ken! Run for help!" He held up his baton as protection and kept backing down one step at a time.

Ken turned and froze in panic. Abi was standing at the bottom of the stirs also holding two knives; she started to climb one at a time. Ken was shaking as he held out his baton.

As Callum reached Tom he lunged towards him with one knife, trying to cut him on the face, but Tom managed to get his baton in the way and knocked the thrust away. Callum followed up with the other knife and rammed it into Tom's neck, the blood spewed in a fountain in every direction, some landing on the magnolia coloured wall and some splattered all over Callum. Callum followed up with the other knife, slamming it into Tom's chest. Once he felt the knife enter he pushed as hard as he could, right up to the hilt. He then started twisting the knife and cutting; bright red blood was flowing freely out of the wound onto his hands and arms.

Tom screamed and gurgled as blood filled his mouth. Callum pulled the knife out of Tom's chest and plunged it back in, as more blood and gore flew and splattered all over him and the walls and stairs. Tom fell backwards onto the stairs in a death spiral. Abi had got to Ken and was attacking him with both knives. Ken was tiring of trying to defend himself with his baton and did not know what was happening behind him. Callum's razor-sharp, blood covered serrated knife entered the top of his back, severing the spinal cord. Ken gave an agonising scream, spasmed and collapsed on the steps at Abi's feet. Abi was on him in a second, pulling up his head by his hair and cutting his throat from ear to ear. Abi and Callum were both covered in blood as they held up their knives in a ghoulish, victory celebration.

Abi shouted, "That'll teach those fucking interfering wankers to mind their own fucking business."

Abi looked up the stairs at Callum who was a sight in his bra and pants, covered in blood and laughing hysterically.

Behind Callum stood Sharon; she was as white as a sheet, her eyes popping out of her head as she took in the blood-soaked scene. She turned and vomited on the floor and then dashed for the bathroom.

Abi was taking deep breaths as she too surveyed the gory scene.

"They'll be missed very soon; we'll talk in a minute but first let's clean up and get changed."

Abi made for the bathroom and tried the door, it was locked.

"Sharon, open the door!"

Abi could hear the bath running.

"We need to clean up, open the door!"

She turned to Callum. "We haven't got time to fuck around, we need to wash and change, and quickly."

"Mummy, open the door please."

The water was still running.

Callum was becoming very agitated.

"Mummy, open the fucking door please!"

He jumped back as water appeared under the door.

Abi was shocked. "What the fuck! Break the door down! Quickly Callum!"

It was a relatively cheap internal door and Callum charged at it and hit it full on with his shoulder. The door burst open and he nearly fell over as he stumbled into the bathroom. He collected himself and then screamed. The bath was full of red coloured water. He jumped forward and felt Abi move behind him, she turned the taps off as Callum lifted Sharon out of the bath; her wrists were cut, and she was bleeding heavily.

"Leave me, I've had enough." She could hardly speak; she had lost so much blood and it was only a matter of time.

Callum let out a heart rendering scream, "Mummy! Mummy! What have you done?"

He crashed to the tiled, wet, and bloodied floor and held Sharon tight in his arms and began to rock her gently.

Abi was trying to think but couldn't as she took in the awful sight.

Sharon spoke her last words, "I love you Callum," and then she stopped breathing and her head fell to one side. Callum was crying loudly and gasping for breath.

"Why? Why did she do it?" he wailed.

Abi knew why, she couldn't take anymore of her deranged son and the blood and the shit and the entrails and the killing.

Abi put her hand on Callum's shoulder.

Bermondsey Pie & Mash

"Put her on the bed in the spare room, I'll cover her in a minute."

Abi was worried; as soon as the two coppers were missed all hell would break loose in the village. She wondered if they would search the pub, whether she liked it or not. She thought of moving the bodies. She looked at the bath which was still full of crimson water. She quickly unplugged the bath and the water started draining away. She then opened the airing cupboard and pulled out a handful of towels and threw them on the floor.

***

"Two community officers have gone missing in Tadley village."

"What? How can two officers have gone missing?"

"According to the report, they never arrived back at the local nick; they are uncontactable on their radios, so a car was sent out but there is no sign of them."

Karen was worried. "Boian, you don't think we were fooled, do you? Maybe they never left the village and these two stumbled on something. Oh God, I hope I'm wrong, let's keep this to ourselves for the time being. You get the car ready, I'll draw some weapons."

They left the station and were soon back on the M4.

"We seem to live on this motorway," said Boian with a laugh.

Karen was checking over the two Glock pistols and loading the ammunition.

Karen ignored Boian, she was thinking ahead.

"So where could they all be? We're talking about a possible four people: Callum, Tony Bridge, Sharon Travis and now the new girl. It's not like a single person, they need to buy quite a lot of food on a regular basis. We'll check at the local shop first and ask some pertinent questions."

Karen and Boian walked the length of the village on one side of the road and walked back on the other.

"You know what, Boian, there could very easily be an old property out in the woods somewhere that no one knows about. Perhaps we should call in the chopper to have a look for us."

"Good idea, anything's worth trying."

Karen got on the phone to the station.

"Jeff, any news on the two officers?"

"Nothing, your end?"

"All quiet at the moment."

"Speak later," and Karen clicked off.

"Let's go in the shop then."

They walked the ten yards and entered the local shop.

"Morning, Detective Inspector…"

Glynis Coombs, the owner, interrupted her. "Morning, I know who you are, I've answered hundreds of questions with the same answers so I'm sure I won't be able to help anymore."

"We're concerned about the two missing officers, any thoughts?"

"I honestly haven't. I saw them the day they went missing, they were heading over to the pub and it was all normal; I don't know what to else to say."

Karen smiled, "I wanted to ask you a couple of questions. So, do you do deliveries?"

"Of course, it's a steady income for us."

"So, can we have a list of those customers please."

"Of course, I'll look it up for you."

"Has anyone been ordering larger quantities of food than usual? Say, in the last month"

"Not that I've noticed, no."

"Who's your biggest customer then?"

"The pub by miles and they get busier in the summer, so orders have certainly gone up from them."

Karen thought nothing of it. "Thanks for your help."

"What about the list?"

"If I need it, I'll come back."

***

Abi pulled the curtain back again.

"They've come out of the shop and are standing on the pavement, chatting."

Callum was in a foul mood. "Fucking bastards never leave us alone."

"Don't worry, they're confused and don't know which way to turn."

"Why don't we sort them?"

Abi turned and frowned at him.

"Things are bad enough, we don't need any more agro. No, we leave them alone."

Callum muttered, and Abi heard him say, "Shame, that would have been fun."

"They're strolling back down the high street; they've gone into the coffee shop."

"Why don't they just fuck off and leave us alone!" Callum was getting angry.

"Because my darling, they have lost two of their colleagues and want to find them."

Callum laughed, with a sudden change of mood, "They won't find anything, wild animals would already have had a good feed on them two."

Abi turned and spoke at the same time.

"We need to get out even if it's just for a drive, we've been cooped up here long enough."

Callum cheered up immediately.

"Great idea! Where are we going?"

"For a drive, go and put some clothes on."

***

The car pulled into the driveway at the side of the pub. They had gone for an hour's drive and decided to return to the pub because they had become bored by simply driving around country roads. Callum jumped out the passenger side and rushed round to open the door for Abi who was in the driver's seat.

She looked up at him and smiled, "You're only opening the door for me so you can get in my good books and then get in my knickers; I can read you like a book." And she laughed.

"I'm trying to be the perfect gentleman."

"Well, I hope you're not going to be the perfect gentleman once we get to the bedroom."

He laughed loudly. "Are you getting out or not?"

She took her time and looked at him with a mischievous grin on her face.

"What position are we going to start with?"

Callum slammed the door shut and Abi clicked on the key and heard the doors lock.

He looked thoughtful as they made their way to the pub door.

"How about you being on top?"

"Yes, you know I love to be on top."

They hurried up and reached the door; Abi pushed the key in and turned and shoved it open. She was first into the bar, closely followed by Callum. They made for the side entrance to the stairs but stopped as a woman appeared in front of them.

"So, we meet again Abi..." she turned to Callum. "Callum Bolton," she shook her head. "I'm so pleased to see you again."

The pair of them stood frozen; they were so shocked they could hardly speak.

Abi tried to pull herself together.

"How did you get in here? I'm going to report you for breaking in to my property. Now get out!"

Karen smiled. "I'm afraid that's not going to be possible." And she lifted her Glock automatic pistol.

"Both of you sit at one of the tables..." they didn't move. "Move! Now!" and she aimed the pistol at Abi.

Callum was unsure what to say or do; he edged back and decided to leave it to Abi who was much cleverer than him.

A man's voice came from behind him, "Do as you're told."

Callum turned and saw the other police officer, he too was holding a gun. They sat down at the table.

I'm assuming the dead body upstairs is your mother, Callum?"

"Yes, mummy cut her wrists," and he started to cry.

Abi snarled at him, "Shut the fuck up Callum and pull yourself together!"

He opened his eyes wide, Abi had never spoken to him like that.

"And the blood all over the stairs and walls," Karen paused. "I'm guessing belonged to the two police officers?"

Callum smiled, and then started laughing.

"What happened to Tony Bridge, or is that a stupid question?"

Abi was almost in a trance as she spoke.

"He's dead, eaten by wild animals, and Rita Philips and the rail worker at Paddington Station. Oh, it's been such fun and it's not over yet."

Callum was laughing again, maniacally. "Where's all the back-up then, officer Foster?"

It was Karen's turn to smile. She looked over at Boian and threw him a set of handcuffs. "Cuff them together to the table" Boian took out his set and did exactly that and then they both relaxed a little.

"What's going on?" Callum asked looking confused.

"We're waiting," Karen said quickly.

"For what?"

"You'll see soon enough."

Callum shook his head, not understanding what was going on.

"Tell him the truth, officer Foster," Abi snarled.

"There's plenty of time for the truth. So before that, how did you get mixed up in all of these killings?"

Abi threw her head back and laughed. "People need to reach their full potential in life; meeting the lovely Callum allowed me to do exactly that. He really is a very sweet boy."

Callum looked at Abi, "I don't mind going back to hospital. I miss my friends anyway."

Abi turned to Callum. "But I think officer Foster has other ideas for us Callum, not friendly ideas either. What do you say Officer Foster?"

Karen looked at her watch.

"I think that sometimes things just need to be finished and finished for good."

Abi spoke without taking her eyes of Karen. "I told you Callum, this is all unofficial, we're off the radar." She paused and sneered. "Don't tell me, another court case? Right, Karen?"

"Shut up! No more talking! Boian, you watch the two lunatics while I go and make us some coffee."

He nodded and smiled.

Coffee was drunk, and the time went on and on, it got to eight pm and Karen's mobile rang.

"Yes, you're five minutes away; ignore the closed sign on the door, I'll let you in when I see your headlights."

Abi and Callum both sat up and showed some interest. Abi was well ahead of Callum.

"Who's arriving?" She was staring at Karen. "I said, who the fuck is arriving, bitch?"

"Shut your foul mouth! You're no longer in charge! I am!"

"Fucking bitch! If I was free, I'd cut you up for speaking to my Abi like that." Callum spat a huge glob of phlegm which hit Karen on the arm, and that really amused him, and he started laughing again.

Karen just looked at him and said quietly, "You won't be laughing soon."

There was an earie silence and then suddenly, they all heard the screech of tyres and saw the flash of headlights on the window. Karen rushed down the stairs; Abi and Callum were all ears as they heard the front door open.

Again, there was an earie silence and then they heard the front door open again and they heard more than one person entering the pub. Then they heard wheezing and loud breathing; it was a frightening sound and it got louder and nearer as shoe sounds landing on the stairs got closer and closer. Abi and Callum couldn't take their eyes off the door, and suddenly it slowly opened. Karen was the first to enter.

Ben was behind Karen, he was coughing and wheezing; next in was Paul Bolton, he was walking slowly and it looked and sounded like he could hardly breath. Last in was Oliver whose lungs were rattling every time he took a breath. They all had burns, peeling skin, no hair and looked like death warmed up.

Callum's eyes were on stalks and shining brightly.

"Uncle Paul! You don't look well! And where may I ask, is the lovely Lexi?" She's not dead, is she?" and he laughed maniacally.

Paul tried to speak but all anybody could hear was "Bastard."

They had told Paul they didn't need him and that they would sort it. He had insisted on going with Oliver and Ben and nothing anybody said could make him change his mind.

Abi, unlike Callum, knew immediately what was happening.

"So now I think I understand what's going on; déjà vu. Callum how did your father die?"

Callum looked confused and then he too got it. "Uncle Paul and a bunch of thugs held a kangaroo court, they found him guilty and stabbed him to death.

"Is that what's happening Karen? You fucking slag bitch!" She strained at the handcuffs but all it did was pull Callum closer to her.

Callum was beginning to froth at the mouth. He spat phlegm at all of them, screaming loudly.

"I want to go back to Broadmoor, back to my friends! You can send me, and let Abi come with me! We will be very happy together and you'll never see us again!"

"You're wasting your breath darling; these murdering swine are going to do us; these heroes are going to kill us while we're trussed up like turkeys.

Callum was close to having a fit, he started jerking and just kept repeating himself, "Fucking bastards! Fucking bastards...!"

Karen looked at Boian. "Time for us to go."

The room went silent apart from the noises of laboured hissing and wheezing.

Oliver took charge. "So Callum, at last, after all these years, it's time to finish it." Tears filled his sore eyes as he thought of his beautiful sister Katie.

"So much pain and anguish you have inflicted on my family. Just like for your father Tony, the court has sat," he paused and stared at Callum. "And you have been found guilty and must die for your crimes." He turned to Abi. "And you his partner in murder and torture, the same for you."

Abi wasn't going to take things lie down. "You repulsive shit! I hope you die! I hope you all die very soon! if I could, I would cut you all up and drink your blood! Callum, get ready to fight!"

Callum woke from his trans-like state with a start and growled at the three messengers from hell.

Deadly sharp flick Knives appeared from pockets. Ben and Oliver stepped forward as Abi and Callum shrunk back and got ready to kick. It happened quickly as Ben lunged at Abi. She kicked out but missed and the razor-sharp six-inch blade sank into the flesh around her ankle; she didn't scream but kicked out again and hit Ben's arm. Callum had no free arms but leaped forward, landing a kick on Ben's chest, pushing him back. Oliver grabbed Callum's ankle with his left hand and plunged the knife into his thigh above the knee. Callum howled with pain as he dragged his leg back with the knife still stuck in it. They were all breathing heavily, and Ben and Oliver were both thinking it wasn't going to be as easy as they thought.

"You two wankers are pussies!" Abi spat at Ben, and the spittle hit him on the cheek and he wiped it away with his shirt cuff.

Ben held the knife firmly and attacked again. Abi was ready for him and kicked out with both legs, he feinted with the knife, pulled back at the last second, and then swung it in a rasping arc, slicing deep into Abi's left leg. He smiled as he pulled back, knowing they had plenty of time and that blood loss would eventually slow them down and ultimately kill them.

Oliver had no knife and he ran to the kitchen and within seconds, returned with a meat cleaver and a long-serrated bread knife. He was wielding the two weapons while looking into Callum's eyes. Then he struck. The cleaver crunched into an ankle, splitting flesh, muscle, and bone. Callum screamed in agony as searing pains shot through his body. He knew he had no chance of survival and that the end was near but still, he decided to go down fighting.

"Come on, you cowardly wankers, come on you bastards" he taunted and laughed maniacally, trying hard to ignore the searing pain. "Abi, I love you; hurt them as much as you can."

Then he felt something at his neck and his mouth filled with blood, someone had gotten behind him. Then he knew it had to be uncle Paul. He put his hand up to his throat and felt the knife, he grabbed the handle but couldn't stop the cutting. He heard his own death gurgle and slumped forward and then there was darkness.

Paul enjoyed it; he had gotten some extra strength from somewhere and cutting Callum's throat was a joy to him. He stumbled back to join the boys and the three of them stared at Abi.
They knew what they had to do and all three attacked at the same time. Knives slashed and cut at her legs, she became weak and they moved up her body, cutting her stomach open, letting pink wet intestines pour out onto her lap. Oliver struck the fatal blow. The meat cleaver cutting deep into her neck, fountains of blood shooting into the air as she closed her eyes and fell backwards. Blood and intestines covered the floor. It was over.

Paul stood over the two bodies, panting. "They got exactly what they deserved."

They cleaned up as best as they could, and ten minutes later, they were in their car, speeding back to Virginia Water.

Paul pressed speed dial on his mobile.

"Lexi, it's finished." Paul was crying. "I finished him for Katie, we can all sleep now."

"Yes Lexi; we thank God, see you soon."
THE END

OTHER TITLES AVAILABLE FROM AUTHOR CHRIS WARD

THE BERMONDSEY ADULT THRILLER SERIES

1. BERMONDSEY TRIFLE http://tinyurl.com/jxkf746
2. BERMONDSEY PROSECCO http://tinyurl.com/nebwtys
3. BERMONDSEY: THE FINAL ACT http://tinyurl.com/nbuahoj
4. RETURN TO BERMONDSEY http://tinyurl.com/jtmfec6

DETECTIVE INSPECTOR KEREN FOSTER ADULT SERIES

1. SERIAL KILLER http://tinyurl.com/p5ld9dx
2. BLUE COVER UP http://tinyurl.com/mzy5f2f
3. DRIVEN TO KILL http://tinyurl.com/p8f9c4w

SCI-FANTASY

1. OMG JOE WARREN http://tinyurl.com/jtkcusp

TERRORIST ADULT THRILLER

1. THE HUNT http://tinyurl.com/ppshg48

CHECK OUT www.authorchrisward.com